A CERTAIN SEDUCTION

his head. They sat there until half past nine playing the game where he would say a line of poetry and she had to say the next and so on until one of them couldn't remember any more. He nearly always won; he would never pretend to forget; cheating, even to be kind, was something he never did. As she got up to go to bed, he gave her a sip of his brandy.

'Next year you shall have a glass to yourself,' he said.

She remembered him doing the same thing to her brother.

'I shan't want it, it's horrible,' she said, screwing up her face.

'Ah.' He raised a finger. 'But what seems horrible at fourteen, may not at fifteen,' he said.

She laughed and kissed him on the cheek, then went to kiss her mother.

On his way to bed he came in to say a final goodnight, first going to kiss the sleeping Louisa, then coming to her and kissing her forehead and then both cheeks; it was a nightly ritual. When he was away on business, she dampened her forefinger to imitate his lips.

'Now, I don't want you out of this bed until seven o'clock,' he said.

'I promise.' She snuggled beneath the bedclothes. Normally she was the first up, but tomorrow another ritual must be obeyed. Frederick Jarrouse always insisted on being there to watch the delight on his children's faces when they opened the presents he had bought them, and even though she knew what awaited her this time, she was happy to play this game of love and surprise with her father.

She listened to the sound of his heavy footsteps along the landing and her mother's hushed laughter from their bedroom. Then all was quiet except for the sigh of Louisa's breathing from across the room and the intermittent scrabbling of mice in the ceiling. Sometimes the heathland beyond their garden echoed with the screams of rabbits. When she was young, long before Louisa was born and she had to sleep alone in this big room, their screams would terrify her and she'd cry for her father. He'd come and carry her off to put her in the warm hollow between her mother and him, though she always woke to find herself back in her own bed. One night he hadn't come when she cried. The rabbits kept screaming and she couldn't bear it, so she'd run along to their bedroom on her own, covering her face as she passed the picture of Jesus healing the lepers.

Her mother had been cross. She'd sat up in bed, her long hair jet-black in the moonlight, and Josephine could see she was naked and knew that for some reason, that was why she was angry. It's all those silly games you play, she'd said. No wonder she never sleeps. But her father had put on his dressing gown and carried her back to bed on his shoulders. He stopped at the picture of the lepers and told her that Jesus was just about to make them beautiful again so that they could take off the bandages and follow him back to the celestial city where there was nothing but laughter and happiness.

She'd never been frightened of the picture again, but the rabbits' screams still terrified her because she knew that when they stopped screaming it meant they were dead.

The horse was even more beautiful than she'd imagined. Its coat was the colour of ripe corn and its mane and tail thick and silver as the feathers of pampas grass that grew on the back lawn. It was like everything her father bought her; the very best he could find.

She looked up to see her mother and sister waving from an upstairs window. There was never any jealousy over what kind of presents they received. The cost didn't enter into it; her father got what he thought they'd most like. He bent his head to be hugged and kissed, then straightened up and rubbed a hand round his chin.

'Well, I'd better go and get myself spruced up a bit if we're going out. You'd better get tidied up as well.'

'We're only going riding.' She brushed down the front of her jeans and smoothed back her mass of hair.

He frowned at her. 'Your mother's right about you, you're a born ragamuffin.'

She laughed. 'All right, I'll go and get changed after I've got the horses ready.'

She often looked after the horses on her own; being wealthy did not mean being idle in her father's book.

When she'd tacked up the horses and tidied the yard, she went straight upstairs and rummaged round in her wardrobe for proper riding clothes, finally pulling out a pair of cream breeches and a silk polo neck sweater to match. They had been part of her thirteenth birthday present and were tight on her now. She studied herself in the wardrobe mirror a moment, turning sideways. She had always been small; Nella said it was because she was born early and had never caught up. But now it seemed she was starting to catch up. She pulled the sweater out of her waistband and hoped she wouldn't get big breasts like her mother.

When she got outside, her father was unlocking the doors that opened from the courtyard on to their long driveway and she led her new horse over to the mounting block and climbed on its back. He was just about to do the same when they heard the sound of a car coming up the drive.

'Whoever's that?' he said, handing her the reins of his horse and craning his neck towards the entrance.

She recognised the car immediately. It was the man from the auctioneer's who had caught her singing in the storeroom on the day she'd started school. He'd brought back some unsold paintings from a sale.

'I prefer people to make appointments before coming out,' said her father as soon as the man had explained why he'd come.

'I've tried to telephone you three times.' The man looked completely unruffled by her father's sharp tone.

'Well I'm sorry about that, but Mr Barrow knows I always call in on a Monday,' said her father. However annoyed he got with people he usually remained polite.

'Mr Barrow is on holiday,' said the man. 'And we're short of room for storing valuables.'

When her father went off to get the key to the storeroom, he came over and stroked her horse's nose. 'Hello,' he said, smiling up at her. 'No school?'

'I'm having the day off.' She hesitated. 'It's my birthday.'

His smile widened a fraction and a tiny hollow appeared in his right cheek. Out in the daylight he looked friendly and attractive, his eyes sparkling deep blue and his dark hair lifting in the breeze.

A door banged.

'Well, you look very pretty in your riding gear,' he said, glancing round. He touched his hand to the front of the saddle, then patted her leg before walking off to meet her father.

She watched while they took the paintings inside, then the man came out alone and gave her a final smile before getting back into his car.

He reversed through the entrance, something which her father could never do and which seemed to annoy him.

'I think he was trying to avoid turning round near the horses,' she said when her father commented about there being only inches to spare.

But he shook his head and said: 'These youngsters in flashy cars are all the same – think they know it all.'

She was surprised he said that because the man looked only a few years younger than her mother who was thirty-six, and she didn't think the car was flashy. Not that she knew very much about cars, but black things always looked very sombre to her.

'Where are we going then?' Her father's tone had changed and he was his cheerful self once more.

'Up to the quarries and home by Westheath?' she said tentatively. It was a long way, but she knew he would agree wherever she wanted to go.

He pulled a face of pretended pain. 'What are you trying to do to me, eh? Finish me off!'

She laughed. He was always joking about his age or his weight, but even though he was sixty, there were few things that he couldn't do. Last year he'd had tennis courts installed in the back garden and played as long and hard as either she or Lawrence, and whenever he had time, he did most of the gardening himself.

The day was bright, but the weak February sun had little warmth and great gusts of frosty air blew from the horses' nostrils as they trotted up through the pine woods. Their little terrier, Bertie, ambled along behind, making frequent sorties into the dead bracken, then tearing along on his stubby legs to catch them up. The new horse was fast and perfectly schooled. Josephine was a skilled rider; her father had placed her on the back of her first pony before she could walk, and over the years he'd taught her to ride, just as he would Louisa. Her brother was more interested in cars now, but could sometimes be persuaded to join them when he was home. But they never went to gymkhanas or shows, just as they never went anywhere else.

As they approached the site of the ancient flint quarries, they slowed to a walk. The air was spicy with the tang of pine resin, the cathedral-like calm of the woods broken only by the harsh 'churr' of a mistle-thrush. Then they were out in the sun again and the heath stretched before them, its uneven contours patched brown from the scratching of rabbits. She looked across at her father and smiled with sheer happiness; maybe he was lucky, just as the man had said, but she was lucky too. Later, at tea, there would be a cake and she would blow out the candles and wish, and every year it was harder to think of anything to wish for.

Bertie was ahead of them as they emerged from the woods and, when he began to bark at something on the path, they both pulled up. Josephine stood up in her stirrups to see what it was.

'There's a snake – no two. Bertie! Here!' she called. She had never been frightened of snakes. Some years the wet places around the meres and the sandy paths along the river bank were infested with them. Normally they slid away at the vibration made by approaching feet or hooves.

Her father shouted as well but Bertie was too intent on driving away the snakes to pay any attention. 'Stupid dog,' he said. 'He should know better.'

'They look as though they're fighting,' said Josephine. 'Do you think they're sorting out their territory?'

'Bit early for that. Maybe he disturbed a nest of them hibernating. Come here, you idiot dog!' her father shouted. Bertie paid no attention and her father slid his feet from the stirrups. 'I'll have to go and fetch him before he ends up getting bitten. You stay here and hold the horses.'

Just as he leant forward to dismount, Bertie leapt into the air with a shriek of pain and came tearing towards them in a frenzy of yelping. The horses jigged on the spot as he shot between them. Josephine held hers steady but her father's shot forward, rearing to a halt as it came to the first hollow of the quarries. Her father went crashing to the ground, his heavy body landing with a thud.

She jumped from her horse and ran to him. 'Daddy! Are you all right?'

He tried to heave himself up but sank back again. 'I'll be OK in a minute.' He was breathing very fast and rubbing the side of his head. 'Just give me a minute. You go and see if you can find Bertie. We'll have to get him to a vet as quick as . . .' He blew out a long breath and put a hand to his face. 'Go on, quick as you can.'

She stared down at him, biting her lip. She could never remember him being ill or hurt, or anything. The horses were both grazing now and she wasn't sure whether she should try to catch them before searching for Bertie. She turned to look across the heath and then towards the woods, then back down at her father.

'Quickly, Josephine,' he murmured.

There was no sign of Bertie and, after calling his name a few times, she ran back to her father. He had his eyes closed but opened them when she bent down to him. He was staring straight ahead and his voice came out in short painful gasps.

'Go to the farm,' he said. 'Fast as you can. Get help.'

She looked frantically towards the horses, worried that they might dart off if she tried to catch one of them. With a little sob of panic, she started to run and didn't stop until she was at the farmhouse. With barely a moment's hesitation she went straight in through the back door. Her lungs were burning and she had a terrible cramp in her side, but she managed to explain exactly what had happened.

The farmer telephoned for help then took her back to the heath in his Land Rover. As they jerked to a halt, she saw that her father had managed to move a short distance and prop himself against a tree. She smiled with relief and pulled at the door handle, but the farmer put out a hand to stop her.

'I'll go and see to him, you stay here.'

She shook him off and jumped out of the Land Rover. A few feet away she stopped because she saw that her father's head was hanging at a strange angle and his mouth and eyes were wide open.

The horses were still grazing. She could hear the sound of their teeth tearing at the grass and the soft breath blowing from their nostrils. One of them raised its head and shook itself, the movement running in a shudder right along its body, making its tail swish and the bridle jingle like tuneless bells.

She walked on very slowly, falling to her knees beside him, touching his hand, then tugging at his arm. His body fell sideways; he was playing a game – she knew he was.

'Daddy, *Daddy!*' She began to scream at him to stop it. 'It's my birthday . . . it's my birthday,' she said, her voice choking away and lost in the loud wail of the ambulance as it came bumping slowly over the rough ground.

Chapter 2

Josephine lingered on the bridge, leaning over the railing to watch the trout as they darted this way and that, their bodies dark as shadows against the sandy river-bed. In the distance she heard the church clock strike four and knew she ought to get home.

She leant further over the bridge. The water looked invitingly cool and she was tempted to go down and dip her feet in. The walk up to the old quarries and back had made her hot, and she wasn't at all hungry. And her mother would probably have company again.

As she turned into the drive she saw the black car parked in the courtyard. Only the tail-end was visible but she knew who it belonged to.

In the kitchen, Nella was putting cups and saucers on to a tray.

'Is he staying to tea?' asked Josephine, knowing very well that he was – he'd been for tea the last four Saturdays in a row.

'Yes, and we're having it in the dining room.' Nella stopped to look at her. 'So you'd better get tidied up.'

'I'm clean enough.' She glanced down at herself; Nella seldom made any remarks about her appearance: as long as she went to school tidy, nobody seemed to bother.

'Put a cardigan on then.' Nella pulled a disapproving face and placed a white linen tablecloth on top of the cups and saucers. 'You're showing all your middle.'

Josephine gave her T-shirt a downward tug. 'It's meant to be like this. Shall I take that through for you?' she added, knowing Nella was getting flustered because *he* was there.

17

There was no one in the dining room but she could hear voices coming from the study. She shook out the cloth, sliding it into position over the highly polished surface of the table. If the weather was good they usually had their tea out on the lawn, just as they used to when her father was alive. But her mother's visitor always came to the house dressed in a suit and tie; he didn't look as though he would want to sit out on the lawn. She heard her mother laugh and glanced over her shoulder to see her coming across the hall, with Christian Irving, the man from the auctioneer's, close behind her.

'Has Nella put an extra cup out?' said her mother, coming over to rest a hand on her shoulder. 'Only Christian came to bring me a copy of the sale brochure and I've asked him to stay for tea.'

Josephine nodded and went on laying the table.

'Hello, Josephine.' Christian had followed her mother into the room.

'Hello,' she murmured without looking up.

'Have you had a nice walk?' he asked.

She shrugged. 'All right, thank you.'

'What's the matter, darling?' said her mother.

'Nothing.' She looked up, forcing herself to smile. How could she explain? How could she say, I don't want you being happy with that man who is going to sell all Daddy's beautiful things. I don't want him coming here and looking at you and making you forget Daddy.

Solange gave a little frown of concern, but her face was rarely serious for long; the arch in her top lip, where a glimpse of perfect teeth was always visible, gave her a naturally happy expression. Josephine had the same mouth, the same full upper lip and big dark eyes, but when she was unhappy it showed.

'I'll go and tell Nella you're ready,' she said, turning away.

After tea, Louisa insisted that Christian come and see her kittens. Normally she was even shyer than Josephine, but he seemed to have won her over with his gentle show of interest in her. Today he had brought her chocolate and she began to unwrap it as she led him out to the stables where the kittens slept curled in a nest of straw.

Josephine had to go with them. Louisa always wanted Josephine to come with her, whether it was outside, upstairs, or even just into the next room. In the months following their father's death, when Solange had spent whole days alone in her bedroom, Louisa had clung to her, and Josephine, in a different way, had clung to her little sister.

Louisa snapped off the end of her chocolate and handed it to her, then shyly offered a piece to Christian. He took it and turned to Josephine, his eyebrows raised.

'You told me you didn't like chocolate. I would have brought you some. What do you like?'

She shrugged; she'd only said it because she didn't want him bringing her presents.

'Nothing, thank you,' she said.

He laughed. 'You don't like anything?'

'I didn't mean . . .' She stopped because she could feel herself beginning to blush. He was always twisting round the things she said, and it always had the same effect on her.

He smiled down at her and put his arm round her waist, his hand resting on the bare skin between her T-shirt and jeans. She pulled away and walked on ahead.

There were great puddles across the cobbled yard and he picked Louisa up because she had come outside in her slippers. Nella wouldn't have let her do that, but their mother often didn't notice such things. As he ducked down through the door of the stables, Louisa put her arms round his neck. He stroked her dark curls and stood her on a bale of straw.

'You may not be as devastatingly pretty as your sister, but you're far more agreeable,' he said, his voice purposely loud.

Josephine pushed past him to get back outside. How was she going to bear it if her mother married him? That's what Lawrence had said would happen. Last weekend when he came home, he'd asked her to tell him what had been going on, and when she'd started to relate the ordinary, everyday things that happened through the week, he'd laughed at her and said, I'm talking about our mother's love affair, stupid.

But she couldn't talk about it even to Lawrence. The only person she could open her heart to wasn't there, never would be, and if he had been, none of this would have happened.

A week later when her mother made the announcement at breakfast, Josephine fled from the room. Halfway up the stairs she could hear that her mother was crying and saying, I don't know what I'm going to do with her, she never used to be like this. Josephine threw herself on her bed and cried too.

Lawrence came up, about to shout at her as he'd done a

couple of times lately, but seeing her so upset he sat on the edge of the bed and talked calmly to her.

'You can't expect Mother to stay on her own for ever, Phina: she's only thirty-seven.' He paused as though he was thinking of words to convince her. 'Dad would have wanted her to be happy, you know that.'

She lifted her head from the pillow and looked at him accusingly. 'He wouldn't want her to get married again,' she said, rubbing a hand over her tear-streaked face. 'He wouldn't want her to love anyone else.'

Lawrence gave a gruff sigh of impatience. 'And that's the trouble, isn't it? He was far too possessive. Now neither of you can manage without him.'

She buried her head in her arms again but he went on.

'You never go anywhere or do anything, and how many times have you come home from school crying because someone's teased you? Things have got to change.'

'I don't like him,' she protested tearfully.

'Well Mother does – and that's the important thing. You're just being selfish. You can't have Dad back and the sooner you realise that and start thinking about Mother for a change, then the better it will be for everyone.'

She put her hands over her ears.

'Listen, Phina.' He pulled one hand gently away. 'I can't say I'm all that struck on Christian. He's a bit arrogant and I think he's too young for her. But they obviously love one another. And anyway, she can't manage this place on her own and I can't keep coming home all the time. She's doing the right thing getting married again.'

Her mother came to join them. 'Why can't you be happy for me, Phina?' she said. 'It doesn't mean I shall forget Daddy.'

But Josephine knew she would; every time she saw them together she thought it. The day she came across them unexpectedly in the stable next to her mother's aviary, she was sure her mother had forgotten him completely.

They were talking very quietly, looking through the wire at the birds. Christian had his head bent to hers in a particularly tender way, as though he didn't want to miss a word of what she said. Then he pushed her back against the wall and kissed her. Josephine couldn't move for a moment. She stood in the doorway and watched her mother's hands creep to the back of his neck and her fingers, glittering with the rings she always wore, entwine themselves in his hair.

And in those few seconds she felt that her father was truly dead, that her mother no longer had room in her heart for his memory – or for her. She backed away, but caught her arm against the door and it slammed shut. They turned to look and she stood there with stupid hot tears running down her face. Christian said something to her mother, then came over to her.

'Come on, Josephine, don't be miserable.' The softness of his voice was all it needed and the tears became a flood. She put her hands to her face and went to run off but he caught hold of her.

'Please don't be unhappy,' he said. 'You make me feel as though I shouldn't be here.' He bent his head close to hers, just as he had done to her mother only a few moments before. 'Do you want me to go away and never see your mother again? Is that what you want?'

It was too hard to say yes, too hard to say anything. When he pulled her head against his shoulder, the need for comfort overwhelmed her and she stood there and cried against him, tears that were nothing to do with him but were for the great bleak hole that her father's death had made in her life.

Her mother married him at the end of July and, after the ceremony, Josephine and Louisa took their bridesmaids' posies and laid them on their father's grave. Josephine shed the first tears she had for weeks, and she wiped them away quickly because the photographer was waiting and she didn't want to upset her mother. But she spoke to her father in her head, just as she did when she went up to the quarries and stood by that lone birch tree where he'd died. In some ways it seemed he'd been dead far longer than eighteen months, but in another way, because she still missed him so much, it felt as though he'd hardly been gone any time at all. And sometimes, if she let herself become immersed in thoughts of him, it felt as though she would only have to push open the storeroom door and he'd be standing there, waiting in the semi-darkness to show her the dancing figures.

But she must think of him no more today. All sad thoughts must be banished from her mind so she could smile for the camera. She watched her mother standing close to Christian, perched on high heels because he was so much taller than her, the sunlight adding a glow to her dusky Latin skin and glinting off her jewellery. But nothing sparkled like her smile. She never wore make-up and the brightness picked out the tiny lines around her eyes and mouth, but she still looked young, younger than she had for a long time. And so happy.

If he can make her look like that, thought Josephine, then Daddy won't mind. He'll forgive her for being in love again.

Later there was champagne on the lawn back at home. No guests, only a friend of Christian's who had acted as best man, and a meal out in a private room at a nearby hotel. Then they all went home together.

For a moment, clambering out of the taxi and running across the darkening courtyard with Louisa squealing and gripping her hand in case the bats got them, Josephine felt almost happy. It's going to be all right, she thought. Nothing is going to change.

But in the hall, the lights blazing, Josephine watched as Christian kissed Louisa goodnight – lifting her up to cuddle her as he was always doing – and felt suddenly left out. He looked up and smiled at her.

'I suppose you're too big to give me a kiss,' he said.

'Of course she's not,' said Solange.

She hesitated, then went up to him and touched her lips to his cheek, careful to avoid the dark shadow where he shaved. Something about his face looked different tonight.

'Sweet dreams, Josephine,' he said, and she saw her mother take his arm and head him towards the stairs.

Lawrence went and walked up close behind him.

The next morning he didn't appear until midday. When he came into the kitchen asking Nella for coffee instead of the tea she always made, Josephine had the strangest feeling, knowing he was going to be there every day from now on. He looked as though he had just crawled out of bed, his eyes half closed and the shadow on his chin grown black as the boyish wisps of hair that fell over his forehead. His shirt was undone and hanging out of his trousers, the cuffs minus the usual gold cuff-links. For the first time she noticed how small his hands were for someone so tall.

He smiled at her. 'I bet your head's pounding too, isn't it?' he said.

She admitted it was. Lawrence had warned her yesterday she'd suffer if she had any more champagne. But she'd never tried it before and had taken an instant liking to it.

'Your first hangover.' He smiled again, and she heard Nella give one of her disapproving sniffs.

It felt harder to talk to him than it had for weeks. His presence in the kitchen amongst all the familiar things of her life disturbed her. Even the way he looked disturbed her. Unwanted images of her mother and him came into her head: her mother naked with her hair falling about her shoulders, just as she'd seen her that time with her father. And Christian, so much younger than her father, kissing her as he'd done in the stable that day.

She wanted it to be like yesterday: smiling in the sunshine outside the church with the feeling that things weren't going to be so bad after all. Instead, for reasons she couldn't explain, she felt as though her life had been turned upside down once more.

But when Lawrence came home again a couple of weeks later and asked her, how were things, and how was she getting on with Christian, she answered, truthfully, that everything was fine.

'So it's working out all right, is it?' He was trying to start the lawnmower and screwed his head round to her as though seeking confirmation.

She nodded and smiled. 'Except for the garden. I don't think he likes doing that.'

'That's pretty obvious.' The lawns had become very overgrown. Christian had started them half-heartedly a couple of times but never finished. The previous evening he'd told Lawrence they'd get up early and do the lot. But now Lawrence was struggling alone while Christian lay in bed.

'I think he had too much to drink last night,' said Lawrence. 'Does he often drink that much?'

She shrugged. 'Sometimes.' They always had wine with dinner now, but she was usually in bed early because Louisa wouldn't go to sleep without her, and she had no idea what he did later on in the evening.

'And does he often speak to Nella like that?'

'Now and again.' That was something she did know about, the way he snapped at Nella if she tried to tell him what to do. Her mother said Nella shouldn't interfere, she was too fond of that. 'I don't think Nella takes any notice of him.'

'He doesn't speak to Mother like it, does he?'

'No, never.' She looked towards the house where her mother's bedroom curtains were still drawn, then added quietly, 'I think she's really happy.'

'Well, that's the main thing,' he said as the mower chugged into life.

Later, Christian came to help, but they couldn't do as much as they'd planned because it had rained heavily during the week and the lower slopes of the lawns were still too wet to be cut. They stopped for lunch at midday and Christian began drinking again, finishing off a whole bottle of wine to himself because nobody else wanted any. Afterwards they lazed about on the lawn, but Lawrence was soon bored and badgered Christian into playing tennis with him.

'He thinks he'll beat me because I've had a couple of glasses of wine,' said Christian, tapping Josephine on the head with his racquet as he passed her. 'But he's got a surprise coming.'

She looked up at him. He sounded slightly irritable and there was a hint of colour on his face, a slight flush across his cheekbones.

He won every game, and Lawrence came off the court hot and bothered from defeat. The temperature had soared into the nineties.

'God, this heat is killing,' said Lawrence, flinging down his racquet and stripping off his T-shirt. 'I'm going for a swim in the river. It should be deep enough after all that rain.' He looked at Christian. 'Coming? If you can swim, that is,' he added.

'I can swim even better than I play tennis,' said Christian, looking amused. 'I went to a school where we had to jump in a freezing cold lake at six every morning.' He crouched down beside Solange, an arm round her shoulders. 'Why don't you come with us?'

'Oooh, no,' she said with a shiver. 'I can't swim and I hate the water. I'll help Nella get the tea ready for when you come back.'

He looked over his shoulder at Josephine. 'What about you?'

She in turn looked at Louisa. 'Do you want to come paddling?'

Louisa jumped up, scattering the daisy-chains they'd been making. 'Can I put my bikini on?'

'Of course you can,' said Christian, snatching her up and swinging her into the air. 'You can't go swimming with your clothes on, can you?'

Josephine suddenly wished she could change her mind. The thought of being in front of Christian in a bikini made her shyness of him return in full force. Up in her bedroom she lingered over getting changed and finally put back on her T-shirt and skirt over her bikini.

By the time they got to the river, Lawrence and Christian were already in the water, and she sat on the bank while Louisa paddled. Only a thin strip of cloud saved them from the full glare of the sun. The hot air was thick with the heady scent of meadowsweet, and the pungent stench of decaying reeds drifted up from the river's edge.

'Come on out here, it's really deep,' called Lawrence, but she shook her head.

Then Christian came and stood in front of her. 'What's the matter?' he said.

'Nothing.' Her shyness grew to see him in swimming trunks, the dark hair on his chest and legs glistening with moisture. 'I'll come in when I'm ready.'

He pulled a face and kicked a spray of water over her, then stooped to pick up Louisa and carried her off.

Josephine watched them laughing and splashing about in the water, and thought of other summers when they had swum there with her father. Christian looked towards her a couple of times, then he came out to her again.

'Come on, misery,' he said, hauling her to her feet.

'Don't,' she said, digging her toes in the sandy earth.

He laughed and suddenly lifted her up and ran into the river with her, tossing her into the deepest part. She stood up, blowing the water from her nose.

'You . . . you bloody pig,' she shouted at him. 'I've still got my T-shirt on.'

'That's the first time I've ever heard you swear before,' he said, laughing at her again and tugging at her ponytail.

She dived away from him and pulled off the soaking T-shirt and hurled it towards the bank. It fell short and caught in an overhanging branch. Louisa shrieked with laughter and Josephine found herself laughing too. Soon she was swimming with them, forgetting herself in the sheer pleasure that came with having fun once more. It felt like she was a child again, showing her father how she could do underwater somersaults or racing with him to the bridge and back. When Louisa began to complain of being cold, she lifted her up and cuddled her, overflowing with sudden affection.

'I'll take her out,' said Lawrence. 'I'm getting a bit cold as well.'

Christian followed and she watched the three of them go to the bank. Lawrence began drying Louisa, while Christian sat with a towel round his shoulders, taking swigs from a bottle of cider they'd brought with them. She flopped down in the water again, floating on her back, her eyes closed against the sun while tiny rainbows danced between her lashes. Then Lawrence was calling to her.

'I'm taking Louisa home. Christian's going to wait for you.'

She stood up. Louisa waved to her as they climbed up the grassy slope to the lane and disappeared behind the parapet of the bridge.

'Are you going to stay in there for ever?' Christian called to her.

'I'm just coming.' She started to wring the water from her ponytail. It dribbled down her back and she felt suddenly cold herself.

'Come on, Josephine,' he called again. He was standing up now, holding out the towel for her, a huge beach towel patterned with blue dolphins that she'd been bringing to the river for as long as she could remember. For a moment, staring towards the bank, the sun in her face, she had an image of her father waiting for her, holding the towel just as Christian was doing. She ran forward, splashing through the muddy shallows, and he caught her in the towel. It was warm, as if he'd spread it out in the sun as her father used to do, and she stood there and let him wrap it tight round her, shivering in its softness. He began to rub her shoulders with it.

'It's nice to see you happy,' he said, cupping her neck with the towel.

She looked up at him and smiled and for a moment the years fell away again and she leant her head against his chest. He cuddled her, drawing her close, then suddenly ran his hands down her thighs and pulled her hard up against him. The contact with him sent a shock of confusion through her and she twisted away, her hands against his chest. For just a second he held her, then let her go so abruptly that she stumbled backwards, the fallen towel tangling between her legs.

'Careful,' he said, briefly putting out a hand to steady her.

She snatched up the towel and went to sit on the ground away from him, pulling the band from her hair so that it fell round her in a great wet mass. He sat down as well, staring in front of him, silent and still.

'Come on, we'd better get back,' he said after a few minutes.

He spoke to her only once on the way home.

'Put your sandals on, you'll cut your feet,' he said as she clambered up to the lane.

She hardly realised that she still carried them. She glanced up at him, but he went walking on ahead as though he didn't care whether she put them on or not.

Solange came down the lawn to meet them and Christian took her hand. A dried and dressed Louisa immediately ran up to take his other hand. Josephine trailed behind them but, halfway to the house, Solange turned to wait for her.

'Have you had a good time, darling?' she asked.

Josephine swallowed and squinted up at the sun-bleached sky, but stupid and confusing tears welled in her throat and she could only nod and hurry on.

Over the next few weeks, Josephine did her best to avoid Christian and was careful never to be alone with him. He was back at work, so they only met during the evenings, and at weekends he spent his time with Solange and Louisa, lazing about indoors or on the lawn. Josephine rarely joined them. She filled her days as she always had, helping Nella or playing with Louisa, and in the evenings she would curl up alone in her father's study, flicking through his books or just sitting there dreaming. And often she walked up to the quarries. But for some reason she could no longer hold those silent conversations with her father.

For the first time ever, she was glad when the new term started. She threw herself into her school work and even started to join some of the other girls on Saturday trips to town, walking up to the village to catch the bus. The discovery that she could find enjoyment away from home came at just the right time, giving her new interests, diffusing the painful welter of emotion that had been building up inside her. Her shyness still held her back, and more often than not she'd watch on the sidelines as the other girls chatted to boys or pranced around in clothes shops trying on the latest fashions. But it meant that what happened at home became less important; other things were beginning to fill her head.

And at home, things were easier. It was two months since that afternoon they had gone swimming. Once or twice recently Christian had made teasing remarks to her as he used to, and he had started to bring her chocolate, just as he did Louisa. He left it on the desk in the study and she felt they were little gifts of apology for something that he had not meant to do. He no longer worked in the afternoons – why she didn't know and didn't ask – and he started to come and pick her up from school now and again. Her friends made remarks about him, saying how nice it must be to have such a young and good-looking stepfather. One of the older girls even joked, did he take her straight home? Once upon a time, this would have had her in tears, but now she laughed as though it was nothing. But secretly she embroidered on it.

When Lawrence came home at half-term, he commented on the change in her.

'You've got a lot to say for yourself,' he laughed when she chattered on about something to do with school. 'I've never known you so full of it. What have you been up to?'

'She's got a secret boyfriend,' Christian butted in. 'She goes off on long walks and out every Saturday.' He raised his head from the sofa where he was stretched out full-length, his usual position for the evening. 'She rushes off to catch the bus, all dressed up. You wouldn't know your little sister these days.' He sank back down, smiling to himself.

Lawrence glanced at him, then looked back at her as if to say, ignore him. Josephine knew they'd had a row earlier. She'd come back from her walk at the tail-end of it and could see that her mother had been crying. Lawrence and Christian had barely spoken at dinner and although Christian was talkative again now, the atmosphere was tense and her mother had gone to bed early with a headache.

'I just go to meet some of the girls from school, that's all,' she said, looking at Lawrence.

'Well, I'm glad you're getting out. I'll give you some driving lessons up at the old airfield when I can; then you'll be ready to take your test when you're seventeen and we can get you a car. You can't keep relying on buses.'

'I've offered to take her, but she doesn't want me to,' said Christian, pointedly, as though he guessed the remark was meant for him.

'Oh, are you up in time?' said Lawrence.

Josephine saw Christian mouth a swearword at him, but Lawrence ignored him, told her not to forget to put the guard round the fire, and went off to bed. She jumped up, about to follow him, but Christian caught the hem of her skirt as she passed him.

'Hang on, Josephine. Please, just a minute.'

'What?' she said, tugging her skirt away from him.

'It wasn't me who upset your mother. Go and ask her if you don't believe me. Lawrence hadn't been in the house five minutes when he started going on about the state of the place. Anybody would think it's falling down around us.'

'He worries about it.'

'That's not my fault. I didn't marry your mother to become some kind of handyman. She doesn't expect me to either.' He turned on his side to face her, then patted the seat in front of him. 'Sit here and talk to me for a minute.'

'What about?' she said, perching on the very edge of the sofa.

'Anything.' He paused. 'But most of all I want you to say that you've forgiven me for what I did that day at the river.'

She was stunned; it was the last thing she expected him to say.

'I'm truly sorry. I know it upset you, but I'd been drinking and I hardly realised what I was doing.'

She stared into the fire where a smouldering log had burst into flame.

He craned round to look at her, bringing that vaguely perfumed smell that always lingered about him. 'Am I forgiven?'

She nodded and he slipped an arm round her waist.

'And I'm sorry for teasing you earlier. I know where you go and I understand.' He gave her a little squeeze. 'It should be so easy for us to get on. You're just like your mother. All you want is to be loved and happy, isn't it?'

Her legs and face grew hot from the blazing log but she didn't move. He squeezed her again, prompting her to answer.

'It's difficult for me,' he went on. 'I can be as affectionate as I like to your mother and Louisa, but I have to be careful with you, don't I?'

Still she didn't answer. He took his arm from her waist and settled himself more comfortably, hands behind his head.

'Tell me what you get up to on Saturdays,' he said. 'I bet you do meet boys.'

'Sometimes we do.'

'And have any of them asked you out on your own?'

'Yes. But I don't particularly like any of them.'

It was true; she'd been asked out on a number of occasions, but despite the fact that she stood out as naïve and immature against the other girls, all the boys who joined their crowd seemed childish and uninteresting to her.

'Perhaps you're too fussy. You want them to be tall, dark and handsome like me.'

She jerked her head round and saw that he was laughing at her, his cheek deeply indented and his blue eyes glittering as they always did after dinner and wine.

'I'm only joking. I expect you compare them all with your father, that's the trouble.' He sat up, swinging his feet to the floor and putting his arm round her waist again. 'I'm going to bed.' He leant his head briefly on hers and drew her against him for a moment before standing up. 'Your mother will be wondering where I am. I might not be much good at mending broken windows, but I am good at making your mother happy.'

She sat there listening as he bolted the front doors, heard the creak of the stairs as he went up, and finally his footsteps along the landing above her head. Silence hummed away in her ears; she stared into the fire but saw nothing, and all she could think of was what he would soon be doing to make her mother happy.

Chapter 3

The next day, there was another row. Christian stormed out
and didn't come home until past midnight and Lawrence went
back to Cambridge. It was Christmas Eve before they were all
together again.

The atmosphere was strained at first, then Christian agreed
to go with them to the midnight service at the village church
and the tension eased.

'At least he tries to please Mother,' Lawrence said to Josephine as they went out to the car.

'He doesn't usually go,' she said. She wished he wasn't
coming. People would stare at them with him there. She knew
very well what the gossips said about her mother: widowed
just over a year and married again to a man much younger
than herself, and she didn't want to sit there with him under
the scrutiny of local people.

As they squeezed into the narrow pew, she glanced up at
him, expecting to see his face creased with annoyance at the
attention they were getting. Over the months she had learnt
how quickly he could fly into a temper over things like this.
But he smiled at her, tall and smoothly handsome, as confident
as if he owned the place. And in an odd way it boosted her
own confidence, made her feel protected against those prying
stares.

Back at home, Nella had hot mince-pies waiting. Lawrence
put chestnuts in the glowing ashes under the fire basket, while
Christian poured them all drinks. Last year had been so awful
with none of them wanting to celebrate; a dead, unhappy
Christmas after all the years when it was the most important

31

day of all. Josephine felt a twinge of sadness remembering how they used to sing carols, the room full of her father's cigar smoke and sweet with the scent of the fruity punch that he always made. She looked across at her mother, wondering if she was thinking of it too, but her mother was looking at Christian. He was sprawled in an armchair, Louisa curled on his lap asleep, an empty glass at his elbow and a moody stare fixed on his face.

He'd been like this ever since the rows with Lawrence: one minute irritable and almost unapproachable, the next doing anything to please. Yesterday he'd gone out and bought them a television, saying he was going to bring them into the twentieth century for Christmas. Now he looked bored with it all.

'Can you take Louisa up to bed?' said Solange gently.

He smiled at her as though he'd been perfectly happy all along, and eased himself carefully to his feet, Louisa cradled in his arms.

'Phina, you go up as well and undress her.'

She followed him up, watching while he lowered Louisa into bed.

'I shouldn't bother to undress her, you might wake her up,' he said. 'Just take her shoes off.'

He waited quietly while she unbuckled Louisa's shoes and took out the plastic slides from her hair. She put the slides on the dressing table, then went to pull the curtains.

The back lawns were bathed in light from a moon that was almost round; just a tiny section was missing, as though it really were made of cheese and some night creature had nibbled away at it. She smiled to herself and thought of her father again, and how he had taken her outside one moonlit night to show her the noises she could hear were only hedgehogs foraging for slugs in the flowerbeds.

'Once, when I was little,' she began, her heart suddenly so full of memories that they overflowed, 'I heard something rustling about outside and I thought the garden was full of goblins . . .' She stopped as a scraping sound came up from below the window. 'What was that?' she whispered, a hand against her chest.

Christian came and looked over her shoulder just as a large dog fox emerged from the shadow of the house. It padded down the lawn, stopping halfway to look back, its head raised as though it knew they watched. Josephine was spellbound by it; even with its mange-patched coat it looked extraordinarily beautiful, its brush tipped with silver in the moonlight. But more than that, it had appeared at just the right moment, adding perfection to her memories.

'It's looking at us,' she smiled, turning to Christian.

'Don't be silly,' he said. But he was smiling too and he suddenly bent his head and kissed her on the lips.

Almost at once he straightened up with a murmured, Happy Christmas, Josephine, as if to explain what he'd meant by it. She stared at him, saw him lick his lips and could feel their moist softness sweet with the taste of wine. He smiled again and reached out to ruffle her hair, but she turned away and watched the fox disappear in the dark at the edge of the lawn.

Christmas Day was dominated by the new television. Louisa could hardly take her eyes from it, and although Lawrence had remarked that if they had wanted one they'd have got one before, he too sat glued to it.

Josephine watched with them, but by the afternoon, when they still sat there, surrounded by discarded wrapping paper, dirty plates and leftover food, she grew increasingly restless and fed up with being shushed every time she spoke. She sat on the corner of the hearth, feeding bits of Christmas paper into the fire and watching the flames shoot up in bright iridescent colours.

'Pack it in, Josephine, you'll set the chimney on fire.' Christian raised his head from where he lay stretched on the sofa with Louisa, a can of lager beside him, the last of a four-pack that Lawrence had bought him.

She looked straight at him, then put on another piece. Lawrence reached out and snatched the paper away from her.

'Stop causing trouble,' he muttered.

'Why don't you go and make some tea, dear?' Solange said to her.

'In a minute.'

Christian raised his head again. 'Now,' he ordered.

'I'll do it,' said Solange, patting his shoulder.

After her mother had left the room, Josephine looked at Christian and said: 'You don't like your present, do you?'

'What?' he said, screwing up his face. 'What are you on about now?'

She had bought him a red T-shirt on a Christmas shopping trip to town last week. The money her mother had given her was fast dwindling when she'd realised she'd got nothing for him and lingered in the menswear department of the store where she'd bought the other presents, unsure what to do. He only wore expensive clothes – Nella was always saying she was half afraid to iron his shirts. The T-shirt had been on top of a box of oddments. Why she picked it up, she had no idea; she'd never seen him either in a T-shirt or in anything red.

It lay on the floor now, still in its polythene bag.

'You don't like it, do you?' she repeated, tossing a piece of screwed-up paper at it.

'Of course I do, stop being so childish.'

'I know you don't,' she persisted, poking her foot at it. 'I bet you never wear it.'

He sighed and swivelled round to face her. 'What's the matter with you? I've said I like it.'

She had a burning urge to carry on arguing with him; it was all mixed up with a feeling of boredom and wanting to laugh and cry; she'd had it all morning and the wine at lunch had made it worse.

All at once he sat upright and began unbuttoning his shirt. Lawrence looked over his shoulder to see what was going on.

'Your sister is going to have one of her tantrums if I don't do this,' said Christian.

Lawrence frowned and turned back to the television. Josephine stared into the fire, deciding that she hated him and she'd never buy him another present as long as she lived.

'Are you satisfied now?' he said, getting up and coming to crouch beside her.

She knew he was wearing the T-shirt but wouldn't look at him.

'You can be an absolute pain in the arse, do you know that?' he said, getting up to go and help Solange who had come in with the tea.

She heard her mother say: 'Oh, that really suits you, Chris. Don't you think so, Phina?'

'Will you please be quiet?' said Louisa loudly. 'I can't hear the television.'

Christian laughed and went back to sit with her. Solange handed round the tea, then joined him and he stretched out again, his head in her lap. Josephine stole a glance at them and found him watching her, his eyes half closed but fixed on her. He reached down for the lager and, as he moved, Solange laid a hand on his cheek. With a little turn of his head, he captured one of her fingers in his mouth, but she took her hand away, looking up briefly as though his action had embarrassed her.

'Do that to me,' said Louisa, crawling across to put her hand on his face.

'Stop it,' said Solange, more sharply than she normally spoke. 'I thought you were watching television.'

'Give me a kiss instead,' said Christian, tweaking her nose. 'A big Christmas one.'

Louisa laughed and pressed her lips against his.

Josephine got up from the hearth, nearly knocking over her cup of tea, and stumbled through the clutter of things that lay across the floor.

'Where are you going?' said Solange.

She stopped, her hand on the door handle. 'Have I got to be interrogated every time I leave the room now?'

'I was just going to say could you take some of the dirty plates and things out with you,' said Solange. 'That's all.'

'I'm sorry,' Josephine muttered, and went back to gather up the plates. She took them to the kitchen and washed them. Nella had gone up for a nap; the kitchen was clean and tidy; there was nothing more to do. On the draining board were a number of empty bottles, beside them her father's old Cognac which Lawrence had found at the back of the chiffonier earlier. It was still a third full and she poured some into a wine glass and wandered through into the dining room with it, going to sit by the window. The first mouthful made her shudder and scorched her throat, but after a few more careful sips she was able to drain the glass. It settled so warmly in her stomach that she was tempted to go and pour herself some more. She looked out to the courtyard where the corners were already growing dark, despite the brightness of the day. Just an hour or two of daylight were left. Her father used to say the brandy helped him sleep and she waited, expecting to feel drowsy, wondering why she felt more awake and restless with every minute that passed. Suddenly she jumped up and went back to the sitting room.

'I'm going for a walk,' she announced, standing in the doorway.

'What, now?' said Solange.

'Yes. We always used to go for a walk on Christmas Day.'

Solange's face softened. 'But that was with Daddy. You don't want to go on your own.' She leant across to tap Lawrence on the shoulder. 'Do you want to go for a walk with Josephine?'

'Not now,' he said, without taking his eyes off the television.

Christian sat up. 'I'll go with her.' He disentangled himself from Louisa and stood up, stopping a moment to finish the remains of the lager, then went off to get his coat.

When he came down, Josephine hadn't moved an inch.

'Go and get ready then,' he said. 'Unless you've changed your mind.'

'No, no, I haven't,' she said quickly.

'You don't know what you want to do half the time,' he muttered.

'Where are we going then?' he said as they walked down the back lawn.

'I don't mind.' She was a few paces ahead and pushed through the gate, leaving it to swing behind her. Out in the lane she quickened her pace but he caught up with her in a few strides.

'Josephine, I don't much like walking, I only came to keep you company, so can you snap out of this mood and be a bit more sociable.'

'I'm not in a mood.'

'You're in something. What's upset you?'

'Nothing.'

He looked down at her, his eyes searching her face. 'Is it me?'

She didn't answer but, when they came to the track that turned up to the quarries, he vaulted over the stile in front of her and stood there barring her way.

'What's going on in that head of yours,' he said softly, putting his hands on her shoulders. 'Is it because I teased you about the T-shirt?'

She sat on the top bar, her cheeks burning despite the frosty air. The urge to cry was there again. She wanted to lean forward and let herself fall against his chest so that he would catch her and fold her up in his arms. I'm lonely, she wanted to say. I want to be Louisa – I want to be my mother.

'I want to . . .' she began, without realising she was saying it.

'Tell me,' he said quietly, taking her face in his hands. 'What do you want?'

She shook her head and jumped from the stile, then started to run. The track was hard as rock, the ruts frozen. There wasn't a sound anywhere except the sharp cracks as her feet broke the ice – and, behind, the thud of his heavier steps as he followed her. He called out once for her to stop, that it would be getting dark soon, but she ignored him and ran on, branching off down a little path that wound along the edge of the heath. It was bordered by silver birch and covered with soft humps of dead brown grass that muffled all sound. She slowed down, her lungs aching with the cold air, and finally came to a halt as the path petered out on to the heath. It stretched before her, white and empty as a tundra landscape, the hollows shadowed dark blue by some trick of the light. She looked up at the sky, breathtakingly vast, the afternoon sapphire slowly turning to navy and soon to be lit by a million stars.

She knew Christian had come up behind her. It was like last night when they had watched the fox; another magical scene spread before them, and when she turned round he kissed her just as he had done last night. But this time he didn't stop and ruffle her hair, he caught hold of her and began to kiss her roughly until her lips were bruised and her head swam. She did nothing, not even when he pulled her down on to the soft dead grass and lay on top of her. It wasn't desire for him; it was the yearning to be held and caressed and have someone say they loved her more than anyone else. And she knew instinctively that all these things would come if he desired her.

He pulled her coat open and slipped his hands up under her clothes.

'This is what you want, isn't it?' he said against her ear. He raised his head to look down at her, his mouth open, his breath blowing shallow and fast in her face and beads of sweat glistening across his brows.

He started to kiss her again and slid his hands up to cover her breasts. The sensation as his fingers moved across her skin was totally unexpected; it felt both exciting and repugnant and made her want to put her arms round his neck and push him away at the same time. For a moment she lay completely still, her eyes closed, her arms flung out sideways.

Then she felt his hand slide down to the zip of her jeans.

'No, don't,' she said, grabbing at his wrist.

He pushed her off and caught hold of the zip.

'Don't. Stop it.' She struggled against him.

'It's a bit late for saying no.'

'Let me go or I'll tell my mother.' She began to cry, and he shook her so hard that her head slammed on the ground. She struggled frantically now, screaming and hitting out at him.

He let out an angry sigh and rolled away from her. 'You give out all the signals . . . You knew what would happen, don't make out you didn't.' Then he was on his feet and dragging her up, shaking her once more. 'You'll end up getting raped, do you know that?'

She stood there panting and crying and desperately ashamed at the terrible mistake she'd made.

The walk home was a nightmare, trailing along beside him because he kept a grip on her, and knowing she would soon have to face her mother. He didn't say a word until they were at the back door when he stopped and brushed down the back of her coat and pointed a finger in her face.

'No more hysterics, Josephine. This has all been your own fault.' He paused and pushed open the door, lowering his voice. 'And if you say a word to your mother, I shall tell her exactly that.'

'Leave me alone.' She shook him off and ran straight upstairs.

Up in her room she curled on her bed, pressed her face into the pillow and cried until she thought she'd never be able to stop. But it didn't make her feel any better; nothing could turn the clock back. She heard Christian come up and guessed he was getting washed and changed by the sound of water running through the pipes. Then he went back down.

She started to undress, intending to get changed herself, but the thought of going downstairs with the others made her feel even worse, and she went to lie on her bed again. When she heard footsteps along the landing she quickly pulled the bedspread over her, covering herself just as Christian came into the room.

'You'll have to come down,' he said. 'Your mother's asking where you are.'

'I don't want any tea.'

'You have to come down,' he repeated. His voice was calm but there was an undercurrent of anger. 'I can't have her coming up and finding you like this.'

'You needn't worry – I won't tell her.' She tried not to start crying again but couldn't help it.

'You're making a fuss about nothing. Now get dressed and come downstairs. I'll give you ten minutes, then I'll be back to get you.'

She washed her face and did as he said, because she believed what he'd said – that he'd come and get her – and whatever happened she mustn't cause a scene in front of her mother.

In the dining room, Nella and her mother were setting out the table. The Christmas cake was in the middle, decorated with sprigs of holly that they'd picked in the lane, and a crudely carved wooden angel. The angel was one of the few possessions that her mother had brought with her when she came to England, and every year she put it on the cake saying it reminded her how lucky she was. Last year, the angel had been left off, but now it was back, its painted face as bright as ever.

'We thought you'd fallen asleep,' said Solange.

'No, I . . .' She stopped and rubbed her fingers over her lips, forcing herself to smile. 'I was just getting changed.' She looked across at Christian who was over at the chiffonier pouring drinks. His usual white shirt had replaced the red T-shirt and the back of his hair was damp and combed.

'You walked a long way then, I hear,' said Solange, straightening the wooden angel, then looking back at her.

'Yes . . . I'm sorry . . . we didn't realise it was getting so late.'

'It's all right – I wasn't worried about you.' Solange gave her a puzzled look, then smiled. 'I think you've worn Chris out,' she said. 'He won't want to come with you again.'

Christian turned round now and came to the table. He knocked against the tree on his way, sending a shower of fake snow on to the carpet. Louisa laughed and looked up at him, but he took no notice.

Nella brought in the last of the tea things and, as they were all settling at the table, Josephine saw her mother give Christian a concerned look. He answered with a faint smile but she knew the undercurrent of anger was still there.

No one was very hungry after the huge lunch they'd had, and after a few minutes Josephine said: 'I've got a headache, I think I'll go to bed.'

'You've been drinking too much,' said Lawrence. 'That's why your head aches. All that wine at lunch-time – and was it you who's been at Father's brandy?'

She nodded, pressing her forehead into the heel of her hand.

'Leave her alone,' said Christian. 'She's not a baby.'

'She's too young to be knocking it back like you.'

'She doesn't have that much,' said Solange anxiously.

Christian drained his glass and refilled it, looking at Lawrence with hostile eyes.

Josephine still sat at the table, rigid with the effort of holding back her tears.

'Make up your mind,' said Christian, banging his glass down. 'I thought you were going to bed.'

Louisa suddenly burst into tears and Josephine could bear it no longer but started crying herself.

'Go on then, go,' Christian shouted at her.

Lawrence jumped up. 'Stop shouting at her.'

Christian went to pick up the bottle again but it slipped from his hand and a river of dark red snaked across the cloth. Nella grabbed a serviette, then caught the bottle as it rolled towards the edge of the table.

He held out his hand but Nella kept hold of it. 'I don't think you ought to drink any more,' she said quietly. 'You're going to spoil Christmas.'

He snatched the bottle from her and tilted it to his lips.

'He already has,' muttered Lawrence.

Christian looked as though he was going to laugh, then he threw the bottle at Lawrence. Solange gave a little cry, but it bounced off Lawrence's shoulder and fell to the floor.

Josephine put her hands to her head. 'I hate you, I hate you,' she screamed, running to the door.

Christian was up immediately and caught hold of her. 'Shut up, you hysterical child,' he shouted at her.

'Take your hands off her, you bastard,' said Lawrence.

Christian swivelled round to look at him. 'What did you call me?'

'A no-good drunken bastard,' repeated Lawrence. 'I know how much of my mother's money you're getting through. And I know some other things which I shan't repeat in front of her.'

In one swift movement Christian had grabbed him by the front of his jumper and rammed him against the wall, his fist raised ready to hit him. Lawrence toppled sideways and fell on to the Christmas tree. The whole lot crashed to the floor, fairy lights and chocolate figures scattering everywhere. He scrambled up and went for Christian, but Solange had rushed to them, crying and begging them to stop.

Josephine was screaming, her hands over her face. She heard Louisa start screaming as well, and looked up to see her mother clinging to Lawrence, and Christian just standing there, his arms hanging by his sides as though he didn't know what was happening. Then all at once he stormed off, slamming the door so hard that more of the decorations fluttered down on to the floor.

Nella went and opened the door a fraction, then closed it again. 'I don't know where he is now,' she said. 'We'd better wait here until he calms down.' She turned to Lawrence and started to cry herself. 'Whatever would your father say?'

Lawrence took his mother's hands from his arm and held on to her wrists. 'I'll throw him out, Mother. Let me throw him out.' He swung round to the table and snatched up the knife they'd used to cut the cake.

Solange collapsed in a frenzy of renewed crying, begging him not to do anything, and in the end Lawrence shouted, 'All right, Mother, I won't retaliate, I'll put up with seeing you married to a no-good drunkard who attacks me for protecting my sister.' He paused for breath, angry tears streaming down his face, then slammed out himself.

There was complete silence for a moment, then they heard Lawrence run upstairs. A couple of minutes later Christian was in the doorway.

Solange picked up Louisa and went to sit over by the fire, her back to him.

He stood there breathing deeply. 'Just say the word, Solange, and I'll go. I'll go right now if you tell me to.'

Nobody spoke; only Louisa turned round to look at him, her face wet and sulky, her thumb in her mouth.

'Just say it,' he repeated.

Solange began to cry again, and he went over and put his arms round her and Louisa, burying his face in Solange's hair.

Josephine could hear that he was crying too and saying over and over that he was sorry. She pressed her knuckles against her mouth and ran from the room. Nella followed her, calling to her, but she ran off upstairs and locked herself in her bedroom. It was all her fault. Pain welled up in her until she felt her heart would burst open with it. How was she going to bear it in this house with him now?

Chapter 4

The following weeks were the most awful since her father's death.

Lawrence had gone, saying he wouldn't be back while Christian was still there, but within a few days her mother was acting as though nothing had happened. Josephine felt totally isolated, unable to look at her mother without being swamped with guilt and misery. Day after day she wandered off on long frozen walks or shut herself in her room. Christian hardly spoke to her; all his attention was concentrated on Solange and Louisa once more.

He made a special fuss for Solange's birthday in the middle of January, bringing her a beautiful negligee set of cream lace and a huge bouquet of flowers. And as they settled down to dinner he produced a bottle of champagne. Josephine knew he had curbed his drinking since Christmas – her mother was continually pointing this out to Nella – but after dinner he poured them all large glasses of the champagne. She was about to refuse it, leave the table once she'd finished her meal as she'd been doing every evening, but something about the look on his face as he leant across and kissed her mother to say happy birthday jarred against her frayed nerves. She emptied her glass in quick gulps, then refilled it without being asked.

'Not too much now,' said Christian.

Josephine looked at him defiantly and lifted her glass again.

'You heard me.' He looked uncomfortable but gave a little smile and added, 'You know it makes you act silly.'

'Oh, do you think so?' Her voice was high and strained and she saw her mother look anxiously across at him, but he just frowned as though to say, humour her, you know what she's like.

It felt as though they were united against her. 'Well, it doesn't make me violent and attack people for nothing,' she said, losing control of her voice as she spoke.

'Josephine, please . . .' Solange begun.

'You'd forgive him anything,' Josephine shouted before she could finish. 'Anything.'

Christian half rose from the table. 'Now stop this,' he said. 'Apologise to your mother.'

They stared at each other for a moment. His eyes darkened with the shadow of approaching anger but she no longer cared.

She gripped the stem of her glass. 'You apologise to her,' she said and flung the champagne in his face.

He lunged at her across the table. She jumped up, screaming at him to leave her alone, threw the glass at him as well, then fled and locked herself in her bedroom. Solange came up after her and then he was there telling her to calm down and it would all be forgotten. But she refused to open the door and the next day she went to Lawrence.

She arrived on his doorstep in a downpour of sleety rain. He had a girl installed there and she knew he didn't want her to stay but said she could sleep on his sofa for the night.

The girl was kind to her, taking her side when Lawrence went mad at her for hitchhiking most of the way.

'You can't expect her to stay at home if he's the ogre you make out he is,' the girl said.

Lawrence calmed down and went to phone their mother while the girl helped Josephine dry herself and lent her some clothes. Josephine said little more than that there had been a row, but she felt the girl guessed there was more to it than that.

'How old are you?' she asked.

'Sixteen next month – then I'm leaving home.'

'Where will you go?'

Josephine shrugged, tears suddenly near.

'You could get a living-in job as a nanny,' the girl said kindly. She lowered her voice so Lawrence wouldn't hear. 'Pretend you're eighteen. You're just the sort of girl professional people want to look after their kids. I did it for a while. They want well brought up, well-spoken girls. They don't worry so much about academic qualifications. And they like those from families with a few bob, so they don't have to pay too much,' she added with a laugh.

'What are you two plotting?' asked Lawrence coming back in.

'I was just saying to your sister, she could get a job as a nanny. If she went to London . . .'

'London! Can you honestly see her in London?'

'She'll be OK if she gets in with the right family.'

They sat and talked about it for a while and Josephine began to feel better. She'd never thought very much about her future before, always believing she would work with her father one day. But in the last half-hour Lawrence's girlfriend had opened up a whole new world of ideas and possibilities.

'I'd have to have a good look at the place first,' said Lawrence.

'You could write references for her,' said the girl.

'Tell lies you mean,' said Lawrence.

Josephine wrote her first job applications that evening. Once the idea was in her head, she couldn't wait to carry it out. Lawrence's girlfriend helped her, taking her out to buy magazines for the adverts and telling her how to word the letters. Lawrence left them to it but made one stipulation: she had to go home and explain it all to their mother.

'I'm not having her worried to death about you – she's got enough on her plate as it is.'

Josephine agreed and he took her home the next day, dropping her off at the front door because Christian was there.

She wrote a couple more applications, telling the same lies, that she was eighteen and that she'd worked in a nursery during the school holidays. It was the first time she'd ever lied to get what she wanted, but after Christmas Day lying seemed a minor sin.

Shortly before her sixteenth birthday in February, she received her first reply and a request to go to London for an interview.

Despite her promise to Lawrence, she still hadn't told her mother what she was intending to do. There was an uneasy truce in the house but little conversation between Josephine and her mother and none at all with Christian. She kept to her room, as she had done before, and told only Louisa about her secret plans, disguising them in stories.

★ ★ ★

On the day of the interview she spent an hour getting ready, changing her clothes three times and getting in a panic with her hair. Finally she crept into her mother's room and borrowed a bright red stretchy wool dress that fitted any size, tied her hair back in a ponytail and put on long silver earrings.

'Take the earrings off, Phina,' said Lawrence when he came to pick her up. 'You're going to be a nanny not a model.'

She nearly changed her mind there and then, but he bustled her into the car, saying he hadn't come all this way for her to have second thoughts. A couple of hours later, when they pulled up at the end house of a Victorian terrace in north-west London, she was so nervous that she was shaking.

'It doesn't look all that big,' said Lawrence. 'Not for someone who's paying to have their child looked after.'

She'd hardly got out of the car when a man came down the path to meet her.

'You must be Miss Jarrouse,' he said, putting out a hand. 'I'm Ross.'

The advert had read: 'Wanted – live-in help to look after six-year-old girl. Must be patient, kind and fit as Tessa is very lively. Would suit student or similar as plenty of free time including weekends.' She knew from his letter that he was thirty-four and ran his own building business and that his wife had died six years ago, but the picture she'd formed of him had been of someone older, smart and well spoken. Ross Challenor didn't look much older that Christian, wore dirty jeans and had rough hands and a London accent.

'Is that your brother?' he asked, pointing to the car.

'Yes. He's going to collect me later.'

'Tell him to come in.' He smiled. 'Set his mind at rest.' Before she could answer, he was beckoning to Lawrence.

'Like your car,' he said, looking towards Lawrence's Porsche. 'What do you do?'

'I'm at university,' said Lawrence stiffly.

They followed him round the back of the house, through a yard with all kinds of building materials and a lorry and Range Rover parked side by side.

'I'll tell you what's what as we go,' he said, stopping for a moment. 'Do you mind if I call you Josephine?'

'No,' she said, beginning to feel a bit more at ease, though she could see Lawrence was looking down his nose at the place. On the way there he'd said to her, 'I'm not so sure about all this now. It's like being a servant.'

They came first to a large conservatory, one end obviously used as an office, with filing cabinets and drawing boards.

'That's the trouble with working from home,' said Ross. 'It takes over. I restore old buildings,' he added as Lawrence peered at one of the drawings. 'I do all the plans and quants as well as getting out on site.'

Lawrence raised his eyebrows slightly but said nothing. Josephine wished he'd be more friendly.

They went next into a huge kitchen extension. Everywhere looked clean, if a bit untidy.

'It's much bigger than it looks from the front,' said Josephine, trying to make conversation.

'At the expense of the garden I'm afraid,' said Ross. 'Have you got much garden?'

'Two acres,' said Lawrence.

'I thought you might have,' said Ross, smiling.

He led them into a long hall, stopping at the first of two downstairs rooms.

'I'm moving in down here,' he said. 'You – or whoever gets the job, will have their own bedsitter upstairs next to Tessa. And the bathroom up there would be yours. Come and have a look.' He led them upstairs and showed them two spacious, well-decorated rooms, one obviously his daughter's bedroom, the other complete with sofa and television, and another smaller room strewn with toys.

'The situation is this,' he said. 'I have a girlfriend. We go out a lot, she comes to stay, I go and stay with her. And I want to keep this part of my life separate from Tessa at the moment. I don't want her disturbed if I come in late. Do you know what I mean?'

Josephine saw Lawrence pull a face but she nodded and said, 'Yes.'

He took them back downstairs. 'Come and have something to eat while we wait for Tessa,' he said.

Lawrence refused, saying he was meeting someone and that he'd come back later.

Alone with him, Josephine was seized with shyness, but he talked away about his daughter while he took bowls of salad from the fridge and chicken pieces from the oven.

'Wine or lager?' he asked. 'Or would you rather have coffee?'

She asked for wine. It was cool and slightly sweet and she

sipped it quickly, seeking the confidence alcohol brought her.

'I've got a woman who comes in to clean for me. She did all this,' he said, waving a hand towards the plates. 'She usually does the vegetables for me in the morning and I cook stuff like sausages for Tessa and me.'

'I could do that.'

He looked up surprised, then smiled. He had the kind of face which always seemed on the verge of smiling. 'So you can cook, can you?'

'Yes, I like cooking.'

'Even on the wages I'm paying?'

'Yes, I wouldn't mind. The wages sound fine to me.' She smiled back at him. 'Considering my income is exactly nil at the moment.'

They sat at the table after they'd finished eating and he told her more about Tessa, topping up her glass as he did so. He explained how his parents had helped look after her up until recently but that his father was ill and they couldn't manage so much now.

'Someone brings her home from school at the moment but that would be part of the job. Do you drive?'

'No, I don't.' She was glad Lawrence had gone. 'I'm going to learn though. My brother's going to teach me and I expect I'll get a car when . . .' She broke off, remembering again she was supposed to be eighteen.

'It doesn't matter: the school's not far and all the other things she goes to are quite near. She goes to brownies and ballet, so you'd have to take and collect her. You'd just have to see her to school in the mornings, then you'd be free until you collected her. I look after her at the weekends or she goes to my parents.'

He looked at his watch.

'She'll be in shortly. What do you think then?'

'I would like the job.' She wasn't sure whether she should sound eager or not.

He leant his elbows on the table and tapped his fingertips together, looking straight at her. 'I have to be honest. I do have a couple of reservations about you.'

Her heart sank.

'I had in mind someone who'd be studying – you know, head down with their books in the evening. I don't want someone who'll be wanting to go out all the time.'

'Oh, I wouldn't,' she said quickly. 'I never go out.'

'Weekends would be OK – but I wouldn't want any blokes coming back here.' He smiled. 'Or any lovelorn boys coming down from Norfolk.'

'I don't have a boyfriend.'

'What's the matter with them up there?' he laughed.

She felt herself start to blush and pretended to be brushing something from her dress.

He stared at her for a moment. 'What sort of name's Jarrouse?'

'French,' she said, glad the subject was changed.

'Is your father French?'

'My grandfather was.'

'Can you speak it?'

'Yes,' she nodded. 'I could teach your daughter.' She thought he looked interested. 'I could teach her how to cook as well – I'm quite good at it.'

The interested look turned into laughter. 'French, cookery! She's only six.'

She felt herself blushing again, sure she'd said the wrong thing, but he just looked amused, then stood up listening as a car pulled up outside.

'I'll be quite happy if she just picks up a bit of your accent,' he said, smiling over his shoulder as he went to the back door.

As he pulled the door open, a small girl rushed in. He hoisted her up in his arms. She had the same soft brown curls as him, but her face was tiny and pinched, almost pixie-like, whereas his was broad and healthy-looking.

She was shy at first, then asked Josephine if she had a pony.

'I read her your letter,' said Ross.

'Oh,' said Josephine remembering that she'd listed her hobbies as walking, riding and reading. 'I used to have one,' she said.

'Have you got a cat?'

'Yes, we've got lots.'

Tessa looked intrigued and came over to her, asking question after question, especially interested to hear about all the kittens at Waylands.

'That's enough questions, Tess,' said Ross, looking at his watch. 'Josephine has to go home in a minute.'

'Can I come and see your kittens?' persisted Tessa.

'You could have one if you like.'

'Yes!' she said excitedly, clapping her hands.

49

Ross came and swept her up, cuddling her and nuzzling her curls.

'You've done it now,' he said, grinning at Josephine over the top of her head. 'I hope you're going to supply the cat food as well.'

On the way home, she said to Lawrence: 'Do you still miss Dad?'

'Of course I do. What made you say that?'

She shrugged. 'He had the same hair as Dad. It just made me think of him.' She put a hand to her throat, feeling for the locket with her father's picture and flicked it open to have a look.

Ross had told her he'd got some other girls to see and he'd phone her at the end of the week. Two days after the trip to London, he phoned and said the job was hers if she still wanted it.

'I think you bribed my daughter with the kitten,' he said, then added, more seriously, 'Tessa means everything to me. I want someone I can trust and I feel that you've been brought up with all the right values – that's not very common these days.'

The time had come to tell her mother.

'You're not going,' Solange said when she was halfway through explaining. 'I'm not having you living in a house with a single man, not at your age.'

'Mother, he's got a girlfriend,' said Josephine. 'And anyway I'm upstairs with his daughter.'

'It makes no difference,' said Solange. 'It's not right.'

Christian stood there listening but said nothing. Josephine looked from one to the other of them, burst into tears and walked out, going to Lawrence once more.

He brought her straight back home, marched her indoors and told Solange that she was going and that was that.

'It's a lot less risky than her hitchhiking to me every time your husband upsets her,' he said.

Solange cried and Lawrence paced about the room as though he wanted to tear his hair out. 'I'm fed up with all this. I've got my finals this year; how can I study with all this going on?'

'I wish Josephine was at school studying,' Solange sniffed.

'Well she's not and she's never likely to be after all the nonsense Father filled . . .' His voice faded away, then he sat with his mother and took her hand. 'Don't worry, I'll keep an eye on her. It's about time she did something with her life anyway.'

Josephine sat in her usual place in the hearth, hating all the fuss, hating to see her mother crying again, and on edge in case Christian came back from wherever he'd disappeared to. But when she heard her mother begin to discuss it calmly with Lawrence and ask about Ross Challenor and what the house was like, she wondered whether she really wanted to go after all.

And later that evening, after she'd gone to bed, her mother came up and sat with her, tried to tell her about things she should have talked about long ago. But Josephine found it embarrassing and painful; the secret of Christmas Day stood like an invisible barrier between them.

'Don't worry about me,' she said, forcing a smile. 'I'm not stupid.'

'But you're very attractive and you have no experience of men – that's what worries me. They're not all as wonderful as your father, you know.'

'I know that,' she murmured, rolling the hem of her night-dress between her fingers.

The fox came again that week, attracted by the scraps that Nella had thrown on the roof of the back porch for the birds. When Josephine went to pull up the bottom sash of the window as she did every night, he was standing on his hindquarters against the wall of the house. Leaning out over the sill, she felt as though she could almost touch him, just a few inches and she could run her fingers through his dark red fur. It seemed a marvellous thing to happen on her last night at home, a parting gift. She woke Louisa and when they went and looked from the window together, the fox had somehow got onto the porch roof and was eating the scraps of food. He paid no attention, even to Louisa's loud whispers; he munched away, as dainty and relaxed as if he were the only creature in the world. Then, with a great yawn and a long tongue flicking out to wipe round his muzzle, he leapt to the ground, shook himself, and padded off across the lawn, just as he had done on Christmas Eve.

'Is he really a goblin?' said Louisa, her eyes wide, the curtains held protectively across her face.

'Yes,' whispered Josephine. 'I think he is.' It was a cruel thing to say to Louisa, who would have to spend her nights alone from tomorrow, but she felt driven by a longing to grasp at childhood memories, knowing that everything was about to change.

PART 2

Dancing with the Magician

O body swayed to music, O brightening glance,
How can we know the dancer from the dance?

W.B. Yeats

Chapter 5

She left in tears, because both her mother and Louisa cried and her first night away she cried herself to sleep with homesickness.

But during the next couple of weeks there were times when she felt happier than she had for a long while. In fact it was difficult not to feel happy in that house: the big sunny conservatory where an assortment of people were always coming and going, the kitchen where Betty the cleaning lady sat with her every morning asking her questions about her family over a cup of coffee, and upstairs her pretty room where she could retreat whenever she liked.

The homesickness faded; so did the pain of Christmas Day. She threw herself into looking after Tessa, burying all that had happened under the layers of happy days that made up her new life.

Tessa was an affectionate, biddable child, a bit whiny at times, but easy to coax out of any bad temper and a lot less spoilt than Louisa. Josephine had brought the promised kitten with her, sealed in a cardboard box on the back seat of Lawrence's car. It had mewed loudly all the way there, but Tessa had been delighted with it and it had broken the ice in those first uncertain moments of Josephine's arrival.

Ross worked long hours but went out of his way to make her feel at home when he was there. And he never lost patience over the numerous mistakes she made as she struggled to understand so much that was alien to her.

He seemed concerned that she had nothing to do but hang around the house when Tessa was at school and, despite his remarks at her interview, he asked her if she would like to go out with his sister one evening.

'She's a bit older than you but she knows everyone round here. You might be able to make some friends. I don't want you getting lonely and going off back home,' he added.

She wasn't particularly keen on the idea. She hadn't met Miran, but had heard his mother moaning fondly about her and had got the impression she was one of those extroverted people who always made her feel so stupid. And when Miran bounced into the house on Saturday evening in a mini-skirt and halter-necked top, announced the kitchen smelt of cats, then told Ross he looked a mess and it was about time he got a haircut, Josephine's heart sank.

Ross seemed quite unperturbed, treating her in the same easy affectionate way he did Tessa.

'Where's this party then?' he asked her.

'The Rising Sun.' Miran sat on the kitchen table swinging her legs. 'Well, go and get ready then,' she said to Josephine. 'We don't want to be too late, it gets crowded in there.'

'I am ready,' said Josephine, feeling her heart sink even lower. She had put on a pale blue velvet dress that her father had brought back from France for her mother. It had long tight sleeves and tiny pearl buttons all the way down the front and he had always said how it suited her.

'Oh . . .' Miran paused for just a second, then smiled and added quickly, 'It gets very hot in there – that's all I was thinking.'

Josephine saw Ross raise his eyes briefly to the ceiling. 'She looks very nice,' he said. 'Not everyone wants to go out showing their arse like you, Miran.'

Miran laughed, then turned her attention back to Josephine. 'Well, let me do your hair,' she said, kindly. 'Did you know I'm a hairdresser?' She jumped from the table and pulled out a chair and told her to sit down.

Tessa came to see what they were doing but Ross tutted, shook his head and walked off.

'Don't take any notice of him,' laughed Miran. 'Now then,' she put a hand each side of Josephine's head. 'What can we do with this?'

'What the hell are you doing to her?' said Ross, coming back into the room.

'Just giving her a trim,' said Miran brightly, tossing a hank of Josephine's hair at least ten inches long into the bin.

'Don't let her bully you, Josephine,' he said.

'It's all right, I don't mind.' Over the past ten minutes Josephine had decided she liked Miran after all. Underneath the bubbly exterior she had the same kind way of speaking and same easy-going manner as her brother. She also looked like him with her deep brown eyes, ready smile and curly brown hair, though hers was highlighted with blonde streaks.

'Come and look at yourself in the mirror,' Miran commanded, leading her through to the hall and switching on the light.

Josephine ran her hands through her newly cut hair. It was still quite long but looked very different, floating round her shoulders in a soft dark cloud. She fanned out her fringe which Miran had also cut, thinning it out into spiky fronds.

'Go and get my make-up bag, Tess,' said Miran.

When Tessa came running back with it, she took out a brush and stroked blusher on to Josephine's cheeks, then put a smear of blue shadow on her lids.

'That'll do,' she said. 'Don't you normally wear make-up?'

'Sometimes.' Josephine didn't want to admit that she never did.

'Well, you don't need much with your colouring.' She smiled over Josephine's shoulder, then gave Tessa a little push. 'Go and tell your dad we're late and we need a lift.'

The Rising Sun was so packed they could hardly get in the door.

'It's a private party really,' said Miran as she led the way, squeezing past the swell of people at the bar and waving to a group of girls at a corner table. 'They hold a lot of them in here.' She pointed to a curtained archway where the beat of music throbbed away in the darkened interior. 'It's all the theatre people – actors and dancers and everyone.'

Seated at the table with Miran and her friends, Josephine looked round. The Rising Sun was all polished mahogany, midnight blue velvet and tasselled light-shades. The walls were covered with large black and white posters of ballerinas and sad-eyed clowns, with here and there signed photographs of film stars from a previous era. Some of it was a bit shabby: the light-shades were stained with smoke and the arms of the leather-covered benches worn down to the wood, but it all seemed to add to the atmosphere.

'How are you settling in with Ross then?' Miran asked her.

'I really like it there,' said Josephine. 'I'm on a month's trial so I hope he thinks I'm all right.'

'Oh he will, don't worry. Ross is a darling. He can be a bit of an old woman at times, but it takes a lot to upset him. Mum and Dad like you.'

'I like them as well.'

'What about Cheryl?'

Josephine shrugged, not wanting to say that Ross's girlfriend was the one she liked least and the only one she'd clashed with. It was only a few days after she'd arrived. Ross's parents had brought sweets for Tessa but he said she wasn't allowed to have them until after her dinner. She'd cried, and later, when they were on their own, Josephine had let her have one, making her cross her heart and cut her throat that she'd eat all her meal. Tessa had thought the cut my throat bit was funny, and had repeated it to Cheryl and told her about the sweet. Cheryl had immediately taken Josephine aside and told her in no uncertain terms that she wasn't to go behind Ross's back spoiling Tessa.

'You have to get to know her,' Miran said. 'Nurses are often a bit sharp. Probably all the death and illness they see – everything else seems trivial.'

Music had suddenly started to come from an overhead speaker, and Miran raised her voice above it.

'I think Ross might marry her, though I don't think she's the right one for him. She's very career minded, and all he wants is a house full of kids and somebody to look after him.' She put her hands to her ears and shouted across the table to one of her friends.

'Shall we try and get in there in a minute?'

'Wait until that lot at the bar go in,' her friend shouted back. 'They're probably waiting for the food, then they'll all try and get in at once.'

'We're quite skilled at this,' said Miran, turning back to Josephine. 'It's worth it though.' She smiled and clicked her fingers, jigging to the music. 'There're some tasty guys among that lot.'

Josephine looked automatically towards the bar where people stood in little groups. Some were in evening dress, some quite casual and others looking as though they were about to go on stage. But they all seemed to share a similar aura, something vibrant and colourful which lifted them above the ordinary. She felt excited and happy, drunk on the atmosphere and the vodka which Miran had bought for her.

Her eyes travelled along to a group at the end of the bar. They were young, about her age: three girls and a boy. Beside them a man about twenty-five or so leant on the bar talking to them. Out of all that bright crowd, he was the most striking. He had hair the colour of deep red wine cut in layers down to his shoulders, flawless cream skin and narrow slanting eyes. He wore tight jeans and a black leather jacket adorned with brilliant gold studs. One of the girls in the group said something to him and he smiled, his eyes almost disappearing beneath long dark lashes, then he moved slightly away and took off the jacket. Josephine saw that his left arm was bound with leather straps from shoulder to wrist. She watched, fascinated, as the girl took the jacket from him. One of Miran's friends was asking if she smoked and she swivelled round briefly to say no thanks, then turned straight back, unable to take her eyes off him.

'You're wasting your time looking at him,' said Miran.

She jerked back round again, smiling self-consciously. 'I wasn't, I was just . . .'

'Oh, don't worry, all the girls look at him,' said Miran. 'But he's in love with himself.'

'Stare at his picture instead,' said one of her friends, pointing to the wall.

Josephine glanced round. Above what looked like an advertising poster for a ballet were a row of coloured photographs. They were all of him in different dance sequences, some with other dancers, a couple on his own.

'Is he a dancer?' she asked.

'Was,' said Miran. 'He had a motorbike accident.'

'Do you know him then?'

'I know *of* him. They call him the "Magician".'

'The Magician?'

'Yes, it's to do with some show he was in, he . . .' She broke off and gathered up her coat and bag. 'Come on, they're moving. We'll try and slip in.' Miran grabbed her arm and steered her towards the archway. There was a surge of people going into the room now and they drifted along with the crowd.

'See,' said Miran as soon as they were through. 'It's easy

when you know how. You just wait until they get a whiff of food.'

The party was in full swing. Coloured lights flashed across the room, catching faces and drifts of smokes in its long beams. Waiters ferried in plates of food, dodging between groups of people talking and couples dancing, while the music throbbed away, drowning out all other sound.

She followed Miran to a long table where they loaded up plates, although she'd eaten earlier and wasn't very hungry. The atmosphere in here was heady, and she leant against the table and watched Miran and one of her friends laughing with two men. One of them was telling her a joke. It sounded very crude and he kept leaning forward to whisper parts of it in her ear. Once Miran looked round to see where she was and mouthed, 'All right?' at her. She smiled and nodded but was beginning to feel distinctly not all right.

Miran was led away to dance. A man came up and asked her but she refused, suddenly feeling very sick and unsure of herself and burning hot in the velvet dress. She went to the ladies, splashed cold water over her face and stared at herself in the mirror, surprised at the girl who smiled back at her with such huge sparkling eyes and different hair. No more to drink, she said aloud.

Miran was still dancing when she went back in. It was hotter than ever and she walked to the far side of the room and sat on some steps below the stage, where the draught from a fire door blew pleasantly cool across her face.

People were still coming in through the archway and she saw the group of youngsters who'd been at the bar. She straightened up a little to get a better view. The man with red hair was a few paces behind them and, as they came through the crowd of dancers, she saw that he walked with a bad limp and that he held his left arm awkwardly across his chest.

He came to lean against the stage only a few feet away from her, while the others went off to the table, coming back with plates of food. They offered him some but he shook his head, and then one of the girls went off and came back with a drink for him. It was tall and fizzing and Josephine watched him drink, saw the movements in his throat as he swallowed each mouthful.

After a while, the youngsters drifted off to dance. She watched them now, fascinated by the way they moved and the way they always stayed close together, even if they were dancing with someone else. When she looked back at the man, a woman was rushing up to him, her arms held wide.

She was old, her face deeply lined, but still very beautiful and immaculately made-up. She wore a strapless evening dress and a choker of black velvet.

He bent to kiss her, first one cheek then the other.

'Where have you been?' she said, her voice mockingly stern and strongly accented. 'Nobody has seen you.'

'I've been busy,' he said. 'I've bought a house.'

'I know. I heard you got your money at last.' Her face became serious. 'I hear a lot about you.' She paused and lowered her voice. 'Not all good, Nicky.'

He looked into the woman's eyes and smiled and she put a hand on his strapped-up arm. 'I worry about you,' she said. 'It's not good to do these disappearing acts.' She slipped both arms round his waist now. 'Come and say hello to my new husband. He manages the group that are playing here tonight.' She gave a little laugh. 'They are entirely disgusting but I'm sure you'll like them.'

As they turned the woman looked towards the steps and noticed her.

'Oh, is this your new pupil?'

He looked puzzled, then turned to look at her as well. 'Not that I know of,' he said, his face breaking into a smile once more.

The woman caught Josephine's arm and gave a little laugh. 'So sorry, my dear. But you were looking at him with such adoring eyes, I thought . . .'

'Was she now?' he said.

Josephine thought she would die of embarrassment.

'And Alice said she was small and dark,' the woman went on.

'She's dancing with the others,' he said, his eyes still fixed on Josephine.

'You must introduce me later. Now then, come along. I want you back in circulation, new house or not.'

As they passed her, he stopped and bent his head down to her and said softly: 'You'll get a stiff neck sitting in that draught.'

She gave a tiny smile but didn't look up until he was walking away. Despite the limp he held himself very upright, and with the cascading layers of bright hair, he appeared quite tall, though she guessed he was no more than five foot eight or nine.

A spotlight came on, people clapped and then started to sing happy birthday. Across the room she could see a woman cutting a cake. Champagne sprayed into the air amidst cheers and laughter and, above her, she heard the noise of footsteps thumping around on the stage. Suddenly the steps were vibrating with the sound of loud music, the drum-beat deafening in her ears. The floor became jammed with people dancing, a hypnotising whirl of movement and colour. After a few minutes the music changed to a slow ballad, and limbs that had been moving wildly found their way round necks and shoulders as couples entwined. She folded her arms tightly across her chest and imagined that he came and asked her to dance and she wasn't wearing the velvet dress but something sexy and alluring like Miran.

'Wakey, wakey.' Miran was standing in front of her. 'Come on, we're going back to the bar.'

Miran's crowd of friends seemed to have grown; some men had joined them and they were in high spirits, creating a small party of their own. Someone brought her more drink and she found herself joining in their talk and laughter.

'He's back, Josephine,' said Miran, nudging her and nodding towards the door. 'She fancies that guy they call the Magician,' she said to the man beside her.

'Shut up,' said Josephine.

'What, Nicky Frey?' said the man, leaning across to her. 'I don't blame you, love. He's just had a big insurance pay-off. I could almost fancy him myself.' He laughed and swivelled round and called out; 'Nicky, here a minute. I've got a young lady wants to meet you.'

'I don't,' she hissed. 'Stop it.' But in the drunken atmosphere, with the dimmed lights and deafening music, she forgot her shyness, and when he came across to see what was going on, she found herself smiling at him.

He perched on the edge of the table.

'Not you again,' he said teasingly.

'She's from the backwoods of Norfolk,' laughed Miran. 'She doesn't know how dangerous it is to chase after strange men.'

'I'm not chasing after anyone,' said Josephine, trying to imitate the same lighthearted tone.

'What a shame,' he said. 'I wouldn't mind being chased by you.'

Miran raised her eyebrows. 'There's an offer for you, Josephine.'

She laughed because she couldn't think of anything to say and he reached across and took her hand. 'Come and have a drink with me,' he said.

Miran's face changed slightly. 'She has to come home with me. She's not used to London.'

'I'm not abducting her,' he said. 'Though I'd like to.'

Josephine laughed again. Even through the haze of intoxication she guessed that he always talked like this.

He took her to another table and bought her more vodka and she decided it was the best evening she'd ever had in her whole life. When he asked her how old she was, she added another year to the lie she'd already told Ross and said she was nineteen.

She was sure he liked her. He didn't say a lot but kept smiling at the things she said, which came more easily after each drink. And he'd taken her hand, holding it between his own and running a finger gently round her palm. She drained her glass once more and looked at him.

'You've got gold eyes,' she said. 'I've never seen anyone with gold eyes before.'

Nicky took the glass from her. 'I think you've had enough.'

She nodded; her head was spinning and she had an overwhelming desire to let it drop on the table. 'I feel sick,' she said, leaning back against the seat.

He stood up. 'I'll take you out in the fresh air. Stay where you are and I'll go and get your coat.'

The seat felt as though it were swaying in time to the music. She spread her hands to steady herself and closed her eyes. When she opened them, Miran was looking down at her.

'I'll take her to the Ladies.'

'I want to go outside,' she murmured, worried that he might disappear if she went off with Miran. 'It's so smoky in here.'

'Give me her coat,' she heard him say.

'I'm responsible for her.' Miran sounded a bit annoyed.

'So what?'

'I don't want her going off with you.'

'I'm not a monster,' he said. He sat down with her and put an arm round her shoulders. 'Who do you want to go with?' he asked.

'With you,' she said, letting her head fall against him.

Outside, the frosty air hit Josephine like a slap in the face. It blew away the sickness and sharpened her wits but still left her pleasantly uninhibited.

'I think I've had too much to drink,' she said as if it had just occurred to her.

'You were drinking too quickly. It'll wear off.' Nicky put his arm round her shoulders, tucking his hand under the warm collar of her coat. 'Are you really nineteen?'

She chewed her lip, trying to think what she'd been saying and wondering if she'd made a complete fool of herself. 'No, eighteen,' she said finally. 'I didn't realise what I was saying.'

'You don't sound too sure now,' he laughed. 'Come on, we'll walk to my house. That'll sober you up.'

'To your house?' She stopped. 'How far is it?'

'Not far. Don't you want to?'

'Yes, yes I do,' she said quickly. 'I like walking.' She glanced up at him, wondering why he seemed to smile at everything she said.

Within a few minutes, she had no idea where they were. They had turned off the main road, leaving behind the noise of traffic and the lights from shop windows and were now in a quiet residential street with trees between the lamp-posts and tall three- and four-storey houses on either side.

She was quite a fast walker and he kept pace with her despite his limp, but she noticed that now and again he put a hand to his thigh as though it troubled him. When he suddenly stopped and leant against a long brick wall she thought there was something wrong until he said: 'Here we are. My fortress.'

The wall was high and she looked towards its top, but could see only a tangle of overhanging branches and beyond them the spire of a church, pointing up into the frosty sky like the tip of a sharpened pencil.

He took her by the shoulders and held her in front of a wrought-iron gate. The bottom was shaped like a shield, the top a complicated pattern of black bars. She peered between them but couldn't see much because the moon, although full and bright, was behind the house, and the front garden lay in deep shadow.

There was a large padlock on the gate and he touched his

hand to it. 'We can't get in. I haven't got the key with me. I haven't moved in yet and I have to keep it well locked up. I've got some expensive equipment in there.' He gave her shoulders a little squeeze. 'Unless you want to climb over.'

She thought he was joking, but he walked to the end of the wall where it joined the fence of a neighbouring strip of wasteground. With a little spring, he was on the fence, then heaved himself on to the top of the wall with his good arm and sat there smiling down at her.

It was very quiet and, for a moment, looking up at him, she felt caught in one of those dream sequences which can seem so real even after waking. She shivered and placed both hands on the wall, feeling almost drunk again, and nearly leapt out of her skin when the church clock began to strike the hour. The sound echoed around them, smashing the silence.

He laughed and reached down to haul her up beside him, then lifted her down the other side as though she were no weight at all.

Now the house was in full view. It rose three storeys, a narrow white house with long windows whose tops arched like those in a church. It had a sad, neglected air, the walls stained and some of the windows boarded up. But the carved stone fillet at the eaves and the crazy zig-zag of an old fire escape that wound up the side gave it a strange charm.

'It's beautiful – and sort of frightening,' she said. 'Is it really yours?'

'Yes.' He sounded surprised. 'Don't you believe me?'

'You look too young to have a house like that.'

'It's nothing to do with age, it's to do with cash. My accountant says it's a heap that will eat up all my money.' His voice grew quieter. 'But I wanted it. It's perfect for what I want.'

'It suits you,' she said.

He laughed and turned to face her. 'Am I beautiful and frightening then?'

She shrugged and smiled, not sure how to answer, wanting to tell him that, yes, she did think he was beautiful, and that the only thing that frightened her was that this night would soon be over.

'You're beautiful,' he said, suddenly hugging her and lifting her off the ground with one arm. 'You're beautiful and funny and I don't want to take you back to your friend.'

'We don't have to go back yet – she'll wait for me.'

'You're going back. You've had too much to drink, you've lied about your age and it's freezing.'

But he led her to the fire escape and sat down on one of the cold metal steps, pulling her down on the one below. She sat there between his legs and leant her head back against his chest and he wrapped his arms round her.

Almost at once he said: 'We'd better go back.'

She didn't move and he leant forward and kissed her on the cheek and she thought back to Christmas Day and wished he would kiss her like Christian had. She swivelled round to face him and put her arms round his neck. There were security lights dotted round the walls and she saw him smile and shake his head. Then he was kissing her, his mouth open, his hands tangled in her hair. She tightened her arms round him. The clock struck again; just one heavy note but again it made her jump.

She felt him shiver and reach up to take her wrists. He held her away from him and touched his forehead to hers.

'You don't want your friend going home without you, do you?'

'I don't care.'

He sighed and took her hand and pushed it under his leather jacket and under his T-shirt.

'Can you feel that?' he said.

'What? Your heart?'

He pressed her hand more tightly against his chest so her fingers were splayed out against his skin. 'Yes, it's pounding. That's what you've done to me.'

She could feel nothing except the smoothness of his skin and guessed that he was teasing her, but it didn't seem to matter and she went to put her arms round his neck once more.

'Come on,' he laughed, holding her away again and resting his arms on her shoulders. As he moved, a stud on his jacket caught the chain of her gold locket and it snapped. He grabbed it as it fell and held it towards one of the lights.

'Who's this?' he asked, opening the case.

'My father.'

He held it nearer the light to study it, then looked at her.

'Where do you get all that beautiful black hair from then?'

Josephine smiled. 'My mother.'

He looked at it once more, snapped it shut and slipped it in his pocket.

'You can't keep it,' she laughed, reaching for it. 'It's valuable.'

Nicky caught her wrist. 'I'll get the chain mended for you. You can come and see me when I move in here next week and I'll give it back to you then.'

When she didn't reply, he shook her arm. 'Will you?'

She nodded and he laughed aloud.

'What's funny?' she said, smiling at him.

'You,' he said, standing up and pulling her with him. 'I don't usually have to ask girls twice.'

It was more difficult to get back over the wall from this side, and he had to climb on the branch of a tree to get on to it.

'I think I'll leave you in here,' he said, sitting astride the branch. 'You can be my prisoner.'

'I'll get over the gate.'

'You won't, it's got spikes across the top.'

She went to reach for the branch but it was too high for her.

'Stop it,' she said suddenly, looking back over her shoulder at the house with its sinister boarded windows and the fire escape caught in a shaft of ghostly moonlight.

He pretended to jump over the wall and she gave a scream of fear mixed with laughter.

'Coward,' he smiled and reached down for her.

She clambered up beside him, grabbing his arm to steady herself, and felt the buckles of the straps through his sleeve. She'd noticed he never straightened it, but it still seemed to have great strength.

'I really like your house,' she said, fingering his sleeve.

'And what about me?'

'And you,' she smiled.

On the walk back he was very quiet, and she looked up at him a couple of times and told herself he probably had hundreds of girlfriends, that this evening meant nothing to him and he would have forgotten her by tomorrow. The nearer they came to the Rising Sun, the more downcast she felt.

People were drifting out on to the pavement now. He was holding her hand but loosened his grip as he stopped to talk to someone. Miran came out with a couple of her friends and called to her.

He was still talking and she slid her hand from his, sure he would hardly notice, but he swung round and caught hold of her again.

'You will come and see me, won't you?' he said, his narrow eyes stretched wide.

She nodded; Miran tugged her away, and he was lost in the crowd.

'Where the hell have you been?' said Miran. 'We've been waiting to go.'

'We just walked to his house and back.'

Miran looked at her sideways. 'I think there's more to you than meets the eye. Still, as long as you've sobered up a bit.'

'Yes I have.'

But back indoors, she felt a little thrill of intoxication again. She would have to go and get her locket; it was too precious to her not to get it back.

She was about to go upstairs when Ross called through from the kitchen. He was making coffee, dressed only in jeans, his hair tousled, his eyes heavy-lidded and a sheen of sweat across his shoulders.

'Have you had a good time?' he asked.

She knew Cheryl was there; she'd heard her cough as she came past his bedroom and the urge to smile and say, yes thanks, have you? rose to her lips. She bit back the words but had no control over her smile.

'It was good,' she said. 'I really enjoyed myself.'

He raised his eyebrows slightly. 'You look as though you did.'

The next morning she had a splitting headache and was embarrassed to find Ross still there when she brought Tessa down to breakfast. Parts of the evening were a blur in her memory and she couldn't remember exactly what she'd said to him last night. She was only glad that Cheryl had gone.

'You're looking a bit subdued,' he said, leaning on the sink as he finished a cup of tea. 'Bit different from last night.'

'Am I?' she muttered.

He laughed and drained the cup. 'I'll get all the details from Miran,' he said winking at her as he left.

But they didn't see Miran for nearly two weeks.

'She's got a new bloke,' Ross said. 'We won't see hide nor hair of her until the novelty's worn off.'

She finally showed up one evening on her way from work. Cheryl was there and they were all in the kitchen eating a Chinese takeaway that Ross had brought in with him.

Miran came singing through the back door and straight up

to Josephine, putting an arm round her neck from behind and whispering, 'Well? Any developments?'

Josephine shook her head and tried to laugh it off. Hardly an hour had gone by when she hadn't thought about him, cursing herself for not having the courage to go back to his house and then deciding that it was out of the question; he was sure to have forgotten her and it would all be too embarrassing.

Miran gave her ponytail a little tug. 'Never mind. We'll soon find you someone else. I've had people ask about you.'

Ross looked up. 'What are you up to now?' he said.

Miran went and perched on the table beside him. 'Nothing to do with you. I've come to see Phina.' They all called her that now. 'Do you want to come to a hen party with me tomorrow night?' she said, stretching across the table towards Josephine.

'I wouldn't know anybody . . .'

'Miran, do you have to sit on the table when we're eating?' Cheryl interrupted.

'What's up! I've got clean knickers on.'

Josephine laughed and Cheryl glared at her and stood up, starting to gather up the empty foil cartons.

'I have to be here on Friday nights anyway,' Josephine said.

'Ross won't mind.' Miran leant over and hooked an arm round his neck. 'Will you?' she said, making kissing noises at him.

'No, we're not going out,' he said. 'But what is this party?' He eyed Miran. 'Make sure Josephine knows what she's letting herself in for.'

'It's just a friend who's getting married. Drinks and nothing else. She's made us all swear no kissograms, no male strippers.' She laughed. 'But we have planned a little surprise for her. Anyway,' she added, 'we're going down the Rising Sun: they don't allow things like that.'

'Not much they don't,' said Ross. He smiled across at Josephine. 'Still, you enjoyed yourself there last time, didn't you? Go on, go with her.'

'All right,' she said, getting up to help Cheryl because she could feel her cheeks growing hot.

Miran had told her not to dress up and that she'd probably wear jeans, but the only jeans that Josephine had brought with her were stained and worn from walking and gardening. She spent all day Friday worrying what to wear, veering from sheer excitement at the thought that she might see Nicky Frey again, and then sunk into the depths of gloom thinking he might not even notice her.

The agreement with Ross had been that he would pay her in cash at the end of her first month and then they'd have a chat to see how it had gone. Midday he came back to the house and gave her an envelope with the money in, saying he had to rush off to take his men's wages round. She counted it out; the first money she'd ever earned in her life and the only time she hadn't had to ask someone for what she needed. After picking up Tessa from school, she went along to a little boutique that she'd passed on her way shopping, often stopping to look in the window.

She tried on numerous things while Tessa dived in and out of the changing cubicle. Finally she settled on new jeans, and a white lacy top similar to the one the assistant had on. While she was paying for them, Tessa wandered off to a rail of children's clothes and put on an embroidered waistcoat with long beaded tassels.

'Can I have some new clothes as well?' she said, running up to Josephine.

Josephine bent to read the price tag. 'All right, I'll buy it for you. It looks really pretty. You can wear it to go to tea with your nanna on Sunday.'

Tessa watched as she got ready to go out that evening. She had put her hair up, pulling little tendrils around her face in the way her mother often used to wear hers, then put on the gold earrings that had caused the trouble on her first day at school.

'Can I have some earrings?' said Tessa. She'd put on her new waistcoat and was busy combing her hair in imitation of Josephine.

'They won't go through your ears.'

'I want my ears done like yours. Can you do them?'

Josephine laughed and bent down to hug her. She felt happy, confident she looked nice, and Tessa's increasing affection for her soothed away the pangs of homesickness that came when she thought of Louisa and her mother.

'I'll do your hair like mine instead,' she said.

A few minutes later a door banged downstairs, and she thought it must be Miran come for her. She took Tessa's hand. 'Come on, come and show Daddy how pretty you look. He's letting you stay up tonight.'

But it was Cheryl. She came into the hall as they came downstairs.

'Whatever have you got on?' she said to Tessa.

'It's new,' Tessa said, her face dropping. 'Phina bought it for me.'

Cheryl looked at Josephine now. 'She looks like a flaming hippy. Whatever made you buy that?'

The excitement she'd felt all day evaporated.

'I like it,' Tessa protested. 'I'm going to wear it to Nanna's.'

'You're not going out in that,' said Cheryl.

Tessa burst into tears and Ross came through from the downstairs shower room to see what all the fuss was about. Josephine was kneeling down beside Tessa, her own eyes stinging with tears and feeling that her whole evening had been spoilt.

At that moment Miran came calling through from the kitchen.

'You go,' said Ross. 'I'll see to Tess.' He stooped to lift her up and Josephine walked off, her face averted, knowing if he asked what was wrong, she'd cry.

When Miran said, 'Wow, you look terrific,' then added with a laugh: 'There could be magic in the air tonight,' it only made her feel worse, because she was suddenly sure the lace top was too low-cut and her hair looked awful.

And when it came to half an hour before closing time and there had been no sign of him, she wished she'd never come: never come here, never come to London, and never left her mother and her sister and the home that she loved so much.

'Cheer up.' Miran nudged her and she looked up – and saw him. He had just come in with two men. She watched as he limped up to the bar with them, deep in conversation. A few minutes later another man came to the door and called him away. At the last moment he saw her.

He came straight over and sat down opposite her, his head to one side. 'You didn't come and see me.'

Miran turned momentarily but Josephine hardly noticed.

'I've got your locket mended,' he said. 'I bought a new chain for you.'

'Thank you,' she muttered.

'Will you come and get it?' He leant across the table, smiling into her eyes.

'Send it to her,' said Miran, turning round again.

'Nicky, are you coming or not?' the man called from the door.

He ignored him. 'Do you want me to send it?'

'It might get lost,' she said.

He laughed and lifted her hand to kiss the tips of her fingers, then stood up and was gone.

'You look like the cat that got the cream,' Miran said to her, raising her voice to cover the laughter that had erupted as the girl who was getting married began to unwrap a present they'd given her.

Josephine smiled happily and looked across the table. She wasn't quite sure what the girl had just taken from the pile of discarded paper, but had a good idea what it was. And when the girl stuck it in her mouth, to a round of applause, she laughed along with the others.

On the way back, Miran said to her: 'Well, at least you're going home more or less sober this time.'

'I've still enjoyed myself.'

Miran hesitated, as though she was deciding whether to speak or not, then she said, 'I know it's none of my business, but mind how you go with him.'

'Of course I will.'

'And I shouldn't say anything to Ross – I think he sees himself as a second father to you – he can be a right old fusspot.'

The next morning when Ross called her into the conservatory where he was working on some plans, she thought of Miran's words, especially the father bit, and felt a sudden little skip of happiness. Everything seemed to be wonderful again.

He looked up, his face serious and said: 'Your month's up then, isn't it?'

She stood there, unsure of him for a moment, then he smiled and said, 'I'm very happy with you, Josephine. And my mum reckons Tessa's manners have improved overnight. So – ' he spread his hands – 'are you going to stay?'

'Yes, please,' she said, biting her bottom lip to stop herself smiling too much. 'Yes. I love it here.'

'Great.' He stared at her for a few seconds. 'By the way. Don't go spending your money on Tessa. It was very sweet of you, but she has too much already.'

She'd forgotten about the upset yesterday and stood there, the smile fading. He looked at his watch then back at her. 'And

I don't pay you enough for that anyway,' he added jokingly. 'Now how about making me some coffee.'

As she was making the coffee he came into the kitchen. 'Do you want to come over to my parents with us tomorrow? Mum's always on about you.'

She had toyed with the idea of going to get her locket, changing her mind a hundred times about how long she should wait before going so that she didn't appear too eager. But it seemed a complicated excuse.

'Thank you . . . I'd love to,' she said finally.

She'd enjoyed the weekend so much that, going to bed on Sunday night, she hardly thought of home. Cheryl had been working and Ross had taken her and Tessa to Windsor, to see the castle. And on Sunday Tessa had worn her waistcoat and been told by her grandmother how swanky she looked. And over it all, like the icing on the cake, was her decision to go and get her locket on Monday.

Chapter 6

The house was difficult to find. It was only when she spotted the church with the tall spire that she realised she must have passed the right turning and was now going in the opposite direction. She circled back, keeping her eyes open for the long brick wall.

When at last she found it, she saw how she'd gone wrong. The house was at the end of a cul-de-sac and on that night he'd led her to it through an alleyway at the opposite end of the road. She couldn't actually remember walking through the alleyway, and now she peered down it. It was cobbled, and dark even on this bright March morning, and petered out beside a row of ancient cottages in front of the church. That was why the church clock had sounded so loud. She stood there a moment trying to get her bearings – and gathering courage to go through that iron gate.

The garden looked as though it hadn't been touched for years. The trees were tangled and uncared for and, beneath them, a dark forest of weeds and mossy pavings, not a spring flower in sight. And in daylight the house looked even more dilapidated, the walls marked with age and the fire escape that had appeared almost magical tipped with moonlight, an ugly rusting scar against its side.

As she walked to the front door, picking her way between scattered piles of building materials, she could hear the sound of loud rock music echoing up from below. She realised the house must have a basement, although there was no sign of one, no windows below ground level.

She rang the doorbell and waited. Rang it again and decided

that either it was impossible to hear it above the music, or he wasn't there. Just as she had decided to go, a girl's face appeared at a narrow window beside the door and it opened a fraction.

'Can you come back . . .' she began. 'Or are you Josephine?'

'Yes, yes I am.'

The girl smiled and pulled the door open wider. 'He's in the studio,' she said. 'Follow me.'

Josephine recognised her as one of the group who'd been with him that night at the Rising Sun. She was dressed in leotard, thick tights and leg-warmers, her blonde hair caught up in plaited ponytail.

She followed the girl along a high-ceilinged hall, the plaster chipped and the air filled with the smell of mould and damp. At the end was a new-looking door painted in garish purple.

'Be careful on the stairs,' said the girl, pulling open the door.

The stairs were narrow and very steep but they were thickly carpeted and well lit by shaded wall-lights each with a different coloured bulb. At the bottom was a circular lobby where natural light filtered down from a domed glass ceiling way above. The walls were covered in pictures: framed photographs of dancers, many of him, and the words 'Magic Spell' were emblazoned in small lights above them.

The girl smiled over her shoulder as Josephine looked at them, then pushed open double louvered doors, holding one ajar for her. The whole basement had been converted to form a large dance studio, complete with barre and floor-length mirrors. There were no windows, just long fluorescent bulbs, and in their light she could see that the studio had been built some years ago: the wooden floor was darkened with age and marked with scuffs and stains and the mirrors had patches of silver showing through the glaze. But on the far wall was a huge screen which looked brand new, and there were wires and speakers connected up to what appeared to be film and sound equipment.

The music was so loud that she could feel the floor vibrating beneath her feet, and the screen flickered with images of dancers that were caught and thrown backwards and forwards in weird reflections between the mirrors.

Limbering up at the barre were the two other girls and the boy, the group she'd seen before. The girl who'd brought her down joined them.

Nicky was there with them and came over to her immediately. 'I've come for my locket,' Josephine said, tapping the base of her neck. She felt disorientated and nervous. The room seemed airless and filled with a strange, sweet smell.

'I shan't be long,' he said. 'Sit down and watch the video.' He pointed to a great heap of giant cushions over by the wall. There were no chairs, there was no furniture at all. She went to the wall and leant against the barre, watching as he walked back to his pupils. He was barefoot and wore only jeans and a black leather waistcoat and the black strapping on his left arm. His shoulders and upper arms were powerfully muscled, the skin the same perfect cream colour as his face. She thought of that night he'd brought her here, how he'd taken her hand and pressed it against his heart, but now he paid no special attention to her – he would just give her back the locket and that would be it.

There was a shuffle of feet as the group came to the middle of the floor.

'Just the first sequence,' he said, his voice barely audible above the music.

She'd noticed before how quietly he spoke and now, listening to him again, she thought how gently and carefully he gave instructions to them and how intently they looked at him as they listened. She watched, fascinated by them, fascinated by the atmosphere of shared intimacy, the secret smiles that passed between them as they took up their positions. But when they started to dance it was like a burst of power exploding as their bodies moved in tempo with the pounding beat of the music. He stopped them only once, going to stand between the blonde-haired girl and the boy when they faltered as he lifted her above his head. He placed the boy's hand on the top of the girl's leg.

'Hold her properly,' he said, his voice serious. 'Or you'll end up breaking her neck.' Then he bent his head close to the boy's and pushed back the fringe of hair from his forehead in a gesture that seemed almost fatherly. 'Now you're sleeping with her, you're frightened to touch her,' he said, smiling into the boy's face. 'It's the time when you should dance together best.'

The girl giggled and tossed her head, looking away. It seemed to Josephine that the room had grown a degree warmer, and that the sweet smell had increased with the rise in temperature. She could see its source now. Beside a door in the corner of the room was a small black marble plaque, and on each side burned a number of candles in brass sconces. The smell came from their smoke.

There was a break in the music and they came to a halt, panting and flexing their limbs. 'That's enough,' he said. 'We'll have a longer session tomorrow. I've got someone to see.'

Four pairs of eyes were turned on her for a moment. Then they went to the far side of the room, flipping off ballet shoes as they went and pulling on jeans and sweaters from a heap on the floor.

'Sorry to make you wait,' he said, coming over to her again. 'But I didn't know you'd come in the morning.' His tone was warmer now, and he put a hand on the wall beside her. 'I thought you would come in the evening.'

'I couldn't. I look after a little girl. It's my job.'

He smiled at her the way he had in the pub. 'It doesn't matter – as long as you came. I've got your locket.' He patted the pocket of his waistcoat but didn't take it out.

His pupils were about to go, when the blonde girl came running back.

'Nicky,' she said, standing close beside him.

'Alice,' he said in the same tone.

She smiled. 'You haven't forgotten we're going for a costume fitting, have you?'

'No, I haven't forgotten.'

'You promised you'd come this time.' She looked at Josephine. 'And we're going straight there now.'

He put his arm round the girl. 'If I promised, then I'll be there.'

'See you in a minute then.' She gave a coquettish little smile and ran off after the others.

He turned his attention back to Josephine. 'I have to go out. Did you say you couldn't come out in the evenings?'

'I can at the weekend.' Her heart was racing. She stared at his mouth; his lips were soft and full like a woman's.

'I can't wait that long,' he said, smiling and massaging his shoulder as he spoke. 'Come and have lunch with me tomorrow. I eat in a place just round the corner. Go back through the alley where I brought you before and you'll see it. It's called Sapphire's. You can get back to the main road that way. Meet me there at twelve.'

'What about my locket?' she said quietly.

He fished it out of his pocket and held it in front of her, but drew it away when she went to take it. 'I'll give it to you tomorrow,' he said. 'I have to go and get changed now. You know how to get out, don't you?'

She waited a moment, thinking he might kiss her, but he didn't. He had already disappeared into the far corner of the studio by the time she reached the louvered doors.

She found Sapphire's easily, though she couldn't remember seeing it the night she'd met him. It was small, no more than a café, with curtains at the windows and simple-looking decor; but there was something exclusive and expensive-looking about it. Walking up to the main road, she planned what to wear and decided on her blue velvet dress. She remembered him saying how much he liked the pearl buttons that night she had sat drinking with him at the Rising Sun.

The next twenty-four hours seemed like a hundred, and she was early going to meet him. But he was waiting, sitting at a small round table, his left leg stretched into the gangway, a glass in front of him.

He got up and pulled out a chair for her and asked what she wanted to drink. Unsure what to ask for, she said: 'I'll have what you've got.'

'It's only fruit juice. Sapphire's licensed, you can have what you like.'

'Fruit juice will be fine.' She longed for a glass of wine, but added, 'I don't normally drink like I did the other night.'

'I realised that,' he smiled.

A grossly fat woman brought the menu, placed it in front of her, then stood beside Nicky, stroking his hair.

'I like your friend, Nicky,' she said.

Josephine looked up, not sure whether she really was a woman. She had blonde twenties-style waves and painted cupid lips, but her voice was a hoarse tenor and she wore a man's baggy suit with a bow at the neck.

'Yes, she's pretty, isn't she?' Nicky smiled across the table at her but she looked away, unsure how to behave, what she should say.

The woman began stroking his forehead now. 'And will I be seeing more of her?' she asked.

'I think you will, Sapph. In fact I'm sure you will. Her name's Josephine.'

'Pleased to meet you, dear.' The woman held out a chubby hand, the fingers loaded with rings. 'I like to know he's not on his own in that dreadful old house.'

Nicky laughed out loud and Josephine began to smile as she took her hand. It all seemed like a game; she just had to learn the rules.

She ordered an omelette because she wasn't at all hungry and it seemed the lightest thing to have. But the eggs were whipped into such a great rich creamy froth that she could eat no more than half. Nicky had sandwiches with a filling that looked like little grey fish, and he watched her as he ate, saying little but prompting her with questions about her job and her home.

As soon as she put down her knife and fork, Sapphire was by her side.

'Have one of my sorbets, darling,' she said. 'They slide down as easily as a nun's knickers.'

Nicky put out an arm. 'Go away, Sapph. Bring her pavlova and keep your comments to yourself. Ignore her,' he smiled once Sapphire had disappeared.

The pavlova arrived, glistening with slivers of kiwi fruit and strawberries. Josephine put a hand to her chest. 'It looks delicious but I don't think . . .'

'Just taste it,' said Nicky.

She smiled across at him and began to eat and, as she lifted the spoon for the third time, he reached out and took her wrist and guided it to his own mouth. There was no one else there and she was tempted to spoon the rest of it to him because it suddenly seemed an exciting and intimate thing to do. But he took the spoon and put it down, then held her hand against his cheek.

'Do you want coffee?' he said.

'No, thank you, I've got . . .' She broke off and picked up the glass of fruit juice because he was making her nervous.

He twisted her arm round to look at her watch. 'What time do you have to pick this little girl up?'

'Half past three.'

'Let's go back to the house,' he said. 'I want to show you the rest of it.'

But when they got there, he took her straight down to the studio, flicking on just one of the lights and then going to turn on the music. She stood by the door, looking at herself in the long mirrors. They were slightly misted and all she could see clearly was her mass of hair, fluffed out from the dampness of the day, and the pearl buttons like a row of white dots down the front of her dress. He came to stand behind her and put her hand on the barre.

'Have you ever learnt to dance?' he said, putting an arm round her waist.

She shook her head.

'I'll show you. Take off your shoes. Now turn your feet out with your heels together.'

She did as he said, her eyes still fixed on the opposite mirror.

'Don't keep admiring yourself.' He gently lifted her hair to kiss the back of her neck. 'Now put your feet apart, keeping them turned out.'

It was difficult and he adjusted his arm tighter round her and put his lips to her ear. 'There are five different positions. Première, seconde, troisième, quatrième, cinquième. But we'll only try one or two to begin with.' He had his head over her shoulder, his mouth against her throat. 'What do you think?'

She didn't answer and he pulled her back against him running his hands up her ribs to stop just below her breasts, then down again, his fingertips joined like an arrow at the base of her stomach. And all the while she could feel his tongue moving against her neck, as though he were tasting her just as he had the pavlova. She closed her eyes and he turned her round in his arms until her back was against the barre. He began to kiss her. It was just light touches of his lips against hers at first, then he put his hand to the back of her head and opened his mouth, kissing her long and deeply. When he drew away from her, she was breathless and trembling. He smiled and lifted her chin so she had to look at him.

'I want to make love to you, Josephine,' he said, pausing to run his tongue across her lips. 'Do you want me to?'

'I don't know.' Her voice came out shaky and small and she buried her face against his shoulder.

He ran his hand gently over her hair. 'That's no answer,' he said, stepping back a fraction and tilting her chin again. 'Don't you like me enough?'

She nodded, wanting to say, I like you more than anybody in the world. Instead she reached up to kiss him. But he held her away and took the top button of her dress between his fingers and flicked it open. He undid two more and waited a moment to see her reaction. When she did nothing to stop him, he undid the rest and slid his hand between her legs.

'Relax,' he whispered, as she flinched away. 'I won't do anything you don't want me to. You can tell me to stop any time.'

But when he moved his fingers against her, the sensation of pleasure was so immediate and surprising that she didn't want him to stop. He began to kiss her again and the feeling grew so intense that she let out a sigh against his lips. And between kisses, he took off her clothes, then stripped off his T-shirt and pressed his naked chest against her. The feel of his bare skin on hers sent tingling spirals of excitement from her stomach to her breasts; warmth and dampness spread between her thighs and he dipped a testing fingertip into her.

'I think you know now,' he murmured.

She went limp against the barre and he let go of her for a moment. When he began to touch her again, she could feel it was no longer his fingers and she twisted away from him. He caught her round the waist and lifted her down on to the cushions.

'Don't you like it that way?' he said.

She didn't answer and he caressed the inside of her thigh.

'Josephine,' he said, looking down into her face. 'You're not a virgin, are you?'

She nodded and closed her eyes and felt him stretch beside her and pull her very close.

'I should have guessed, but . . .' He stopped and kissed her. 'You've got such a seductive look about you.' He kissed her again. 'I knew you were special.'

She wound her arms tightly round his neck, almost delirious with the sensations that he was arousing in her.

'Am I special to you?' he said.

'Yes, yes.'

'Very special?' He had his fingers against her once more. 'Making love is like dancing,' he said, moving them in a tiny circle. 'First you learn the steps.' He traced a line slowly up her stomach and back down. 'Then you need to practise.' He was whispering against her ear and moved his head round to push his tongue into the corner of her mouth.

She felt his finger move slightly into her and reached down to press his hand closer, wanting more. The pleasure increased, uncoiling in her stomach and heating her skin, making her breath come in short, deep sighs.

He looked down into her face again. 'Do you want me to now?' he said, stopping the movement of his fingers for a moment.

She closed her eyes and pulled his head down to hers and whispered, yes, and he pushed his tongue into her mouth and eased her legs apart.

It was like all her dreams of being loved turned into one long, slow movement, and all her feelings and emotions concentrated in that movement. With the first stab of pain, the physical pleasure subsided and almost disappeared, but soon that seemed all part of it, all part of the intensity of her feeling for him. And his sighs of pleasure filled her with such emotion that she clung to him, hugged him tight, feeling that she would do anything in the world for him. He responded by slipping a hand down between their bodies as he moved against her.

'But it doesn't matter how much you practise,' he whispered. 'You can only reach perfection when you find the right partner.'

The cushions floated up around her. Every inch of her body felt affected and the room grew dark before her eyes. She felt poised on the verge of something and bit into his lip with her greed to find it. He jerked back, then collapsed on her with a low moan.

As he slid from her, she put her hands to her face. Her skin was burning, her forehead soaked with sweat, strands of wet hair stuck in her eyes and mouth. He lay stretched on his back, breathing in a succession of long, contented sighs. She rolled close to him and he put out an arm to encircle her, then rubbed his hand across his mouth, holding it up to show a streak of blood.

'You savage,' he said. 'I was as gentle as I could be and you go and bite me.'

She snuggled close against him, knowing that, for some reason, that had pleased him. And he'd called her special. It felt as if she could do no wrong; as if all the damage her heart had undergone was repaired, and that all the spare love that had been so dangerously headed towards Christian had now found its right place.

'What are you thinking?' he asked softly. 'Is it about me?'

'Yes.'

'Are you going to love me for ever, is that it?' he coaxed.

'Yes.'

He laughed quietly and propped himself on one elbow, running his eyes down her body.

'Don't stare at me,' she said.

'Why not?' He pushed her on to her back, smiling, then his face grew serious for a moment. 'I've grazed you with my zip,' he said, touching her thigh, then bending to kiss it. 'I'm sorry. But I never take my jeans off in the light because of my leg – I can't even stand the sight of it.' His voice had become lighthearted again and she wasn't sure if he were joking or not, but he had got up to do up his jeans and she couldn't see his face.

She craned her head to look at the graze. It wasn't much; the skin was only just broken; she hadn't even felt it. The other stains of her blood seemed more important.

'That means you will love me for ever,' he said, coming to crouch beside her. He had picked up her clothes and she reached for them, feeling suddenly exposed.

He laughed and held on to them, then gave her his T-shirt.

'Here, put this on. We'll go upstairs and you can wash and do your hair.'

She looked at her watch. It was just after two.

'How long have you got?' he asked.

'Ages.'

He spread out on the cushions again and she pulled on the T-shirt and stared down at him. With his fan of glossy hair, his slanting gold eyes and the lustre of a creamy pearl on his skin, it was hard to imagine that any part of him was ugly. She wanted to throw herself on him and kiss him from head to toe.

'Go and press down the middle button in the top row,' he said, reaching over to point at the stack of equipment by the wall.

She jumped up and did as he said and immediately the screen came to life.

He rolled over on his stomach, pulling her beside him. 'It's before my accident,' he said. 'You can see what I was like.'

She glanced at him but he had his eyes fixed on the screen.

He was dancing in a group but was obviously the star. His hair was dyed with black streaks and he was thinner than he was now, but apart from that he looked the same – except of course his limbs were not damaged then. It was some kind of live show with singing and flashes of the audience. The music was fast and loud and pulsing with rhythm, the dancers' costumes a mixture of black leather and red silk. She watched entranced as the music died away and he leapt on to a raised platform with one of the girl dancers, stood there a moment embracing her, then jumped down the other side, disappearing in a cloud of smoke as the music burst out louder than ever.

'That was nearly seven years ago,' he said as the film ended. 'I was only nineteen and I beat over a hundred others at the audition for that show. They argued over the last three of us for a week. The director said I wouldn't be flexible enough because I was a classically trained dancer . . .' He broke off, turning to her. 'Ballet, I mean.'

She nodded as though she knew, though she didn't; she just liked listening to him.

He rolled on to his back. 'We had to dance for him again every day that week and then he wanted to see us do acrobatics.' He smiled to himself. 'I was swinging from a trapeze before I could walk – they didn't know that.'

'What, in a circus?' She really was interested now.

'My parents were both circus performers. My mother was a Hungarian gypsy. She could . . .' He stopped and caught her wrist. 'Come on, let's go upstairs,' he said.

She bundled up her clothes and followed him to the far corner of the studio where she'd seen him disappear yesterday. There was a narrow door there and, as he opened it, she could see some writing on the black marble plaque she'd noticed before. But there was no time to stop and read it: he was holding out a hand to help her up a short flight of steps and through another door. It led on to the fire escape and she shivered slightly and looked around, wondering if anybody could see her in just the black T-shirt.

'Don't worry,' he laughed. 'If anybody looks up here, they'll think you're an apparition.'

Halfway up, a gust of wind caught at them, and he turned to smile at her, his hair lifted from his shoulders, his muscular body smooth and white as alabaster. You're the apparition, she thought.

They went right to the top. She could see the church and the row of cottages and whole streets stretching out in all directions. And directly below, visible between the iron slats that formed each step, was a square of concrete that made the drop look dizzily menacing. She gripped the rail tighter, relieved when he opened another door and led her back inside.

It was his bedroom: a huge room packed with furniture and boxes and dark because there were long heavy curtains still drawn across the windows.

He switched on a light and looked at her as though awaiting her reaction.

'I have to keep everything in here because it's the only room that doesn't need work doing to it,' he said. 'The last owner lived in here.' He waved a hand round the room. 'Most of this furniture was his. I had a furnished flat before.' He went to switch on a heater. 'I shall have central heating put in eventually.'

'It's wonderful,' she said, looking round.

There were two sets of floor to ceiling windows, both draped with yards of purple velvet curtains hanging from heavy brass rails, the pelmets covered with the same material, pleated and ruched and faded along the edge to pale lavender. The walls were covered with dark cream paper striped with purple and also faded in places, and the ceiling was an amazing whirl of fancy plasterwork. Most of the furniture was antique, but against one wall, and looking completely out of place in this magnificent room, there was a huge television and more sound and video equipment.

The bed was a four-poster, very old and ornately carved and hung with worn drapery, most of which had been tossed back and tucked behind the great dark headboard. It was heaped with a mountain of duvets and pillows and a huge fur rug.

'I have to keep warm,' he said, seeing her look at it. 'If my leg gets cold it aches.'

She waited, thinking he might say more, but he went over and put on some music.

'Was it like this when you bought it?' she asked.

'Yes. I think the guy who had the studio built decorated this room originally. He was married to a beautiful dancer half his age and wanted to keep her happy.'

'I bet she was.'

'Not for long.' He yawned and smiled. 'She died six months after moving here. There's a plaque downstairs to her memory. I'll show you sometime.'

She glanced at her watch. Quarter to three.

'Where's the bathroom?' she asked.

He nodded towards a door on the far wall at right angles to the one they had come in.

She picked up a hairbrush from the dressing table. 'Can I use this?'

'Let me.' He lifted her on to a small chest of drawers and started to brush her hair but was soon kissing her instead.

'I have to go soon,' she murmured against his lips, looking over his shoulder at the great bed and imagining what it would be like to lie there with him and pull those drapes around them.

His kisses grew more passionate and he slipped his hands inside the T-shirt, pushing his palms up under her breasts and burying his face against her.

'I want you again,' he whispered, and she wrapped her arms round him, excited by his words.

He held her there on the chest of drawers, standing between her legs. She could feel the buckle of his belt pressing into her stomach, and put her fingers to it, wishing she had the courage to undo it.

'Go on,' he said. 'It's one of the three most erotic things you can do to someone – undress them.' He lifted the T-shirt over her head.

'What's the second?' she murmured.

'I'm about to show you,' he said, putting his lips to her breast.

There was no hesitation this time; she was immediately on fire for him, and when he finally undid the buckle, then his zip, she watched him, until he smiled at her through half-closed lids and put his hand briefly over her eyes.

'You wouldn't even look at me across the table at lunch,' he said. 'Now you want to see everything.'

She put her head against his shoulder. 'Do you always do that?' she whispered. 'Even with girls who are on the pill?'

He put his hand on her mouth now. 'Always. Now stop talking,' he said, taking hold of her knees and opening her legs as though he were opening a book.

As soon as he touched her, the sensations of pleasure came rushing on a giant wave and she leant back against the wall, letting him wrap her legs round his waist. She could feel he held back a little, as though frightened to hurt her, but she cared for nothing except to reach the same heights as him. Still he was gentle, and she felt suspended on the crest of that wave, wanting so much to be tipped over. Then he reached forward and pulled her up against him, pushing his tongue deep into her mouth. It triggered the very depths of response in her. She gave a little sob of ecstasy and let her head fall on to his shoulder.

A last shiver went through her and she hung there, idly sucking at the skin of his neck to prolong the feeling. The church clock began to strike but she had not come back down to earth and it was no more than the ringing already in her ears.

'Was that perfection?' he murmured, holding her thighs and rubbing both thumbs against her.

'Don't, don't,' she sighed with a mixture of pleasure and contented exhaustion, holding his hands away from her. 'I can't bear any more.'

'Not ever?'

She gave another long sigh and pressed her lips against his neck again, and he laughed softly; then he drew away from her, a hand to his reddened skin.

'You're intent on branding me, aren't you?'

'Yes,' she said, glancing again at the bed and wishing she could just fall into it with him. 'I want all the other girls who look at you to see it.'

'You're the only girl who's been in here with me.' He enclosed her in his arms a moment, then lifted her to the floor.

Standing there naked, with the rush of blood slowing and the buzzing in her ears gone, she felt suddenly shy and self-conscious. The church clock struck once and she was thrown into panic.

'Tessa,' she said, grabbing her clothes.

There was no time to wash now, no time to brush her hair again. She fiddled desperately with the pearl buttons while he phoned a cab.

He took her down the inside stairs and fetched her coat from the studio.

'Don't panic, it'll be here in a minute,' he said. 'You'll get there in time.'

They went out into the road to wait for the cab and, as it came down from the top of the cul-de-sac, he said: 'Come on Saturday. Come early – before I'm up. I'll turn off the alarms, come round the back way.'

She was climbing in the cab now, checking her watch again.

'You don't have to pay anything,' he said, closing the door behind her. As it drove away, she smiled to herself, thinking that she hadn't even got her locket back.

But the smile faded when she reached the school. She was just a few minutes late but Tessa was in tears.

'Fiona said a man will get me if you don't come,' she sobbed.

Josephine crouched down, hugging and kissing her. 'Tessa, darling, I'm sorry.' She pulled out a handkerchief and wiped away her tears. 'Don't cry, no one's going to get you.'

Tessa gave one last anguished sob and picked up her school bag which she'd dropped on the ground.

'You must always wait for me inside,' Josephine said gently.

'Miss Cook said I could go because you were there.'

Josephine lifted her up and kissed her again. 'Shall we go and get something nice for after dinner?'

Tessa nodded.

'Some cakes. We'll get some that Daddy likes as well.'

'I want an ice cream,' said Tessa, smoothing her hands down Josephine's hair. 'Your hair's messy,' she said.

Josephine laughed and put her down. 'You can have ice cream and cakes,' she said.

Back indoors, she rushed upstairs to get tidied up before starting the dinner. She'd begun to cook for them more and more. Ross still brought in takeaways now and again, and sometimes he and Cheryl went out for a meal, but Josephine usually cooked for her and Tessa. Tonight she was making a meat pie for the three of them because Ross had said it was his favourite.

Tessa, the kitten in her arms, followed her up and watched while she got changed. The pearl buttons were all done up on the wrong holes and she laughed to herself and thought thank goodness Ross hadn't come home early as he sometimes did.

She was back in jeans and T-shirt by the time he came in, her hair in a ponytail and her face washed. But underneath the shiny exterior, her skin still felt warm and creased with lovemaking, and every now and again her pulse would quicken a little with a leftover tremor of desire.

'You look hot,' Ross said as she started laying the table. 'Turn the heating down if you want.'

'It's because I've been slaving over a hot stove for the past hour,' she said, smiling, the words coming more easily than usual.

'Well, it looks worth it,' he said as she put his dinner in front of him.

'And we've got cakes,' said Tessa. 'And I had an ice cream.'

The atmosphere was happy and relaxed. Cheryl had started a nightshift and sometimes came in to see Ross on her way to work, but tonight she hadn't, and after dinner he took Tessa into the sitting room with him. Normally he played with her in the kitchen for half an hour, then it was her bedtime.

Josephine made coffee for them and took it in. When Cheryl was there she would put Tessa to bed and spend the rest of the evening in her room. Even when Ross was out, she usually went upstairs. It was only on the odd occasion like tonight when there were just the three of them that she spent the evening in the downstairs sitting room.

The television was on. It was obviously a programme about dancing, with flashes of different dance sequences and scenes of backstage changing rooms and ballet dancers doing barre exercises. She was immediately interested and sat down to watch.

'Do you like dancing?' said Ross.

I do now, she felt like saying. 'I like the music,' she smiled.

'I want my Jungle Book video on,' said Tessa.

'Let Josephine watch this first.'

'You said I could,' Tessa whined.

'It doesn't matter,' said Josephine. 'I'll watch upstairs.'

'No, she gets her own way too much.'

Tessa started to cry and pulled away from where she was sitting in the crook of his arm.

'Please don't make her cry,' said Josephine.

'She'll get over it,' he said. 'Does your sister behave like this?' he asked, lifting Tessa on to his lap and cuddling her.

'Often,' said Josephine.

'I suppose it's the same situation,' he said. 'Losing a parent – you spoil them to compensate. Still,' he paused, a shadow of sadness passing over his face. 'Tess doesn't remember her mother, so maybe that's a good thing.' He looked up. 'How long ago did your father die?'

'Just over two years ago, on my . . .' She checked herself in time. 'On my sixteenth birthday.'

'On your birthday.' His eyebrows raised slightly. 'How sad for you.'

Normally, just discussing it would bring tears to her eyes, but tonight she felt as though a little flame burned away inside her and that she could talk about anything. When he asked her more about her family, she found herself chatting away about them, about the happy times before Christian had come, the days riding up in the pine forests and the hours spent with her father in his storeroom and study amongst the antique furniture and his books and paintings.

'Don't you get homesick?' he asked.

She shook her head. 'Not now. And I wanted to get away. I . . . I don't really get on with my stepfather.'

'I expect he found it difficult coming to a ready-made family.'

She nodded, wondering why she had mentioned it.

Tessa had fallen asleep on his lap. Josephine went and made them more coffee and they carried on talking. She was tempted to tell him about Nicky – not what had happened that afternoon – she could no more repeat any of that to him than she could have done to her father; she couldn't even go back over the details in her own mind – just to say she'd met someone that she really liked and to talk about him a little. But she remembered what Miran had said – and anyway it would be impossible to say anything without giving away more. Even to think about him made her heart quicken.

He was asking about her mother now and she ran off upstairs and fetched a photograph of her. It was a family group taken at her wedding to Christian. Why she'd brought that one with her she had no idea; it had probably been the first one that came to hand as she packed.

'Where does she come from?' he asked.

'South America, but my father met her in Martinique. She was brought up in an orphanage there by French nuns.'

'Quite a background,' he smiled.

'His father left him a house there and he went to sell it. She was working there as a cleaner.' She clasped her hands round her knees, remembering how her father had told her about the first time he saw her mother. In her present state of mind, the story felt more romantic than ever and she was lost in the beauty of it as she spoke. 'She was only sixteen but he fell in love with her when he heard her singing as she did the sweeping up. He said she looked up as he came in the door and he fell in love with her in that moment.' She bit her lip and hugged her knees tighter, thinking of that evening when she had first seen Nicky.

She looked up. Ross was still holding the photo and had obviously said something to her.

'Sorry – I didn't hear you.' She gave an embarrassed little smile, knowing she had been talking too much and lapsing into dreams.

'I said, she's very beautiful.' He smiled back at her. 'Still, I guessed she must be.'

She felt herself start to blush, but for once she didn't care because the glow of happiness and excitement was still there and again her lips curved upwards.

'You've done nothing but smile this evening,' he said. 'What have you been up to today?'

She shrugged and tried to look serious. 'Nothing much.'

'Well, as long as you're happy here,' he said, getting up with Tessa in his arms. 'We don't want her flitting off now, do we, Tess?'

Tessa stirred and said she wanted to watch her video, but he laughed and carried her off to bed.

Josephine sat there a while longer, dreaming of Saturday.

Chapter 7

But by Thursday evening, her happiness had a great cloud over it.

Cheryl had called in on her way to work and Josephine had just made some coffee for her when Miran stuck her head round the kitchen door. She was as lively as usual but within a few minutes it was obvious she wanted to talk to her on her own.

She'd noticed before how Cheryl hated Miran to make a fuss of Ross in any way. In fact Miran had told her that Cheryl didn't like any other woman near him. 'One of the other applicants for your job was a Scandinavian girl,' she'd said. 'She soon put the mockers on that. You're just lucky she didn't see you before he gave you the job.' Josephine thought it was all a bit ridiculous; Cheryl was a long-legged blonde with a superb figure and it was obvious that Ross was in love with her.

Now, as Miran stood behind him, arms round his neck and asked him about a new foreman he had just employed, Cheryl picked up her coffee and went off to the sitting room.

'I suppose she sees enough men's bodies all day without me going on about them,' laughed Miran.

Ross got up to follow Cheryl. 'You do get a bit much at times,' he smiled. 'And anyway, he's married.' He put a hand out to Tessa to go with him.

'That's got rid of them.' Miran hoisted herself on to the worktop next to where Josephine was piling plates into the dishwasher. 'It's you I want to talk to.'

Josephine closed the dishwasher door. 'Me?'

'Have you seen that dancer guy again?' Miran said, watching her face.

'Yes.' She paused; something about Miran's tone alerted her. 'I went out to lunch with him on Tuesday.'

'Are you seeing him again?'

She gave an uncertain smile. 'Why?'

'Because . . .' Miran pursed her lips and looked away for a moment as though she was searching for the right word. 'I think he's a bit heavy for you, Phina.'

'What do you mean?'

'I've heard some rather nasty things about him.'

'What?' She felt suddenly cold.

Miran reached out and put her hands on her shoulders. 'I wasn't checking on you or anything, it just came out in conversation. I was telling someone about you and him and she said he was a nutter and to warn you to give him a wide berth.'

Josephine took a step back away from her. 'Why, what has he done?'

'Apparently, a few years ago, he threatened to kill some girl. The police had to be called out because he threatened her with a knife.'

Josephine swallowed. 'What for?'

'I don't know.' Miran shrugged. 'There weren't any charges brought against him. But I always think there's no smoke without fire – and he does have a bit of a bad reputation.'

Josephine took another step back. 'Why didn't you tell me that before? I was with you when I met him.'

'I didn't want to spoil things for you – you were having such a good time that night at the Rising Sun. And anyway, I didn't even know about the knife business then.'

'Well, I'm not listening to tales. I'll ask him about it myself.'

'So you are seeing him again?'

'Probably.'

'Look, Phina, you're living in my brother's house and you're responsible for his daughter. He'd get rid of you – make no mistake about that. He's the most easy-going person you could wish to meet, but when it comes to Tessa . . .'

'I haven't made any definite arrangements.' Her brows drew together and she went to gather the last of the things off the table.

'Good.' Miran jumped down. 'How about making up a foursome sometime then?'

'I have to be here in the evenings – I don't want to get involved with anyone.'

She was relieved when Ross told her that he, Cheryl and Tessa were going out for the day on Saturday. Although she was free to do as she pleased at the weekends, so far she had spent them all there and, with Miran's warnings on her mind, she had decided to say she was going shopping.

Tessa was downstairs with Ross and she slipped away before eight, taking a bus to the turning past the Rising Sun and then the shortcut through the cobbled alleyway. As before, she noticed how quiet it was here, how it seemed so distant from the main road when it was only a few minutes' walk away, and how once she entered that cul-de-sac, the rest of the world got left behind.

She went round the back and in through the kitchen as he'd said. It was in an appalling state: no modern fittings and almost impossible to imagine that anyone had ever prepared food there. A huge wooden table stood in the centre of the floor and two cats were standing on it, licking a milk bottle where the cream had burst through the foil top. They fled when they saw her and she turned to watch them disappear into the tangle of brambles outside the back door.

The house had a confusing layout, with doors that looked as though they led into rooms but which lead into cupboards instead, and two separate flights of stairs. The first, she soon discovered, had been blocked off at the top. The other led in two stages up to the second floor. She was unable to resist peering into some of the rooms. Most were in a very bad decorative state and looked as though they had been unused for years; even the squares on the wall where once pictures had hung, were covered in cobwebs and dust. But despite this, she still thought it had a certain charm. Her father would have loved it. He would have created images of the past in the empty rooms; sniffed into corners for the auras of those who had lived here before, and listened for the echoes of their footsteps down the hallways.

Up on the second-floor landing there were just three doors, two of which had been painted. She tried the first but it was locked. It was then that she noticed the narrow cable that ran along the top of the doors, disappearing down the wall and into the floor, and remembered what he had said about an alarm system. She tried the second door and knew immediately it was his because of the wave of warm air that enveloped her as it opened.

He was still sleeping. The curtains were closed, pulled together and overlapped so that the sunlight filtered through only in a dim purple beam. She crept round the bed and stood there looking down at him. His wild hair was spread on the pillow and his matching lashes fluttered slightly against his cheeks. She peered a little closer, but he didn't move. On the bedside table were two bottles of tablets, one with the lid off. She tilted it with a forefinger to read the label.

'They're painkillers – for my leg.'

She jumped and smiled and realised he'd been awake all along.

'You did it perfectly,' he said, stretching his right arm above his head and yawning. 'I wanted to open my eyes and find you here.'

She sat down beside him and he reached out to press down a button on a black box above his head, then put his arms round her waist as the room filled with music. She saw he still wore the leather straps and touched one with her finger, thinking of Miran's words and knowing she must ask him about it.

'Aren't you getting in with me?' he asked, spreading his hands round her ribs.

She should ask him – ask him before she committed herself any further.

'I've still got the third erotic thing to show you,' he said, smiling up at her.

She pulled off her shoes and moved closer to him.

'Do you usually get into bed with all your clothes on?'

'No.' She laughed but couldn't bring herself to get undressed in front of him, even in the semi-darkness.

'Well, I can't lift that sweater over your head,' he said, stretching out on the pillows. 'But I'll close my eyes if it makes you feel better.'

She felt as though she were doing a striptease, as though he watched her from behind those pale closed lids, and as though, once more, it was all part of a game. But she didn't care now. And when he lifted the heap of bedclothes to let her in, she no longer cared about what Miran had said, or about anything except her desire for him.

'Show me what the third thing is,' she said as he began to kiss her.

He held her chin in his fingers a moment. 'Do you know,' he said, 'I've never met a girl as inexperienced as you who gets turned on so quickly.'

'It's you. It's your fault.'

He fixed his eyes on her. 'I was rehearsing for my first show,' he said, his voice pitched even lower than usual. 'I had to lift a girl like this.' He pushed back the duvet and lifted her above him, holding her there while he carried on talking. 'The choreographer wanted it to represent the sex act and he told her to imagine she was about to be lowered on to . . .'

She put her hands to her ears, smiling. 'Don't,' she said.

'He said it so that she would have the right expression on her face.' He lowered her a fraction. 'I had to hold her there for a count of fifty.' He lowered her a little more. 'But I can't do that any longer.'

She closed her eyes and gave a little moan as he lowered her the rest of the way.

It was so hot in that great bed that she emerged dripping with sweat and wanting to throw off all the bedclothes. But he wouldn't let her and she knew it was because of his leg and climbed up to sit on the pillows beside his head, a piece of the drapery wrapped around her.

'It's nine o'clock,' she said as the church clock began to strike.

'Ten,' he corrected. 'Do you lose all count of time when you're with me?'

'Yes, I do.' She sighed, remembering Tessa waiting for her and then Miran's words were back in her head and she blurted out. 'You didn't really try to kill someone did you?'

He made a noise of weary impatience and sat up beside her. 'What have people been saying about me now?'

She repeated what Miran had said.

He slumped back down. 'If you're going to believe everything you hear about me you might as well go right now,' he said.

For a moment she was devastated and stared at him, wishing she had said nothing.

'But I don't want you to do that.' He reached up and stroked her cheek. 'So I'll tell you what happened and then I never want to talk about it again.'

She sat silent, waiting. He sat up again, massaging his

shoulder, then his leg beneath the duvet, and finally reaching for the bottle of tablets.

'Don't look so worried,' he smiled. 'I'm all right once I've exercised. I spend two hours every day exercising, then I'm fine.' He swallowed two of the tablets then settled down again, his head against her leg, his arm hooked round her knees. 'While I was in hospital after my accident, my girlfriend walked out on me. We'd been together since we met at ballet school when we were both fifteen, and she decided she couldn't wait three months for me – or rather she thought she might end up with a one-legged lover.' He looked up at her. 'Do you think I had reason to get a bit upset with her?'

'Yes – how cruel of her.'

'She made silly excuses, like she didn't approve of my friends – the ones who stood by me – and that I was so changed she didn't know me. It was a load of bullshit and I went berserk at her. I probably did threaten her, I don't remember what I said. The police came and, yes, I did have a knife, but that was nothing to do with it. It was for self-defence. All the time dancers like me get insulted and goaded by brainless thugs. Most of us are ten times fitter and stronger than any of them but . . .' He paused and looked up at her. 'I'd been in hospital for three months. I could hardly walk, let alone defend myself. That's why I had the knife. But we were both quite well known and the papers loved it. Jealous lover and all that. They'd have been delighted if I'd killed her.'

He was silent for a while. She wanted to know more, about the accident, about everything, but he looked dejected and angry and she felt angry herself, angry at Miran for repeating things without finding out the truth.

'It was four years ago,' he said finally. 'But people always believe the worst of me and go on believing it.'

'I don't,' she said. 'I don't believe any of it. I can't imagine you hurting anyone.' It was on her lips to say she loved him but all of a sudden he pulled her into his arms.

'Who told you?' he asked.

'The people I work for.' She didn't want him confronting Miran; saying it like that didn't pin the blame on anyone in particular.

'Ignore them,' he said. 'Don't speak to them about me or listen to anything they say. When you come here, to me . . .'

He lowered his voice and put his lips against her ear. '. . . When you're here, we'll forget about the rest of the world.'

She put her arms round his neck. 'I do already,' she whispered back; then in a tiny voice which she could barely hear herself, she whispered that she loved him.

He just held her and then the clock was striking that awful gong sound again and he said he must get up because he had to go and meet some people later and he must do an hour's exercise first.

'I won't be out long,' he said. 'You'll wait here for me, won't you?'

Then he asked her to go down to the studio and bring him back a carton of milk from the fridge in there. She pulled her clothes back on and did as he said, going down the main staircase, then the narrow stairs into the basement. It was very quiet and eerie in there, especially with the candles burning away in the corner, and she ran across to the fridge and got the carton as quickly as she could.

When she got back upstairs, he was dressed in black tights and sleeveless T-shirt and standing in front of a long mirror combing his hair. She went up behind him and put her arms round his waist and he spun round and pinched her away.

'You must never touch me when I'm dressed like this,' he laughed.

She laughed too and the last wisps of that black cloud vanished completely.

'Can I pull the curtains now?' she asked.

'If you like,' he said, going to a cupboard and taking out a box of porridge oats.

She watched in amusement as he made his breakfast with the oats and cold milk.

'Is that because you haven't got the kitchen fixed?'

'No, I never eat cooked food,' he smiled. 'And I don't drink tea or coffee, so I don't need a kitchen.'

She looked at him, wondering if he were joking.

'If you want anything while I'm away, go round to Sapphire's and get it. She'll put it on my bill.'

While he ate, she wandered round the room looking at things she hadn't noticed before. In a corner there were a pile of cases and boxes. He said they were things which needed unpacking and putting away and perhaps she could do it for him while he was out. She readily agreed; it was just the sort of thing she liked doing, especially when all his belongings looked so interesting.

'Not now,' he smiled as she started to poke around in one of the boxes. 'I want you to come down with me while I exercise.'

In the studio he put on music and one of his dance videos for her and switched on a couple of the lights. The huge room no longer felt eerie but, despite the beat of rock music and the light from the modern fluorescent bulbs, it had an atmosphere of enchantment, as though anything might happen there. She curled on the heap of cushions, alternatively watching him and the screen, already enchanted herself.

She was amazed at what he could do, how effortless his movements and how supple his body became after a few minutes of exercising at the barre. Then he came to the centre of the room, stopped to tighten the straps on his arm and performed a series of acrobatics, ending with a cartwheel executed with one hand. She clapped and he flopped down beside her and lay there panting, his eyes closed, the sweat glistening on his skin.

After a few seconds he rolled over to watch the rest of the video. Again it was of him dancing; this time a variety of different sequences. And in all but one he was the star, and even in this he stood out because of his looks and talent. She glanced at him; he seemed hypnotised by the screen and she thought, if I could have one wish in the whole world it would be for you, so that you could dance again.

He turned suddenly to find her staring, kissed her and smiled.

'I'd better go and get changed now. Could you go and see if the milkman's been? He should have left some cartons of fruit juice.'

She did as he asked and took the cartons up to him. He had on jeans and a blue shirt and was standing in front of the mirror looking at his neck. She sat on the bed and watched him.

'They'll think I've shacked up with a vampire,' he said, pulling up the collar of his shirt. 'Or a sex-crazed schoolgirl.'

She laughed and he turned round, smiling at her. 'Perhaps I should just hibernate in here with you for a week,' he said, taking his leather waistcoat from the back of a chair. As he lifted it, her locket fell to the floor. He picked it up and opened the case as he had that first night.

'Would you wear a picture of me?' he asked. 'And never take it off?'

She nodded and hugged her arms round her legs, chin on her knees and he hooked the chain over the top post of the bed. 'I'll do it later,' he said.

He was gone for over two hours. She sorted through the cases and boxes. They were full of his stage costumes and make-up, music cassettes and photographs, and a pile of stage and theatrical magazines. The photographs were in bundles, sealed up in envelopes with sticky tape, and she didn't undo them but placed them in a drawer, then hung the costumes up in the wardrobe, placing each carefully on a separate hanger. They smelt of him. She held the sleeve of one to her nose and sniffed. It reminded her of the time her father had come home with a chest full of clothes that he said had been shut away for two centuries. He'd opened the lid and she'd crouched down beside him, her face inches from the heap of faded silk and satin. It's the perfume of life, he'd said, the most beautiful perfume of all. She could smell nothing but mustiness and knew it was like the dancing figures in the wood – it took practice to learn how – like making love – first you learn the steps . . .

A sudden feeling of loneliness came over her and she wished Nicky were back, nervous to be alone in this house for too long.

'I bet you've been all over the house poking into everything,' he said when he finally returned.

'I have not! I haven't even left this room.'

'I know,' he said, holding up a key. 'I locked you in.'

She looked at him, half smiling, not knowing whether to believe him and he laughed.

'You'd believe anything,' he said. 'It's the back door key. I turned off the alarm system earlier, so I locked up instead.'

She wasn't sure what he meant about the alarm system, but it all seemed too complicated to worry about, so she opened the wardrobe and showed him what she'd done.

'You shouldn't have bothered,' he said softly. 'I shan't wear them again.' He ran his hands across the hangers then turned and said: 'Come on, I'll show you round the rest of the house, then we'll go to Sapphire's and get you something to eat.'

They started in the locked room next door. It was cold and

gloomy with only one window, and the remains of an ornate fireplace, part dismantled, the grate filled with soot. Covered with dustsheets were a few pieces of furniture and some framed prints.

'I bought all these from the previous owner,' he said, lifting the sheet and sliding out one of the pictures. 'But I bet the old guy with the young wife owned this one. Look at this lecherous bloke after all these girls.'

'No, they're after him,' she laughed. 'It's Hylas and the Nymphs.'

'Who?'

'It's a Greek myth.' She trotted it out, just as her father had done to her some years ago. 'Hylas went to get water from the pool of Pegae and the nymphs that lived in the pool fell in love with him and lured him down to their grotto.'

'Did he drown?'

'Probably.' She smiled, her head to one side. 'But I think they were nice to him before he died.'

'How nice?' He pushed her against the wall and began to kiss her.

They never got to Sapphire's and, later, entwined together in the big bed, she heard the clock strike and realised it had become dark the other side of the velvet curtains.

He had fallen asleep but woke when she sat up.

'I'll have to go soon,' she said.

'Stay here. Sleep here with me.'

It would have been so easy to say yes – the weekends were her own, she was free to do as she liked – but she knew Ross would worry if she didn't go back. He was always warning her to be careful if she went out on her own, and the night she had gone to the hen party with Miran he had given her the money for a cab home.

'They think I'm coming back,' she said. 'They'll be worried.' She always said 'they' for some reason.

'Phone them.'

She hesitated. What could she say? Ross knew nothing about Nicky, he also knew she had no friends.

'I don't think . . .'

'Never mind,' he said. 'I'll call you a cab.'

There was no change in his tone but she knew instinctively that he was annoyed with her, and while they waited for the cab to arrive, he hardly spoke.

He came down to the front door with her but he was barefoot and she knew he wouldn't walk to the gate. As he pulled open the door, she couldn't stand it and turned to him.

'Don't you want me to come here any more?' she said, her voice barely more than a whisper and almost lost in the gust of wind that blew in from outside, banging the door back against the wall.

He caught the door and stood there, twisting the handle back and forth as though he had to think of an answer, then suddenly he grabbed her and pulled her back inside.

'What do you think?' he said, lifting her in a great hug that made her gasp. 'What do you think?'

She didn't answer him because, once again, she was confused by his behaviour, but he just laughed and hugged her tighter and said, 'Come tomorrow. Come early again.'

There was no one around when she got back. In the kitchen there was a note propped on the table. It said: 'Your mother phoned – you can call her back up until eleven. Please leave the conservatory light on for us, Ross.'

It wasn't eleven yet but she didn't feel like calling this late in case Christian answered. That kiss on Christmas Eve which had aroused such a confusion of feelings now seemed totally abhorrent to her. She didn't even want to think of the rest, and certainly didn't want to speak to him. She decided to call in the morning.

She made herself sandwiches, starving because she'd had nothing to eat all day, and as she ate she remembered: she hadn't phoned her mother on Friday. They had got into a routine: her mother called her on Monday evenings and she rang back on Fridays. Ross never minded her using the phone; often he would say, have you spoken to your mother this week?

Josephine heard the Range Rover pull into the yard, then Cheryl call out, 'She's back', and she slipped quickly off to bed.

In her eagerness to be off the next morning, she forgot all about her mother again, and it was Sunday evening before she finally spoke to her.

Solange sounded almost tearful. 'I was worried about you. I keep thinking of you going out in the evenings and all the awful things that happen in London.'

Josephine tried to assure her. 'I hardly go out at all,' she said. 'I'm sorry I forgot to phone on Friday. I have a lot to do here, I can't . . .'

'But you will be coming home for Easter, won't you? Mr Challenor said he thought you would. I told him I'll give you the train fare.'

She hesitated.

'I miss you, Phina . . . so does Louisa.'

'I will come home. But I can't come on Friday: Ross is working and I have to look after Tessa. I'll come Saturday.' Saturday, when she could be with Nicky for the day – and when he might ask her to stay again.

There was a long pause and she heard her mother start to cry.

'Please don't cry, Mother. I'll come home, of course I will.'

The call upset her and she rang Lawrence.

'It's that bastard she's married to,' said Lawrence. 'He's stayed away from home two nights. Nella told me, but I shan't say anything.' He gave an angry sigh. 'I hope it's a case of give him enough rope and he'll hang himself.'

'So do I,' she murmured. Preferably before next week, she thought.

Ross asked her if everything was all right and she forced a smile and said, yes, fine. But a little while later he said he'd been thinking and if she wanted to stay away for an extra couple of days, he'd get his parents to have Tessa. It was on the tip of her tongue to thank him and refuse; but then an idea came to her – she could go to Nicky for the weekend and still have a couple of days with her mother, and tell Ross she was spending the whole time in Norfolk.

'And are you going to say that every weekend?' said Nicky when she explained it to him. 'Am I going to be your secret lover?'

It was Monday morning. She'd gone there after taking Tessa to school and waited in the studio until he'd finished his class.

'If you want,' she said, unable to keep from smiling at him, the concern about her mother forgotten. 'If you ask me to stay, I will.'

'I shall ask you, don't worry about that.' He made a gesture at her with his lips, obscene and exciting. 'Lost weekends when nobody knows where you are. What a good time we're going to have, Josephine.'

Chapter 8

Josephine knew what to do this time; knew what he wanted her to do. And when she crept into his bedroom early on Saturday and slipped into bed beside him, he really was asleep. There was something on the pillow – in the darkness she could just see that it was a rose, a beautiful dark red rose. She leant over and kissed him.

He stirred, coming slowly awake and smiling sleepily at her. 'Mind the thorns,' he said, propping himself on an elbow and looking closely into her face. 'It's to say I'm sorry.'

She knew he meant last week when he'd made her ask if he wanted to see her again and her eyes stung with sudden tears.

'I just like to get my own way.

'You can't always have your own way,' she said, sniffing at the rose.

'Why not?' He laughed and took it from her and held it to his own nose. 'It smells like you. All sweet and smooth and soft and . . .' He laughed again and tossed it on to the floor, then wrapped her in his arms and pulled her on top of him.

They didn't get up until midday, then he went straight down to the studio to exercise and they spent the afternoon there lounging on the cushions, watching videos and eating yoghurt and fruit from the fridge. Late afternoon, they went to Sapphire's and, although she was closed, Nicky tapped on the window and she let them in and fed them. They sat in a corner and Sapphire came and sat with them and fiddled with Nicky's hair and asked what they'd been doing all day. And when Nicky said, what would you be doing if you'd been alone with her since eight o'clock this morning? Josephine had laughed and put her head on his shoulder, intoxicated by the feeling of warmth inside her.

She woke before him on Sunday. He was sleeping very deeply. Throughout the night he had been restless and twice had got up to take painkillers. She crept from the bed and went to the room next door and fetched the picture of Hylas and the Nymphs and stood it on the dressing table so it would be the first thing he saw when he opened his eyes.

And when he did, he looked confused, almost startled, as though he had no idea where he was. It was a few seconds before he even turned his head and noticed her sitting beside him.

'I couldn't think what was happening for a moment.' He sighed and turned his head towards the bedside table and the bottle of pills. 'I think I've had too many of those bloody things – I feel drugged – especially when I open my eyes and find a pond full of naked girls in front of me.'

She laughed and he rolled over and buried his face in her lap. 'And I haven't spent the night with anyone for years – do you know that?'

He was looking up at her now and she didn't know whether to believe him or not. He said a lot of things that she wasn't sure whether to believe: like his father falling from a trapeze and breaking his neck after he'd performed the most daring somersault ever executed by a trapeze artist. After that, she had told him about her own father: how he had fallen from his horse and how she had found him sitting there with his eyes open and couldn't believe he was dead. He'd listened intently, even saying what a shame that her mother had sold the horses. When she finished telling him, he was silent for ages, staring into space. Then he swung round, smiling and said, what exciting ways to die, and it made her think he hadn't really experienced losing someone he loved.

'Is that really true?' she asked now.

'Everything I tell you is true.' He moved away from her and reached out for the pills, tipping the lot into his palm and counting them. 'Did I disturb you much in the night?' he asked.

'I don't mind – I don't mind anything you do.'

'You're an angel, Josephine.' He gave a long contented sigh, put one of the pills in his mouth and the rest back in the bottle. 'Will you go down and get some milk for me?' he asked.

She was beginning to realise that he always got rid of her before he got out of bed, because of his leg, and she began to wonder what it looked like. And as she made her way down to the studio she wondered again about what he'd said: that no other girl had stayed the night with him for years.

As he mixed up the raw oats with the milk she asked, 'Have you never lived with anybody then?'

He lifted the carton to his lips and finished the rest of the milk.

'You ask too many questions,' he said, throwing the empty carton on to the bed.

'But I want to know all about you.' She picked up the carton and put it in a plastic bag with other rubbish that she had gathered together yesterday.

He didn't answer but lifted the picture from the dressing table. 'We'll hang this on the wall,' he said. 'It can remind me what happens to men who trust girls with pretty faces.'

'And what about the other way round?' she smiled, putting her head to one side. 'What about girls who trust handsome men?'

He raised his eyebrows. 'You want to know about trust, do you? Well I'll teach you about that – later.' His tone implied that she definitely wouldn't want to know what he was going to teach her, and she laughed and backed away from him.

'Why later?' she said.

'You'll find out.'

And when it was dark, he took her down to the studio again and led her to the door that opened on to the fire escape.

'Now, do you trust me?' he said.

She was wary, but said she did.

'Then will you walk up there blindfolded if I promise to follow right behind you and catch you if you trip?'

She looked up to the top. The handrail ran only alongside the steps. On the last one which finished beside his bedroom, there was no rail in front; if you carried on walking you would plunge over the end. It seemed no more than slightly daring; she could keep hold of the rail and pull off the blindfold if she got scared.

'All right, I'll do it,' she said.

He switched off the security lights, watching her as he did so, but she said nothing. Neither did she protest when he turned the music up full blast and shouted above it: 'So you can't hear whether I'm still behind you or not.'

He used his T-shirt as a blindfold. 'Now,' he said, close to her ear and waiting a second as though he wanted his words to have full impact. 'I'm going to tie your hands behind your back so you can't take off the blindfold.'

'No!' She immediately pulled if off. 'I could fall. I could be killed.'

'Then you don't trust me.' He stared at her. 'Do you?'

'I do.'

'Then do this for me. Show me you do.'

Her heart was pounding as fast and loud as the music, and she felt caught on a sudden tide of excitement. She looked up into his face and he smiled as though he knew he had won. Without a word he tied the blindfold again, then bound her wrists together with his belt. He lifted her on to the first step and she began climbing very slowly. It was difficult to balance with her hands tied, but she could feel a slight vibration under her feet and knew he was behind her. About three-quarters of the way up by her estimation, she stopped and said loudly: 'You'd better catch me.' The vibration went on and she realised it could not be him or he would have passed her; it must be the music giving the impression of movement. She went up two more steps and then was seized with sudden panic and turned round. 'Nicky!' she shouted. 'Nicky!'

She felt him grab her from behind, laughing and hugging her in a frenzy of movement. He pulled off the belt and the blindfold.

'I was in front of you all the time,' he said. 'I passed you when I put you on the first step.'

She hit out at him. 'It's not funny, I could have been killed.'

'I wouldn't let anything happen to you.' He was kissing her now, his lips moving over every inch of her face while he pulled her T-shirt free from her jeans.

As she sank down on the metal steps with him, it seemed as if the world consisted only of the beam of light from the studio below and the harsh twang of electric guitars echoing up from the sound system.

And the following day when she sat with her mother and Christian in the sitting room at Waylands and her mother said, 'I was hoping you'd come yesterday, Phina, so that you could come to the evening service with me,' she had to look away, remembering how she had listened to the sound of church bells high on that fire escape with Nicky.

It rained the whole two days she was at Waylands and there was no chance to walk up through the pine forests or wander down along the river, no chance to recapture the things she'd missed so much when she first left. Seeing Christian again wasn't as bad as she imagined it would be. He was moody and quiet the first day, hardly speaking to her at all, and was out at an auction the whole of the next day. Her mother seemed edgy and looked tired and drawn.

Nella told her that Christian had been drinking again, but Josephine made no comment; Lawrence would have to deal with her mother, she couldn't. She no longer wanted to be there. All she wanted was get back to London, and to Nicky. And even to Ross and Tessa. She found herself missing them as well. Waylands seemed filled only with unhappy memories, its huge quiet rooms dismal and cold. Even the gardens, filled now with spring flowers, looked bleak and desolate in the constant rain.

But the first night back in London, her mother's face haunted her, and she cried silent tears into her pillow, confused by her feelings of detachment for the home she had once loved so much. If only that hateful secret did not lie between them; if only she could talk to her mother and look forward to going home. But as she drifted into sleep, she was already hurrying through that little cobbled alleyway, then counting her steps along by the red brick wall, and Waylands faded into the distance.

As spring merged into summer, she went to Nicky every weekend. Sometimes he asked her to come during the week but then she worried about meeting Tessa and she never felt he was quite the same on these days.

The group of teenagers came to his house every weekday morning – or so she imagined, and some days he would go with them to auditions or to meet people. It was a part of his life of which she knew little. Like the two men she had met coming down the garden path one morning. One had tattoos and plaits and the other cropped yellow hair and make-up. Neither had spoken to her, and when she'd asked Nicky who they were, he had said, what men? He'd been shaving and she'd watched his face in the mirror and felt sudden ridiculous jealousy that he should have friends come to the house and not tell her about them. But nobody ever came at the weekends; on those two days he was completely hers.

Her feelings for him became more intense; she wanted to know more about him. Sometimes he answered her questions, other times he would ignore her or answer in such a way that it only created more questions in her mind. And he rarely asked her anything about herself.

Once she asked him about one of the videos they were watching, and he told her it was part of a television series.

'We didn't have television until last Christmas,' she said.

'So you never saw me before that evening in the Rising Sun?'

They were stretched on the cushions in the studio and he lay there, massaging his leg, as she had seen him do so many times before.

'You would have been about fourteen while the show was on,' Nicky said. Like everyone else he still believed she was eighteen. 'You might have been one of my fans,' he smiled. 'It was aimed at early teens. It was about some kids who wanted to dance but hadn't had any proper training. They used to practise in a derelict theatre and dream about being famous. And then I'm the Magician who comes along and – ' he clicked his fingers – 'made all their dreams come true by magic.'

'It sounds wonderful,' she said, rolling over to look at him. 'Do you think they'll repeat it?'

He shook his head. 'No. If I hadn't had the accident, it would have been taken off anyway.'

'Why?'

'It got a lot of bad publicity.'

Josephine waited, knowing it was at points like this when he usually changed the subject.

'Why?' she said again.

'Oh . . .' he sighed. 'Critics who knew nothing about dancing read the wrong things into it. I didn't choose the music but I helped with the choreography and I got the blame for the way I interpreted it.' He smiled to himself. 'I created some brilliant sequences. The kids helped me – they knew all sorts of stories about magic, things they'd learnt at school, like *The Tempest*. I made the mistake of drawing circles on the floor and . . .' he broke off. 'It was all blown up in the papers. Luckily my contract hadn't run out when I had the accident, so I still got compensation for lost earnings – for what it's worth.' His voice had dropped low now and she knew he wouldn't go on, though she longed to know the details of the accident.

'But you would rather still be dancing,' she said very quietly.

'Of course.' He rolled over and lay at right-angles to her, his head on her stomach – he often lay like this. 'Sometimes it's like death.'

She could think of nothing to say. He had closed his eyes and she stroked his hair. It was incredibly shiny, a mixture of many dark, dark reds and almost unreal in texture, like the pearly sheen of his skin. And his eyelashes were unnaturally thick and straight. Lying there, perfectly still, he could have been made of wax. A beautiful broken dancing doll. The words came into her head like the first line of a poem. She whispered them to herself, searching for another line.

His eyes flicked open. 'Do you want to go out tonight?' he said, sitting up. He had never asked her before.

She hesitated, not wanting to move away from this moment, not wanting to be amongst other people with him.

'I don't know your friends – I wouldn't fit in.'

'You don't have to fit in with anybody,' he said. 'I like you as you are.'

'But they're all . . . beautiful and witty and everything,' she finished lamely.

'You should have more confidence in yourself, Josephine.' He traced a forefinger round her face. 'You're as beautiful as any of them and you've got something extra that can't be learnt. You're the sort of girl most men dream of.'

Despite all they did together, he still had the power to embarrass her. She turned away from him. 'Don't be silly,' she said.

Nicky smiled, craning round to look into her face. 'And sometimes I think you know it very well.'

'As long as you dream of me; that's all I care about.' Often she said things like this to him, always hoping it would prompt him into saying he loved her. And always he would laugh and say nothing and she'd look at him and realise how little he ever gave away.

She began to associate his mind with his leg; they became twin secrets, obsessing her curiosity, and early one Sunday morning, while he lay drugged with painkillers, she switched on the bedside lamp and carefully uncovered him.

It was horribly scarred: a raised purple line ran from his thigh to his ankle, crisscrossed on his calf by other ragged lines. It looked as though someone had tried to remove his flesh with a can opener. She stared at it, then ran her eyes up over his body, his flawless narrow torso, widening out at the chest and ending in the smooth-muscled shoulders. How awful to be so perfect and then have part of you destroyed. How specially awful for him. Pity and tenderness overwhelmed her and she bent to kiss the scars, resting her cheek against his thigh.

He moved, raised his head, and she waited, wondering if he'd be angry. But he said nothing, just let his head fall back on the pillows. She kissed his leg again and he took hold of her head and moved it up a little and she knew immediately what he wanted her to do.

'What's the matter?' he said softly. 'Don't you want to?'

All she had to do was say no – he never made her do anything she didn't want to. Half of her did want to. A new experience; something to please him. But still she hesitated. It hadn't taken her long to realise that her innocence was a strong attraction for him, but sometimes she wondered about the other girls he'd made love to and worried that he might wish for someone more experienced for a change.

After a few seconds, she looked up at him and smiled. 'I might not do it right,' she said, then lay her head against his leg once more.

He laughed and hoisted her up beside him. 'No wonder I love you,' he said. Then he kissed her and whispered, 'I'll show you.' But even when he lowered his head and started to suck at the inside of her thighs, finally sliding his tongue inside her until the pleasure was almost unbearable, she could think only of what he had just said – that he loved her.

He began buying her presents, expensive things like clothes and perfume, leaving them on the pillow of his bed as he had done the rose.

One day he gave her an exquisitely pretty camisole top. It was pure white, embroidered all over with tiny blue flowers and very close fitting.

She tried it on as she got ready to go and collect Tessa. She was already wearing a short skirt of soft blue suede that he had bought her the week before and the two matched perfectly.

He lay stretched on the bed watching her, and rolled over to catch her round the waist.

'You look so delicious I could eat you,' he said.

She prised away his hands, laughing at the words. 'I can't go and meet Tessa like this.'

'Of course you can. You'll have all those schoolboys lusting after you.'

'It's a primary school!' She looked at her watch, then at him. 'Wouldn't you care if anybody else was after me?'

'Why should I? I trust you, and there's nothing wrong with someone else fancying you.'

It wasn't the answer she wanted, and she left with a twinge of resentment towards him and annoyance with herself for going to him on a weekday.

Her mother rang that evening, asking when she would be coming home again. She was tempted to say, next weekend, and let Nicky wonder where she was. But, even as the idea entered her head, she knew she wouldn't do it.

'I can't come yet, Mother. It's too far for just a couple of days.' She kept her voice low; Ross still believed she went home every weekend.

'I miss you, darling.' There was a little silence, then she added, 'I'm feeling a bit down because I've had a dreadful cold.'

'I'll come soon,' Josephine relented. 'I promise.'

'Everything all right?' asked Ross as she went back into the kitchen.

'Yes, yes thank you.' She gave a little smile. 'My mother hasn't been very well.'

'Well, go on Friday if you like,' he said. 'My mother can pick Tess up.'

'No, it's all right – my brother will go and see her.'

She looked away, suddenly hating all these lies when he was always so kind to her.

'Why is your mummy not well?' asked Tessa. She was spooning chocolate mousse from a dish and came to stand in front of her.

'She'll be better soon.'

'She's not going to die, is she?' said Tessa, the spoon halfway to her mouth.

Josephine saw Ross look quite stricken for a moment, and she bent down and put an arm round Tessa. 'No, she's only got a cold.' She squeezed her ribs. 'You're getting a fatty eating so much chocolate mousse.'

Tessa giggled and offered her a spoonful.

'You are honoured,' said Ross, smiling again. 'Be careful, Tess, you'll get it all over Josephine's clothes,' he added.

'It's OK, I should have changed.' She stopped and brushed her hands over her skirt. 'It's not really suitable for . . .'

'You look very nice,' he said. 'Just don't go out in my yard like that when the men are there or I'll have a riot on my hands.'

She laughed but knew she was blushing.

'What's a riot?' said Tessa.

'It's what we have when it's your bedtime,' he joked.

'Not yet,' she protested. 'You said we could play cards.'

Josephine had taught her to play Happy Families, and she insisted on playing a game every evening now. Ross dealt out the cards while Josephine loaded the dishwasher.

It seemed to her that Ross tried extra hard to make them laugh tonight, as though Tessa had raked up a bit of sadness and he wanted to forget it. He cheated all the time until he had Tessa shrieking with laughter.

'Phina, he's taken my cards,' she said, crawling across the table to get them.

Josephine laughed as well and caught hold of his wrists to make him drop the stolen cards.

'Pinch him!' shouted Tessa.

'Having fun?'

None of them had heard Cheryl come in. Josephine looked up and felt Ross pull his arms away from her.

'Yes we are!' shouted Tessa, standing on the table now.

Ross lifted her down. 'Bedtime,' he said, passing her to Josephine.

Tessa started to complain but Josephine said she was going to bed as well and would sit with her for a while.

'Oh,' said Cheryl, raising her eyebrows. 'I thought you were going to a party by the looks of you.'

There was an uncomfortable silence, then Tessa said: 'Are you really going to a party, Phina?'

'No, she's not, now go to bed,' said Ross.

Tessa wouldn't settle down, and Josephine knew very well it

was because her father was with Cheryl. She remembered times when she had felt left out when her mother was with Christian – and even much further back, when her father was with her mother. She tried to push these thoughts from her mind; the day seemed to have gone all wrong somehow.

An hour or so after she had gone to bed, Tessa was calling her.

'I want Spikey to cuddle,' she whined.

'Daddy said you mustn't have him in bed.' Tessa had been told before that she couldn't bring the kitten upstairs, but again Josephine knew it was only her jealousy.

Tessa started to cry and Josephine said she could have him for ten minutes and then he had to go back in the kitchen. She could hear the low hum of the radio from Ross's bedroom and guessed he and Cheryl were in there. She crept downstairs and fetched the kitten. Passing Ross's door on her way back up, she heard Cheryl's voice, raised slightly.

'She does it all the time.'

She lingered at the bottom of the stairs, knowing they were talking about her.

'She's the kind of girl who looks for affection everywhere,' Cheryl went on.

'I think she's had an unhappy home life.' Ross's voice was much quieter. 'And Tess loves her.'

'Yes, because she gives in to her all the time. And look how she laughs at all Miran's stupid remarks – she acts like a ten-year-old at times with some of the things she does.'

'Maybe, but she's very capable and willing. She does all sorts of things round the house that I never ask her to.'

'You're just won over by her pretty face and her posh voice.' Cheryl was beginning to sound annoyed. 'But you know hardly anything about her – you didn't even bother to take up her references.'

Ross's answer was lost in a peal of laughter from the radio.

'She's trouble, Ross, I'm telling you . . . you just don't want to see it.'

Josephine crept back up the stairs, stunned and hurt by what she had heard. How could Cheryl say such things about her? She bit her lip, fighting back the tears and grasping the kitten too tightly. It mewed and scratched at her and she stumbled, nearly dropping it. A door opened below.

'Tess?' Ross called. 'Is that you?'

Josephine sped up the last few stairs and into Tessa's room.

'Shush,' she whispered to Tessa, a finger against her lips. But it was too late; Ross came up after her.

'Oh it's you, Josephine,' he said as he opened Tessa's door. 'I thought . . .' He stopped, looking at her for a moment – then he saw the kitten.

'I've told you, Tessa, you're not to have him upstairs.' His voice was unusually sharp and Tessa started to cry.

'It was just for ten minutes,' muttered Josephine, near to tears herself.

'Then it would be a bit longer and a bit longer.' He went and took the kitten. 'You know what she is.'

Tessa buried her head in her pillow and cried more loudly. Josephine couldn't bear it and went to leave but Ross caught her arm.

'I'm not blaming you,' he said. 'I know she can . . .' His voice faded away; he looked uncomfortable, and she knew he suspected she had overheard his conversation with Cheryl.

He gave the kitten back to Tessa. 'Ten minutes, and I mean it,' he said. 'And don't go calling Josephine out of bed any more.'

As she crossed the landing, Josephine could see Cheryl at the bottom of the stairs. She lay awake most of the night worrying that Cheryl would persuade Ross to get rid of her and that she'd have to go home. Nicky had never ever mentioned anything about her staying with him; he seemed perfectly content with things the way they were.

She stared into the darkness, listening to the faint sounds of the radio from below, and wondered what she could have done to Cheryl and why it was that something always happened to spoil her happiness.

Chapter 9

Saturday morning as she walked to Nicky's, she made the decision to question him about their future: not ask him outright if he would ever want her to live there, she couldn't do that – just drop some hints maybe.

But when she pushed open the gate, all the ideas she had for broaching the subject vanished. There was a small boy in the front garden. He was trying to coax one of the wild cats down from the branch of a tree where it stood, back arched, spitting at him. He was a bit older than Tessa, about seven or eight.

'Could you help me please?' he asked, poking at the cat with a stick. 'I just want to give it some milk.' He was well spoken, his voice almost adult in tone – and he was the image of Nicky.

She stared at him without answering. He had the same long narrow eyes curtained with the same mahogany lashes; the same high, slightly crooked cheekbones; and his hair, although nearly black, was highlighted with red in the sunshine and cut in the same long, layered style. Even his clothes echoed Nicky's: he wore denim shorts with leather braces and he had gold rings in his ears.

'I want to tame it,' he said, smiling at her. 'I haven't got a pet of my own.'

The only difference was that he had much darker skin than Nicky, making him look Italian or Spanish.

'It's wild, you can't tame it,' she said almost automatically.

He dropped the stick. 'I'll trap it then. I'll ask Nicky if he's got a box.'

He went racing off up the path and she followed, followed him right up to Nicky's bedroom and watched him leap on to the bed and into the place which was normally hers.

Nicky was sitting up eating his usual bowl of cold porridge oats. He put an arm around the boy's shoulders and looked up at her.

'He's my son,' he said briefly. 'I didn't know he was coming until last night.'

She wanted to walk out. That he should keep such a big secret from her hurt her so much that she wanted to walk out and never see him again. But she couldn't. She just stood there until he held out a hand to her.

'Come here,' he said very softly, and she went to his side and sat on the edge of the bed.

'His name's Nico.' He turned to the child. 'This is Josephine.' Then he carried on eating.

'Why didn't you tell me you had a son?' she said.

'I didn't consider it important.'

'Oh, having a child's not important.' Her voice was stilted with hurt.

'Of course it's important.' He stopped eating and bent over to kiss the boy's cheek. Nico immediately kissed him back. 'He's very important to me. I meant I didn't think it was important to tell you. I didn't know he'd ever be allowed to visit me here and I didn't think you'd ever meet.' He gave Nico his empty bowl. 'Take it downstairs and fill it with milk for the cats if you like.'

When he'd gone, Nicky leant over to kiss her but she turned away.

'It's the girl who walked out on you after the accident,' she said. 'He's her son, isn't he?'

'Yes.'

There was silence and she thought, he's not going to say any more – he's just not going to tell me anything about it.

'If you don't want to kiss me can you let me out of bed? I want to get dressed,' he said finally.

It was all too much coming so soon after Cheryl's accusations, and she covered her face with her hands and cried broken-heartedly.

He pulled her hands away and kissed first her cheeks then her eyelids. 'I didn't realise it would upset you.' He looked into her face then drew her against him.

'I can't bear it when you keep everything secret from me,' she sobbed. 'I feel as though you don't really care about me.'

He stroked her hair and kissed her cheek again. 'Of course I care about you. But I care about Nico as well. I was never married to his mother so I haven't got any rights to see him. She just allows him to visit me when the mood takes her, and I'd never turn down the chance to see him.'

'Does she bring him?' she asked, wiping at her face.

'No, he gets brought and collected by a chauffeur. She's married to a musical director and rich as hell.'

'So you don't see her?'

'No, never. She hates me just as much as I hate her.'

'But how can she hate you? She makes him look like you . . . even his hair's cut the same.'

He sighed and cuddled her. 'It's obvious you don't know very much about hate.'

She wanted to question him more, but Nico came back, and Nicky said he would help him try and trap one of the cats. They spent the first half of the morning in the garden, with Nicky climbing up the trees and then building a complicated trap with strings leading into the kitchen. But the cats soon disappeared over the wall and Nicky suggested they play a game of hide-and-seek in the house. Crouched in a cupboard with Nico, she couldn't resist asking if his mother ever came here.

'Oh no,' he said confidently. 'She'd never come here.'

'Does Nicky ever come to your house?'

'No, of course not.' He gave a little laugh, folding his arms with a shrug that said, don't be silly. 'My other father calls him a crazy bastard.'

The word sounded so incongruous coming from the lips of this well brought up child that she almost laughed herself, then Nicky's uneven footsteps were coming along the hall.

'He wants me to be a dancer like him,' he whispered.

'Are you going to?'

'I . . .' He clutched her and shrieked as Nicky pulled open the door and pounced on them.

Nicky took them to Sapphire's for lunch. The day was hot, front gardens were brimful of flowers, and even the sinister cobbled alleyway was lit by sunshine. It should have been an enjoyable day, a change from the hours spent in the darkened rooms of the house – Nico was a charming boy, with faultless manners and a great sense of fun and Nicky seemed at his best, relaxed and smiling and so obviously devoted to him – but

Josephine could not conquer her jealousy. It rose and fell in varying degrees until the chauffeur-driven car arrived and Nico left. And even then she found it difficult to be herself.

'I'm jealous – I can't help it,' she admitted when Nicky questioned her. 'Not of him – of his mother.'

His brows drew together as though he found her statement ridiculous. 'I've told you, I never see her – we hate each other.'

'If you threatened to kill her for leaving you, you must have loved her very much.'

He gave an impatient sigh. 'So what do you want me to do – threaten to kill you? It's in the past. I don't talk about people you've been in love with, do I?'

'I've never been in love before. You're the only person I've ever loved.'

They were listening to music, propped on the pillows of his bed and he leant over to kiss her. 'What did you say?'

'I said you're the only person I've ever loved.'

'Pardon?'

'I said . . .' She broke off, realising he was teasing her.

He stretched out and lay with his head in her lap. 'Go on, say it again,' he said.

'I love you, I love you, I love you,' she said.

He pushed up her skirt and kissed the bare skin of her stomach, then reached up to undo her zip. 'Perhaps I might kill you after all,' he said. 'If you ever betray me.'

That night, they lay awake talking for hours. He seemed especially tender and loving towards her, and more willing to answer her questions than ever before.

He told her about his mother, how she would thrill the circus audiences by standing on a horse's back while it galloped round the ring, pretending to fall and then recovering at the last second, or lying on the ground while it reared above her.

'She ran off with someone else when I was five. After my father was killed, his mother brought me up,' he said. 'She'd been a dancer in a travelling show but she always wanted to be a ballerina, that's why she sent me to ballet school. She died before I started all the contemporary stuff – but she wouldn't have approved, however rich it made me.'

'Is your mother still alive?'

'I don't think so. I haven't seen her since she left, but I get the feeling she's dead. Sometimes I feel she's watching me from the mirrors.'

He was always saying things like that. Once he'd made up an elaborate tale about the dancer who used to live in the house and whose name was on the marble plaque. He said her husband had killed her and he'd seen her in the studio. And later, when it was dark, he'd asked her to go down there and get milk from the fridge for him. She called his bluff, knowing it was one of his games, but when he came down after her and switched off the lights and shut her in, she had still screamed with fright. And all these games ended in the same way, as though they heightened his sexual excitement.

'Shall we go down there?' he said now. 'You can contact anyone through mirrors.'

'No,' she said abruptly, a vision coming into her head of them making love on the heap of cushions and faces appearing in the mirrors, perhaps her father's. 'No,' she repeated, 'it's too scary.' She took a deep breath. 'Don't you ever get scared here on your own? Don't you ever wish you had someone with you?'

'I came here to be on my own – away from everyone. That's what I wanted – to live alone so I can do exactly as I like. I don't think there's anyone who could put up with me anyway.'

'I would.'

She spoke so quietly she wasn't even sure if he'd heard, but after a few seconds he said: 'I don't sleep well, I don't eat like other people, and now and again I like to indulge in a little wizardry.' He paused, swivelling his eyes towards her. She knew what he meant: his friends that came sometimes and the stuff they took. It never happened at the weekends and he rarely mentioned it, ignoring her if ever she did. Like the other parts of his life, it was nothing to do with her.

Again the seconds ticked away and then he added: 'I need to be alone sometimes.'

He sat up and reached for the bottle of tablets. That was usually the signal that he would settle to sleep for a while, but as he turned to kiss her he said, 'I didn't mean to make you cry about Nico – I'm sorry. Sometimes I don't think of other people's feelings – sometimes I don't want to.'

She kept quiet, sensing he was going to say more.

'When I was lying on the road after the accident,' he went on, 'I heard someone say, "I've got no sympathy for these kids on motorbikes, he was probably going too fast." I was conscious all the time. I was watching my blood run away down the gutter and wanting someone to say I wasn't going to die . . . and I hear someone say that. I couldn't believe it.'

'How did it happen?'

'I was pulling away from traffic lights and a van came up on the inside and cut across in front of me. It wasn't my fault; I never took chances. It was just the image people had of me. I had too much to lose to risk injuring myself. Luckily there were witnesses.'

He shook two of the tablets into his palm and she sat up beside him and wished again that she could think of something to say that would make things right for him.

'There,' he said, hooking an arm round her shoulders. 'You know all about me now.'

But this communicative mood didn't last, and when, the following week, Miran called in with a newspaper and pointed to a small piece headlined, 'Frey Causes Affray at Ballerina's Celebration', she felt once again that he led two lives: one of which she knew nothing about.

She read it through, trying to show only mild interest. Miran had been busy setting up her own hairdressing salon over the past few months and they had seen little of her.

It stated that Nicky had gone into the Rising Sun and ripped all his photographs off the wall a few hours before the start of a celebration party for the opening night of a ballet. She had heard of the ballet *Coppelia*, but not of the ballerina, Elena Martinez. It also said that the barman alleged Nicky had threatened him when he interfered and police had been called, but after intervention by – she read another woman's name – Romana Maron, no charges were brought. There was a picture of him leaving the pub with Alice from the group and the older woman she had seen with him the first night she'd met him.

Ross came in as she was looking at it and peered over her shoulder. 'Oh, him causing trouble again,' he said.

Miran gave her a secret wink. 'Phina had her eye on him that night I took her down there, but I told her he wasn't very nice to know.'

Ross smiled at her. 'You don't go for ponced-up blokes like that, do you, Phina?'

Her cheeks were instantly hot and he gave her shoulder a quick squeeze. 'I'm only joking. I know all the girls like him.' He looked at Miran now. 'I reckon she's got a boyfriend in Norfolk anyway. She's off home every weekend.' He put his arm right round her now. 'I'm only worried that one of these days she won't come back.'

Before she could say anything, Miran had waved a file of papers in front of his face.

'I'm glad I've caught you in such an expansive mood, my darling,' she said. 'I've got all the figures worked out now.'

'Come on then,' he said, stretching and yawning. 'Let's have a look.'

Josephine watched them go through to the conservatory, the newspaper still in her hand. She knew Ross's business was doing well and he was going to help Miran finance the new salon. She felt a sudden flash of annoyance at them and at herself for not having the courage to stand up for Nicky. She wanted to tell them that they didn't understand the first thing about him, and that she wasn't just one of the girls who looked at him, she spent every weekend, not in Norfolk, but at his house, doing things they'd never imagine. But that would mean jeopardising her job and her life in this house where she had grown so happy – it was bad enough with Cheryl trying to turn Ross against her. Once more she seemed caught in a trap of her own making.

It didn't help when she rang Lawrence, hoping to talk, perhaps tell him about Nicky, and he said he thought their mother's marriage was breaking up.

'It's been crumbling since Christmas, and serves him bloody right,' he said. 'The lazy bastard will have to start working for his living again if he walks out.'

'But what about Mother?' she said in a small voice. 'She'll be so unhappy.'

'I know,' he said with a long sigh. 'But she'll get over it.'

'She won't – she loves him.'

'She coped with losing Dad. That was much worse.'

He cut short the conversation, obviously wanting to go, and the need to talk to someone grew until it hurt.

By the weekend she felt restless and excitable, as though something were fermenting away inside her. And for the first time ever she instigated their early morning sex, climbing into bed before Nicky was fully awake and starting to masturbate him.

'How you've changed,' he said, smiling up at her with sleepy, glazed eyes. 'What a great teacher I am.'

'And what a brilliant pupil I am,' she said.

He caught her hand and pushed her down, rolling on top of her.

'Why did you stop me?' she asked, winding her arms round his neck.

'I don't know,' he murmured.

She felt his hands run slowly down her body from her armpits to her thighs, pressing gently into her flesh as though he were moulding her, like a sculptor working his clay.

'I don't know,' he murmured again. 'I don't know why I always want to be inside you.'

They didn't go to Sapphire's for lunch; there seemed to be something electric between them that day which precluded all contact with other people. By mid-afternoon they had exhausted themselves with a mixture of games and sex, pushing what they did to the limits. And once, at the height of passion, Josephine had whispered to him, 'Say you love me, Nicky,' and for only the second time since they'd known each other he'd said it.

'I love you, Josephine,' he said. 'Until death us do part, I love you.'

She watched him do his final exercise session, sated with an emotion that felt almost frightening in its intensity, and when he said he wanted to sleep, she was disappointed, wanting to talk.

They went back upstairs and he drew the thick curtains across, shutting out the sunshine and plunging the room into semi-darkness, then flung himself on the bed.

'Let me sleep, please,' he said, touching her cheek as though to say: be quiet.

But she couldn't keep silent, she had to ask him; the question was burning away inside her.

'Is Nico's mother called Elena Martinez?'

'Yes.' He waited a moment, then turned to face her. 'You read it in the paper did you?'

She nodded. 'Did you see her that night?'

'No.' He gave a sharp little sigh and she knew she shouldn't have started this. 'I didn't go there to see her, I went to speak to her husband.' He made the sound again. 'Under whose roof my son happens to live. I wanted to tell him that unless she stops lying about me, I shall not stop at threats in future.'

'What lies?'

124

He screwed up his face. 'Why do you make me go over all this?'

She felt the tears well up. 'I just want to know.'

'She said that I didn't look after Nico properly last week. That he was left unsupervised in the garden and that I had no food in the house for him and . . .' He broke off and turned over.

'What was Alice doing there?'

'The whole group were there, it's nothing unusual.' His voice softened slightly. 'I used to go there a lot before I met you.'

'Who's Romana?'

'An old dancing teacher of mine. Now stop your questions and let me sleep.'

'I only ask because I want to know about you . . . everything, so that I can understand you better.'

He put his hands to his ears as though he wanted to block her out. 'I don't want you to understand me,' he said. 'I just want you to fuck me.' He moved away slightly, pulling the duvet over his head.

She sat there completely rigid. It felt as though a giant hand were gripping her heart, squeezing it tighter and tighter. Parts of the day flashed before her eyes and she glanced towards his buried head, wanting to drag the duvet from him and pound him with her fists.

Finally she got up and began to gather up things of hers that she'd left there over the weeks. He didn't move. She reached up for her locket which still hung from the bedpost, tugging away at it until she snapped the new chain he'd bought her. Angry tears were streaming down her face and choking in her throat and she wanted to shout at him, if I go I'm never coming back, but knew it would just be a way of getting his attention and that it would mean she had given in once more. She found her shoes and put them on – there was nothing left to do.

She had her hand on the door handle when he leapt out of the bed and stopped her going. It was the first time he'd ever used his strength against her. She cried openly now, kicked him and bit him and scratched him, but he just held on to her until she stopped fighting, then dragged her back to the bed, sitting on the edge with her on his lap.

'I'm sorry, I'm sorry,' he said, pressing his cheek against hers and holding her arms against her sides.

'Why did you say that?' she sobbed. 'You've spoilt everything.'

'I'm sorry,' he said again. 'I didn't mean it, you know I didn't.' He loosened his hold on her and when she made no attempt to get away he folded her in his arms. 'Do you forgive me?' He lifted a lock of her hair and wiped her tears with it, then rubbed it over his shoulder where blood was beginning to ooze from the punctures she'd made with her nails.

'There's nothing to forgive,' she said, the tears starting again. 'You just told the truth.'

'Stop it now.' He gave her a gentle shake and kissed her cheek as though he were pacifying a sulky child. 'I know, we'll go out for the day tomorrow. Anywhere you want. Yes?' He pressed his cheek against hers again and she nodded through her tears.

They went to Windsor. She remembered the happy day she'd spent there with Ross and Tessa when she first came to London, and wanted to capture the same atmosphere with Nicky; prove that there was more to their relationship than just sex and games behind the walls of that brooding house.

But the day was not a success. It started out well – the weather was wonderfully hot and sunny and Nicky was full of smiles and affectionate talk. But he could not walk the long distances she wanted to and, although he didn't complain, she soon realised fresh air and sunshine were not his idea of enjoyment. And she hated the way women looked at him. She tried to ignore it, but some even smiled at him quite openly, and it was obvious that even if he had been on crutches with only one leg, he would still have attracted attention. When two girls in their late teens came up and asked for his autograph while they were in a restaurant having lunch, she almost wished they had stayed at home.

'I didn't realise you were that famous,' she said.

'They just remember my show, that's all.'

She wanted to say: why did you have to look right into their eyes when you spoke to them? Why do you have to smile back so invitingly when women look at you? But she knew she was being ridiculous and that he had done nothing she could reproach him with.

He took her hand as though he guessed her thoughts. 'Come on, let's find somewhere quiet.'

But there were crowds everywhere on such a beautiful day, and in the end they went and sat down by the river so that he could rest his leg. After a little while he pulled off his T-shirt, rolled it up for a pillow and stretched out with his eyes closed. They had chosen a spot in the shade of a huge willow tree but still the sun filtered through, dappling his pale skin with bright patches. She bent her head towards him.

'Don't fall asleep,' she said. 'You'll burn.'

He opened his eyes and slipped his hand round the back of her neck. 'You do still care about me then?'

She sighed. 'Yes, but I can't think why.'

'Let's go home,' he said, brushing his lips against hers.

Yesterday was forgotten.

Chapter 10

But once away from him, Nicky's words kept coming back to her. They were like a wound that wouldn't heal and she went over and over things that he'd said, whole conversations they'd had, searching for clues to his real feelings for her. But her conclusions were always the same: it was true, he didn't want her to understand him – and the rest was true – and it was her own fault because she'd given herself to him far too easily. And now he took her for granted.

She missed a weekend, pretending she was going home, and on Saturday went to the supermarket with Ross and Tessa. It was something she normally enjoyed, but today she trailed along holding Tessa's hand and thought only of Nicky.

Back home, Ross asked her what was wrong, and she said, 'Nothing,' and busied herself stacking away all the shopping for him. Halfway through he told her to leave it and beckoned her into the sitting room away from Tessa.

'I know what's been worrying you,' he said, closing the door.

She stared at him, her mind darting off along different channels.

'You overheard what Cheryl said that night you came down to get the kitten, didn't you?'

'A bit of it.'

'I thought you had,' he smiled. 'I've got to know you over the past six months.' His face became serious again. 'Josephine, I don't know how much you heard and I can't even remember all we said, but let me assure you that I decide who looks after Tess – no one else – and if I'm happy with you that's all that matters.'

'I don't mean to spoil her,' she said with a rush of relief. 'But I don't like to see her unhappy.'

'And I don't like to see you unhappy, so forget about it. Right?'

She nodded.

'I'll soon moan at you when you do something wrong.' He looked at her, his head to one side. 'Cheer up then.'

She forced a smile and wished he'd stop being so kind to her.

By Wednesday she was desperate to see Nicky. It was the first chance she got because Tessa was on holiday from school and she had agreed to look after her during the day, except for Wednesday when she went to her grandparents.

On the way she picked up some shopping for him; she'd often done that: he'd do without something rather than go to the shops himself.

As she walked up the front path, music echoed up to meet her and she went straight down to the studio. Only one of the lights was on, and she stood by the door and watched, unsure whether he had seen her come in. The class looked about to finish; she could tell by their sweat-dampened hair and the heat that filled the room. He demonstrated a movement to them, then stopped to massage his shoulder and tighten the straps on his arm. She had seen him do this a hundred times, but it stirred something in her, and she burned with longing for him.

The music came to an end and they all relaxed, letting their bodies hang limp like a group of rag dolls. Nicky looked towards her now and she was sure he'd known she was there all along. He shook his head like a dog shakes water from its coat and ran a hand through his mane of hair and across his forehead, then went to the fridge and drank from a carton of milk. Finally he came over to her.

'What have you brought me?' he said, peering into the carrier.

'Just some food.' She longed to touch him but held back, wanting him to make the first move.

'Did you have a good weekend?' There was something challenging about his tone and the way he stared at her, and before she could phrase her answer, he added, 'You didn't go home, did you?'

She made the smallest movement of her head, wanting to explain and wanting to say, no, I missed you but I had to do it.

'Don't start playing hard to get,' he said. 'It doesn't appeal to me in the slightest.' He turned and walked off back to his pupils, stopping halfway to say over his shoulder: 'Take that upstairs. I'll be up in a minute.'

She waited there a moment, watched as the group gathered round him. They were laughing together over something, then Alice put her hands on her hips in a defiant gesture and said: 'I'm not doing that.'

She saw the others shrug and look at each other, then Nicky put his arm round Alice and kissed her on the cheek. She shook her head and he kissed her again. She laughed and pretended to hit him. He often kissed his pupils but today Josephine felt a stab of anger, sure he was doing it only to arouse her jealousy. He looked over his shoulder once more and she marched off.

She went up to the kitchen and tipped the contents of the carrier bag on to the table.

The next minute he was standing in the doorway. 'What are you doing?' he said. 'You know the cats get in here.'

She didn't move and he came over and started to gather up the things.

'I'm going upstairs, I have to get changed to go out,' he said, his whole manner offhand. 'Are you coming up with me or not?'

'It's disgusting to keep eating in the bedroom.'

He gave a brief smile and shook his head. 'If you're trying to provoke me, you'll have to do a lot better than that.'

'You tried to provoke me!'

'What, by kissing Alice?'

'You only did it to make me jealous.' Her brows drew together. 'You're always trying to do that.'

He pointed a finger at her. 'Look, I don't lie to *you* about where I spend the weekend. I might have a lot of faults, but I've never lied to you, and I have never slept with anyone else since the first day we met. Anything else I do is my business.'

'So you don't want me in all your life – I'm only allowed in part of it, am I?'

'We'll talk later – when you're in a better frame of mind.' He began to put the shopping back in the carrier.

'When we're in bed, you mean.'

'This is going to end in tears, Josephine,' he said in a warning voice. 'So stop it, now.'

'No it won't,' she said, swallowing hard. 'I shan't cry over you any more.'

'Good, because I don't have the time or the patience to deal with your silly tantrums today.' He didn't even look up and she waited a second then swept the remaining things to the floor.

He looked at her now. 'Pick them up and stop behaving like a spoilt kid.'

'No! I'm not your slave, do it yourself.'

He looked up at the ceiling and took a deep breath. 'I don't need this, Josephine.'

'I don't think you need me either.' The tears were choking in her throat but she held them back. 'I don't know why I come here.'

Nicky left the shopping and walked off down the hall, slamming the door behind him, and she ran out of the back door and down the garden path.

Her anger sustained her for about five minutes, and then she was wiping the tears away the rest of the way home.

The house was empty – Tessa was still with her grandparents and Ross at work – and there was nothing to distract her from thinking about him, going over and over their months together, thinking and crying and railing at herself for getting into this state over someone who offered her nothing. She let out a great tearful sigh as she came to this conclusion: he offered her nothing; and when he was tired of her, that would be that.

Tessa burst through the door just as the phone began to ring, and Ross dumped the fish and chips he was carrying on the table and ran to answer it.

Josephine crouched beside Tessa, admiring the pictures she'd drawn at her grandmother's and all the while wondering if it could be Nicky. She'd given him the number a long time ago, but he'd never called her there and he didn't know where the house was.

'It's for you, Phina.' Ross came to the door. 'It's your brother – he sounds a bit worried.'

Disappointment lurched through her and she answered Lawrence with a curt hello.

'You'll have to come home,' he said. 'I've had a terrible

week. I've tried not to call you, but I can't cope with all this. He's gone. Mother's distraught and Louisa's playing up like merry hell.'

'You mean Christian's gone,' she said. It was a statement not a question. She felt like shouting at him: why do you have to bother me with this now, today of all days? But she took a little breath and said, 'Why? What's happened?'

'He's been accused of raping a girl in the village. Her parents came to see Mother. I've spoken to them and they haven't gone to the police because I think they know that there's more to it than they want to believe. The girl's only fourteen but she's known as a tearaway and a slut – and anyway, she's refusing to say anything against him now.'

She held the receiver away from her ear, staring at the pattern of tiny holes in the plastic, his voice still coming through like a faraway echo.

'Phina?' It grew louder. 'Are you still there?'

'Yes.'

'I think I can persuade them to keep quiet – I'll have to for Mother's sake. I'm taking her to the solicitor tomorrow. The sooner this marriage of hers is over the better. She's hardly stopped crying all week.' He paused. 'You'll have to come home for a while.'

'Tessa doesn't go back to school until next week – I can't just leave Ross in the lurch.'

'This is an emergency, Phina. I'm very, very worried about Mother. And you haven't been home for over four months.'

She rested the receiver against her shoulder for a moment, struggling to control the great tide of misery that had come washing over her.

'You'll have to manage until next week,' she said, putting the receiver back to her ear.

'I can't. I have to go back to Cambridge in a couple of days. For God's sake, she is your mother! Can't you put her first, just for once in your life?'

'All right, I'll come!' she shouted at him and cut him off without saying goodbye.

Ross and Tessa had taken their fish and chips on trays to watch television. Hers had been put to keep warm, but she could eat only a few chips before the tears began streaming down her face once more. She put the rest in the bin, then went up to her room. When Ross came to put Tessa to bed he tapped on the door.

'Can Tess come and kiss you goodnight?' he called. He was always careful not to infringe her privacy on her day off, but Tessa was already pushing open her door.

'Sorry, I didn't realise you'd gone to bed,' he said.

She saw him glance at her, then at his watch, as Tessa came bounding over to her.

'Come on, Tess,' he said after a few seconds. 'I'm looking after you tonight and you know how strict I am.'

Tessa went laughing to him and Josephine could hear him reading story after story to her in her room next door. She listened as he settled her down, heard him reassuring her that there was no one in the wardrobe or under the bed and no horrid men waiting on the stairs, and then she turned her face into her pillow and sobbed with greater misery than she had since Christmas Day.

Ross came and tapped on her door again. 'I'm making some coffee if you want some,' he called.

She pressed her knuckles against her mouth. 'No, thanks,' she called back, stopping before the sobs bubbled over again.

He went downstairs but was back a few minutes later. 'Josephine,' he called through the door again. 'I can't settle down knowing you're up here crying your eyes out.'

It was the final straw, this little show of concern, and she cried broken-heartedly, no longer caring if he heard her.

He opened the door and stood there a moment, as though he wasn't sure what to do. Tessa called out.

'Go to sleep,' he called back. 'Come downstairs, come and have some coffee. Come on,' he coaxed, picking up her dressing gown from the end of the bed. 'I'm a good listener.'

She was too upset to care what he thought now, so she pulled on the dressing gown and followed him down to the sitting room. But by the time she was settled on the sofa with the coffee, her tears had stopped. He sat opposite while he drank his own, looking at her now and again, waiting for her to say something.

'Was it the phone call?' he said finally.

She nodded. 'I'm sorry . . .' The cup started to shake in the saucer and he came and took it from her and put an arm round her.

'Whatever is it?' he asked softly.

'My mother . . .' She stopped to control herself. 'My step-father has left her and . . . and . . . they want me to go home.'

'I'm sorry to hear it.' He gave her a little squeeze. 'But don't worry about anything here – you go.'

And I'll be a hundred miles away from Nicky, she thought. A hundred miles of road and a great row separating us.

'I'll come back,' she said, twisting round to face him. 'I don't mean I'm going for good – you will let me come back, won't you?' The tears started afresh.

'Of course I will.' He held her by the shoulders, looking into her face. 'Come on, it'll be all right. I hate to see you like this. I could see you'd been crying when I brought Tess up – and I saw your fish and chips in the bin.' He smiled. 'Spikey was going mad to get in there.'

She smiled through her tears.

'You must be starving. I'll pop down the road and get us a Chinese takeaway,' he said.

'No, no, I don't want you to do that.'

He put a finger to his lips. 'You keep an ear for Tess, I shan't be long.'

While he was gone, she went and washed her face and brushed her hair. Whatever would he think of her causing all this fuss?

When he came back, he set the foil cartons out on a tray and got cans of lager out of the fridge.

'This is really good for putting a smile back on your face,' he said, pouring lager into a glass for her.

She smiled without thinking.

'See, I told you,' he laughed, and sat down with her, drawing up the coffee table in front of them and dishing out a plate of food for her.

'What happened with your stepfather then?' he said. 'Has he gone for good?'

'I don't really know. My brother's taking my mother to see a solicitor about a divorce – I don't think he could come back.' She paused and stopped eating. 'He's been accused of rape . . . a girl in the village where we live.'

'Oh, I'm sorry.' He looked concerned. 'How awful for your mother. Still, if it's only an accusation, it might not be true.'

She took hold of her bottom lip, twisting it between her fingers. 'I think it is,' she said quietly. 'I think it could be . . . because . . .' Her voice was barely more than a whisper. 'He tried to do the same to me.'

Ross stopped eating and moved his head to look at her, but

she stared into her plate, watching her tears splash into the remains of her food. He took her plate and put it with his own on the tray, then lifted her hand from her lap and held it between his.

'When did this happen?'

'Last Christmas.'

'And that's why you wanted to get away.'

She nodded.

'And what about all these weekends you've been going home?'

Her throat constricted with a great yearning to tell him the truth. But how could she? How could she say, I've been telling you lies all summer, then lower his opinion of her even more by telling him about Nicky. How would it sound to say: every weekend I go to the house of a man who wants me only for sex, but I love him and I can't stop going there. So there you are – see what sort of girl you've got looking after your daughter.

'He's never there.' The words felt like knives in her throat. 'I go to keep my mother company.'

'Oh, Josephine, you poor girl. All this on your mind and yet every Sunday you come back here looking so . . .' He paused. 'Does your mother know what happened?'

'No, no she doesn't. I'll kill myself if she ever finds out.' She collapsed in helpless tears again. 'I wish I was dead. I wish I was dead.'

'Shush, shush,' he said, pulling her against him. 'Don't say things like that.'

'My father would have been so ashamed of me.'

'It wasn't your fault. Shush, don't cry.'

He held her for a long time, occasionally stroking her hair and rubbing his hand up and down her arm. His body was hard and muscular like Nicky's, but there was also something very soft about him, soft and comforting. Their food grew cold and the room became dark. He got up to pull the curtains and switch on a lamp. She immediately missed the warm contact of him and curled her legs up on the sofa. He came and sat opposite her now and poured more lager for her.

'And you've never told anybody about this?' he said.

She shook her head and suddenly it was all spilling out and she told him about Christian kissing her on Christmas Eve.

'I know I shouldn't have gone on that walk with him, but I wanted to.' She pressed her fists under her chin. 'I wanted to be close to him – I felt left out. I wanted him to kiss me again.'

'I think you must have been very confused,' Ross murmured. 'Didn't you have a boyfriend who you could . . .' He broke off and spread his hands.

'No.' She shrugged. 'I hardly ever went out. That was the first time anyone kissed me.' She had stopped crying, almost lost in thought, then looked up and found he was staring at her.

'You mustn't worry about it. You must go home and look after your mother. We'll manage until you come back.'

'You're so kind to me. Nobody's been as kind to me since my father died.'

'It's not difficult to be kind to you, Josephine.'

The strangest feeling came over her. She longed for him to come and sit with her and hold her again. It was a powerful feeling, physical as well as mental, and it drenched her with sudden warmth. He glanced at her, then picked up his can and drained the last of the lager.

'Shall I get you another one?' she said quickly.

'Why not?' he smiled.

She gathered up the remains of their Chinese meal; normally he would have helped – it would have been an automatic reaction – but tonight he sat there staring into the empty fireplace.

Out in the kitchen, she tried to work out how she could say something sympathetic about his wife, sure it was that on his mind. All her troubles had probably brought her death back to him. She scraped the leftover food together and put the plates in the dishwasher, then went to the fridge to get the lager. She felt better; miraculously better considering nothing had been solved. She straightened up, pressing the cold can against her cheek. When she looked round, Ross was standing there.

'I don't think I want it after all,' he said, his face still serious. 'I think I'll go to bed – as long as you're all right now.'

'Yes I am, thank you.' The strange feeling was back, filled with disappointment because it was all slipping away now. She put the can back in the fridge and followed him along the hall. At his door, he stopped.

'How long do you think you'll be away?'

'Not long. A week maybe.'

'Good.' The smile was back in place. 'We'll miss you. Now no more crying, eh?'

'I don't think I've got any tears left.' She stood there, wishing she had, wishing she could be back curled on the sofa with him.

Once more his face grew serious; he looked uncomfortable. He put out a hand as though he was going to touch her cheek, but instead he patted her on the shoulder. 'Goodnight then,' he said.

'Thank you for being so understanding.'

He lingered there, standing in the open doorway, and she had the feeling that it would be very easy to detain him as long as she wanted. It was like a sudden revelation, but she had neither the courage nor the desire to pursue it and with a murmured 'Goodnight', she was off upstairs.

The next day Josephine went home, but was back in less than a week.

Seeing her mother so unhappy brought back all the guilt of Christmas Day. She would go to bed exhausted by sheer emotion as she listened to her mother complain over and over that it was the girl's fault as much as Christian's; what man wouldn't be tempted by a fourteen-year-old who threw herself at him when he was married to a woman eight years older than himself. Then it would be more tears. Even when she was saying she wanted nothing more than to be rid of him, Josephine could think of no comforting words, nothing that would makes things any better. And in the end the strain of it all and her own breaking heart made her long to return to London.

But something was changed here as well. Ross came to meet her from the station, but he seemed slightly ill at ease with her, and back indoors the atmosphere was the same. Tessa greeted her as warmly as ever, hardly leaving her side for a minute.

'Are you going to stay here for ever now?' she asked on her way to bed.

Josephine glanced at Ross before answering, not sure what he would want her to say, but he muttered something about, 'You won't need looking after for ever', and left the room.

When she asked if there had been any calls for her, he answered 'No' in such an offhand way, that she added: 'And nothing on the answerphone for me?'

Normally he would have joked about something like this, teased her about who she was expecting to call: she had got to know his reactions, and his indifferent manner compounded her suspicions that something was wrong. She began to feel as edgy and unhappy as she had at home. Cheryl's appearance a couple of days after she got back sunk Josephine into even deeper gloom: she seemed openly hostile.

'Why isn't Tessa in bed?' she said, the minute she walked in. 'You know she doesn't like to see Ross go out.'

'I didn't know you were going out.'

'What do you think he's getting changed for then?'

'He always gets changed when he comes home from work.'

'Not into a suit, he doesn't.'

Josephine didn't answer, knowing whatever she said would be wrong, but Cheryl wouldn't let the matter drop. When Ross came into the kitchen she said: 'I suppose we're going to be late now while we wait for Tessa to settle down.'

'No you won't,' said Josephine, suddenly on the defensive. She took Tessa's hand and whispered that they'd play hide-and-seek with Spikey if she was good.

Tessa giggled, a hand over her mouth, and whispered back to her. Cheryl looked furious, but Ross ushered her out of the kitchen, his face solemn.

The next day Ross hardly spoke to Josephine and she was convinced that she'd blown it; Cheryl must have persuaded him to get rid of her – and when Nicky finally decided to phone her, she wouldn't be there.

By the evening she was so anxious that she felt compelled to say something. They had just finished eating and she was standing at the sink washing the saucepans while he did a jigsaw puzzle with Tessa.

'You know what you said about only you deciding who looks after Tessa . . .' she began.

'Yeah.'

She glanced over her shoulder and could see he was looking at her as though he wondered what she was going to say.

'Do you still mean that?'

'Get to the point, Josephine.'

'Cheryl doesn't want me here,' she said, resting her hands on the bottom of the sink and watching the suds creep up to her elbows. 'I think she's asked you to get rid of me.'

After a few seconds he said, 'And I think you know why.'

More silent seconds passed, then he sent Tessa upstairs, promising if she went and put her nightie on and cleaned her teeth now, she could stay up an extra half an hour.

Josephine stood motionless, her hands still immersed in the water. 'I don't know why – I've done nothing to her,' she said finally.

She heard Ross sigh. 'She says I'm attracted to you.'

She pulled out the plug, wiping the sink round as the water disappeared, delaying the moment when she would have to turn and face him.

'So what if . . . if she says I have to go or . . .' Her heart was beating faster, her hands shaking a little as she searched for the exact words she needed. She looked over her shoulder. 'What if you had to choose?'

'Don't play with my feelings, Josephine.'

'I'm not.'

'You know bloody well you are,' he said, getting up and leaving the room.

She heard him go into the sitting room and switch on the television. Cheryl was working tonight, she knew, and the following evening they were going to stay with Cheryl's parents in Cornwall for the weekend, taking Tessa with them. She stood by the sink, welded to it by a heady mix of emotions. She had to stay here; she wanted desperately to stay here. She started to chew at her thumbnail, biting into it, and nearly jumped out of her skin at the sound of his voice.

'I'm sorry,' he said, coming in and closing the door. 'I didn't mean to swear at you.'

She looked up. 'I know you think badly of me after what I told you.'

His face crumpled and she felt a little surge of triumph.

'I wish I hadn't told you,' she said before he could answer. 'You were so kind to me that evening, but now you know all about me . . . and now Cheryl thinks you like me, I'm going to lose my job and . . .' She took a deep breath. 'And everything.' If only she could cry as well. But she couldn't because she was flying high on the strangest sensation.

'I don't think badly of you. How could you say that? It's nothing to do with that.'

He sat down at the table, his forehead resting in his palm and his head skewed round so that he was looking at her. 'You really don't understand do you?' He closed his eyes for a moment. 'I don't know how all this has happened – but I know it can't go on like this.'

'I'll keep out of Cheryl's way. I just want to stay here with you and Tessa.'

He pointed at the chair opposite. 'Sit down.'

She did as he said, her heart racing, her hands clenched on her lap.

'You must know that what she said is true – I can't believe you don't.'

'I just want to stay here,' she said stubbornly.

He sighed, his eyes fixed on her. 'It might be better if you went home. Or looked for another job,' he added as her head jerked up. 'I'd help you and I'd give you the best of references.'

The feeling of power was slipping away, just like the water that had drained away down the sink.

She stood up. 'Everything goes wrong for me. It's never my fault but it always goes wrong.' She made for the door but he jumped up and barred her way.

'It isn't my fault,' she repeated, her eyes glistening with tears now.

'Shush, Tess'll be down in a minute.' He put his hands on her shoulders as though to calm her, but they slipped round behind her head and he bent and kissed her. It was a hurried, rough kiss, as though he didn't want to do it and there was no time for her to either respond or push him away. But as soon as he let her go, he caught her again, wrapping his arms right round her and pressing his mouth over hers in a mixture of gentleness and passion. And a little voice inside her seemed to say: this is your last chance. She went limp in his arms and let her lips drift apart.

The sound of Tessa's skipping footsteps came along the hall and he drew away, his face flushed and troubled. Josephine put her hands flat on his chest, looking up into his face.

'Please let me stay,' she said.

Ross went to Cornwall as planned, not saying a word to her until the last minute.

After they were disturbed by Tessa, he'd gone out, not returning until past midnight. He'd left very early for work the following day. It wasn't until he'd come back into the house after putting their cases into the car that he spoke to her.

'We'll talk when I get back,' he said, his face solemn. 'I feel bad about all this – I would have cancelled this trip but I can't disappoint Tess.' He waited as though he expected a reply but she kept silent, not wanting to say anything that would destroy the tenuous hold she had over him.

The weekend was a nightmare of indecision for Josephine. Twice she picked up the phone to call Nicky and twice she put it down again. The third time she got as far as dialling but couldn't remember the last two numbers; she'd never phoned him before and had never written his number down. But in a strange way she felt it saved her pride – he had to contact her first. Then she fell to thinking what was going to happen about Ross. Would he really let her stay just because he'd kissed her? She thought of him with Cheryl. They would be sleeping together; he would confess what he'd done and that would be it – he'd send her away.

When they came home, Josephine waited for two days for him to say something to her, but he was either at work or out, and on Tuesday evening he was very late home. She heard the Range Rover pull up and she got out of bed. She would just go downstairs and ask him what was going to happen – could she stay or not? Before going down, she peered at herself in the mirror. Nicky always said she was the only girl he'd ever known who looked better when she got out of bed than when she got in it. She slipped on her dressing gown and crept across the landing, listening for the sound of the back gate so that she could time it just right. As she opened the kitchen door she heard his key in the lock. Her courage failed her and she hurried across to the sink to pretend she was getting a drink of water.

He looked surprised to see her.

'I'm just getting a drink,' she said, holding up the glass.

He looked dishevelled, his eyes heavy lidded and his chin shadowed with stubble. Without a word he turned to lock the door behind him and she saw that he took a couple of attempts to fit the key in the lock.

'Go to bed,' he said sharply, pulling off his jacket and coming over to the sink.

She moved out of the way and he ran the cold tap and splashed water over his face.

'You said we'd talk.'

'Not tonight.'

'So I've got to spend another night worrying if I've still got a job or not, have I?'

He grabbed a towel and turned round. 'You know very well

that I won't tell you to go.' He was near enough that she could smell the alcohol on his breath. In all the months she'd lived there she'd never known him have more than a couple of pints, but tonight he had definitely had more than that.

She took a step away from him, but he reached out and caught her wrist and pulled her to him. She didn't resist; it was what she had come downstairs for. But his kisses became heated and urgent and he ran his hands down to her hips and pulled her so tightly against him that she could feel he was very aroused. She wrenched away from him and ran back upstairs.

The next morning he was waiting when she got back from taking Tessa to school.

'I'm sorry about last night,' he said.

He had made tea for her and she sat down at the kitchen table with him.

'I'd had a few drinks.' He smiled. 'As you probably guessed.'

'Yes, I did.'

He played with his cup, running his finger round and round the rim, then stopped to look at her. 'I went to tell Cheryl that . . . that I'm in love with you.' He leant back in his chair, watching her and waiting.

All she could think of was how beautiful the words sounded.

He reached out and took her hand. 'And it isn't just physical attraction – forget about last night – I love everything about you. I love the way you do things and the way you say things. Just having you in the house makes me happy.'

She stared across the kitchen and he lifted her hand and kissed her fingers. 'But I know you probably don't want a relationship with someone nearly twice your age. I just had to tell Cheryl because . . .' He stopped and shrugged. 'I didn't want to deceive her.' He ran his thumb across her knuckles. 'She says I'm just infatuated with you and it won't last. But I know it's more than that – we've been living close to one another for a long time now and I can't imagine it here without you. But I want more than that.' He gave her hand a little shake. 'Say something, Josephine. Either you want me or you don't.'

How could she say to him, yes I do want you, but not in the way you want me. I want you to cuddle me, I even like you kissing me – but that's all. Her heart felt suddenly full: full of affection for him and full of pain because she couldn't give him the answer he wanted. If only Nicky loved her like this. She glanced at him but couldn't bear the look on his face. Or if only she could love Ross as she did Nicky.

'I don't know,' she said finally. 'I wish we could just go on as we are.'

'We can't.' He let go of her hand. 'You know we can't. It's not fair on me – I'm only human. I feel a complete bastard about last night, especially after what you told me.'

'I don't think you're a bastard, I think you're one of the nicest people I've ever met.'

'Oh, Josephine,' he sighed and put his arm round her shoulders, resting his head against hers. 'Why did you ever come here?'

She suddenly felt incredibly weary and troubled, worn out by a surfeit of passions and desires that she should only just be discovering.

'I think I want to go home,' she said. 'To sort everything out.'

But going home again solved nothing.

Solange was still very low in spirits. Lawrence had discovered that the girl in the village hadn't been the first of Christian's affairs with young girls and, although Solange had accepted that her marriage was over, she still wanted to believe that he had loved her to begin with, so she would keep talking about him. It depressed Josephine; guilt made it impossible for her to be supportive.

Summer seemed to have disappeared unusually early from Waylands this year, and the gloom of autumn gathered oppressively about its walls. Louisa slept in with her mother now, and Josephine spent long wakeful nights, her heart aching with loneliness. And when she did sleep her dreams were crazily disturbing, filled with music and weird twisted people who laughed and beckoned at her from dark corners. Sometimes they had faces she nearly recognised but, just as the recognition came, she always woke. Once upon a time she would have been terrified, but now her unhappiness seemed to dull all other sensations. At the end of her first week she could bear it no longer. She shut herself in the study and tried to dial Nicky's number again. She tried different variations without success; tried directory enquiries who told her it was ex-directory. Finally she tried Sapphire, but she didn't know the number either.

'Would you give him a message for me?' Josephine asked. 'Will you ask him to call me?'

'Yes, if I see him,' said Sapphire. 'He hasn't been in for a couple of weeks. Have you had a bust up with him, darling?'

'Sort of.' At this point she broke down in tears. 'We had a row and I haven't seen him since.'

'Sweetheart, listen to me,' said Sapphire. 'I should save your tears for someone who's worth them. Don't get me wrong,' she added quickly, 'I adore Nicky, but I don't think he's worth crying over.'

'I just want to talk to him.'

'Well, don't worry, I'll give him your message.'

She waited a week but there was no word from him. Finally she phoned Ross.

Just the sound of his voice was comforting.

'Have there been any messages for me?' she asked after they had chatted for a moment.

'No, should there be?'

'No, I just wondered. Is Tessa being good?' she added quickly.

'Not too bad, but she misses you. So do I – a lot.'

'Do you?' she murmured, surprised how good his words made her feel.

'Are you coming back to me?'

'Do you want me to?'

'You know I do.'

'You haven't changed your mind now you've had time to think about it?' She knew she was stringing this out, making him go on saying these things because she was lonely and miserable, but she couldn't help it.

'No. You being away has just made me all the more certain. I want you to come back – I want you to stay here for good.'

It felt as though a little fight was going on inside her. Part of her said: get out of this now, you've no right to treat him like this. But another part felt desperately hungry for what he offered.

'Did you hear what I said?'

'Yes.'

'I want you to come back and marry me, Josephine.'

There was a great long silence. She could hear the 'pink, pink' of a blackbird out on the lawn and, at the other end of the line, the music from his radio.

'I didn't mean to ask you over the phone,' he said at last. 'But maybe it's best – you can think about it, away from me.'

145

When she didn't answer, he went on: 'I had to say it. It's been on my mind. I want you here.' She heard him sigh and draw in his breath. 'I should have waited and said all this to your face, but if you turn me down, how am I going to deal with it? How could I let things go back to the way they were? I can't, Josephine.'

It wasn't an ultimatum, she knew that. Ross was incapable of playing with her like that.

'Come back and we'll talk,' he said, as though to confirm her thoughts.

She agreed because she couldn't think what else to say without hurting him. But in the days that followed, she realised how difficult it would be to go back and not say yes.

Chapter 11

Josephine went back in the middle of October, telling her mother she was going to look after Tessa during the half-term holiday. And that was all she told her; she hadn't mentioned Ross's proposal, although it was constantly on her mind, vying with her thoughts of Nicky during the long sleepless nights.

Ross came to meet her at the station. It was obvious he had not come straight from work; he was freshly washed and shaved and on his own.

'Tessa's with my parents,' he said. 'I thought we could go out for a meal.'

She was instantly on her guard, chattering away about trivial things, making sure to keep a little distance from him and avoiding his eyes when he spoke to her – all to postpone the question she had to face.

But later, looking at him across the table in the restaurant, a candle flickering between them and her emotions very near the surface, she began to wonder what it would be like to be married to him. He gazed back at her, his eyes chocolate brown behind the yellow flame and his skin still attractively tanned from the summer. His hair was streaked with sun as well and quite long again, curling softly over his collar. Miran had obviously been too busy to come and cut it. She smiled, thinking of the fuss he made, saying she tugged at it worse than their mother had when they were kids. He smiled back at her and she thought, why haven't I noticed before how handsome he is? How Cheryl must hate me.

'What are you thinking?' he asked. 'I keep seeing little clouds flit across your face.'

'That sounds very poetic,' she laughed.

'You make me like it.'

'I was just wondering about Cheryl.' She regretted her words immediately because the cloud was now on his face.

He looked away briefly, then back at her. 'Our relationship was in trouble before I told her about you. We did talk about getting married, but we want different things out of life. Cheryl loves her job, she wouldn't pack up work. And she's not all that keen on kids.' He gave a little smile. 'You don't know these things when you first meet someone.' He looked down at the tablecloth. 'She's very much like my wife – she even looks like her.'

Josephine sat very still. He hardly ever mentioned his wife. Miran had told her she suffered from anorexia and mental problems and had taken an overdose of sleeping pills a few months after Tessa was born. He'd had five years of hell with her, she'd said.

'Karen only thought about her career,' he went on. 'She was a model. She never wanted Tess.'

'I know, Miran told me.' Josephine searched for sympathetic words. 'She said you just want a house full of kids and someone to look after you.'

They immediately seemed the wrong words but he laughed and said: 'Trust Miran.

'Do you want to dance?' he said suddenly. A band had been playing background music while they ate but the tempo had livened now and couples were getting up to dance.

'No – no, I don't like dancing much.'

'I thought all girls your age liked to dance.' He smiled at her and filled her glass with wine. 'Here, you finish this, I've got to drive.'

The music changed to a slow ballad; a woman began to sing. He stood up and took her hand.

'Come on, dance to this with me and then we'll go. I just want to put my arms round you,' he said quietly as he pulled her to her feet.

The words of the song were poignantly romantic, the lights on the dance floor dimmed to a soft glow. He slipped an arm round her waist, the other round her shoulders, and pressed his face into her hair.

'I never felt this way about Cheryl,' he whispered against her ear. 'Nor about anyone.'

She had on a skimpy velvet top. It had come adrift from her skirt and she could feel his hand hot against her skin, his fingers gently caressing her waist. The beginnings of desire stirred in her and, relaxed by the wine, she let her mind drift – and wondered what it would be like to spend the night in bed with him.

When they pulled up back at the house, he made no attempt to get out of the Range Rover, but sat there, his arms resting on the wheel. She hardly dared breathe, knowing that in a moment he was going to ask her the question that had been between them all evening.

'Before I came to meet you,' he began, 'I made up my mind that if you turn me down, I shall sleep in the car tonight and take you back to Norfolk in the morning. I've thought and thought about it, and I can't have you under the same roof and . . .' He looked at her now. 'I don't mind if you don't want to get married right away – I know eighteen's a bit young. I just want to know that you're committed to me.'

She waited a few seconds before answering. 'What if I said yes and then . . . then something went wrong . . .?'

'Like you change your mind?'

She shrugged.

'I'll take that chance.'

There was only one thought in her head now, and the wine and the darkness made the words come easily. 'And if I say yes, you'll want me to sleep with you tonight, won't you.'

'Yeah.' He leant across to kiss her. 'Tonight and every night.'

'Let's go indoors, I'm getting cold,' she said.

In the kitchen he took her coat and kissed her again and asked her if she wanted coffee. She refused, knowing there was only a certain amount of time before the effects of the wine and the excitement of the evening wore off. She glanced at the clock and thought stupidly, one hour until midnight.

The radio was going in his bedroom; he had a habit of switching on music wherever he happened to be, then leaving it.

'This does mean yes, doesn't it?' he said, taking her in his arms. 'I don't think I could let you go now anyway,' he added with a great sigh, hugging her so close she could feel his heart pounding against his ribs.

He slipped the velvet top over her head, then drew her close again, pressing his lips against her neck and unhooking her bra at the same time. She closed her eyes and heard the music grow louder, faster, and felt his hands on her, trembling slightly as he drew the straps over her shoulders. And suddenly she wanted to shout, no, no, I don't want this. It was like a great violent pain in her heart, but she couldn't move and stayed frozen to the spot until he lifted her in his arms and took her to the bed.

'Just tell me two things,' he whispered. 'You don't take the pill, do you?'

'No.'

'And . . .' He paused, his lips resting on her cheek. 'What you told me about not having a boyfriend . . . does that mean you've never done this before?'

'I didn't say that.' The words caught in her throat. 'I don't want to talk about it.'

He was silent for a few seconds; she could feel his breath blowing across her face.

'It's all right,' he said at last, cradling her in his arms. 'I understand.'

The music grew even louder and her reluctance grew with it. But in the urgency of his desire for her, he didn't seem to notice. Almost immediately he was lowering himself on to her. She tightened against him and he stopped for a second.

'I won't hurt you,' he breathed against her ear. 'It's different when you want to . . . when you love someone.'

His words made no sense; they came caught in the panting breath of passion and she wasn't even sure if she heard him right. And he did hurt her, crushing her with his eagerness and pushing into her so hard and deep that she felt almost violated, as though each thrust of his body was for himself alone. Afterwards, he apologised.

'I've been thinking about you so much,' he said. He was holding her in his arms and he drew her head against his. 'I didn't sleep with Cheryl after that first time I kissed you. Our relationship was deteriorating and I couldn't make love to her thinking of you.' He paused to push the tousled hair from her face. 'Sex is very important to me, Josephine.'

She was exhausted both mentally and physically and fell

asleep almost at once. But he woke her in the middle of the night, wanting her again. This time he tried to arouse her first, covering her body with gentle kisses. He stroked her breasts with gentle, searching fingers, then took each one into his mouth, and finally slid his hand down between her legs as though she were made of fragile bone china. But she could feel how hard he grew against her, and when he began to whisper things against her ear, telling her what she should feel as though she knew nothing, it seemed to excite him beyond control and he could wait no longer.

His body felt heavier than Nicky's, and there was the unfamiliar coarseness of the curled hair on his chest and the work-roughened skin of his hands. She didn't want to let these comparisons enter her head, didn't want to notice that his lips tasted differently and he smelt of soap and aftershave, whereas Nicky always had that vague mixture of heat and incense from the studio candles on his skin.

She squeezed her eyelids tight shut and tried to think only of the present and this man who loved her with such passion and could offer her all the things she had been searching for.

Sleep came quickly again; so deep that when she woke it was like crawling from unconsciousness. Feeling Ross's arms still round her, last night came flooding back.

She had a slight headache and sat up, rubbing at her eyes. Ross stirred but didn't wake and she looked down at him. In sleep he looked excessively gentle, his features soft and curved. A tiny pulse beat in the hollow of his neck, and on impulse she bent and kissed it. He opened his eyes, lost for a moment, then smiled up at her.

'I love you, Josephine,' he said, putting his hands up to cup her face. He waited for her response, looking steadily into her eyes.

'I love you too,' she said finally, nuzzling against his shoulder. She felt strangely peaceful. It pleased her and bothered her. It wasn't a lie that she loved him; she could probably have said that quite truthfully many weeks ago. But it wasn't in the way he loved *her* – and whether *she* could ever love him like that, she didn't know. And how she could deal with all the nights ahead, she wasn't sure. But there was something inside her that felt good: protected and wanted. It gave her the urge to curl up beside him with a thumb in her mouth and a lock of hair drawn across her face, just as she used to do when she was small.

'I've got a bit of a headache,' she said.

'Too much wine – I hope you know what you were doing last night.'

She smiled and wound her hair round her hand, rubbing it against her face. 'I know what *you* were doing.'

'That was just for starters,' he said, curving his body round her and kissing her shoulder. He lay there a moment just holding her, then glanced at his watch. 'I'll go and make you some tea, then I'll have to collect Tess.'

'Tea in bed, lovely.' She stretched, about to say, I don't usually get this treatment, but stopped herself in time. How easy it would be to let little things slip out, and how much easier if she had never lied to him.

She watched him dress. His body was tightly muscled like Nicky's but broader, more mature, no sharp angles where the flesh looked too taut for comfort. The comparisons were in her head again and she was glad when he went to fetch Tessa, glad of a little time alone.

Tessa was delighted to see her, bounding up and firing questions at her so quickly she had a job to keep pace with the answers.

'Nanna said Spikey won't ever get any kittens, but he will, won't he, Phina?' she said, standing on the rungs of Josephine's chair, then edging herself on to her lap.

Ross laughed. 'Explain that to her if you can.'

'You're the expert,' said Josephine teasingly. She gave Tessa a little hug and thought how easy it was to slip into the demands of this different relationship.

Ross took the day off and they all went out together. He was constantly touching her or taking hold of her hand, but careful not to display too much affection in front of Tessa. That evening after Tessa had gone to bed, he immediately took her in his arms.

'Let's get married straightaway,' he said. 'Then I can tell Tess you're going to be her new mum – we can be a proper family and . . .'

'Ross, wait.' She wriggled back from him. 'Last night you said you wouldn't mind if we didn't get married for a while.'

'I've changed my mind – I don't want to wait.' He caught her elbows and pulled her close. 'And how will it look to every-body, anyway? Cheryl disappears and you move in to my bed. I don't want my family to think of you like that.'

'We needn't tell anyone.'

'I don't want it to be secret.' He gripped her arms quite tightly. 'I want to be married to you.'

'But I'll have to speak to my mother.'

'Of course you will. We'll go up there as soon as you like.'

'I'll have to talk to her on my own – I'll have to ask her.' She paused, looking sideways to avoid his eyes. 'I'm not eighteen. I'm not even seventeen until next February.'

She felt his grip loosen. 'I was just desperate to get the job. That's the only reason I lied. I had to get away from home.'

'Yeah, I know, you had to get away from your stepfather.' There was something alien about his tone and he let go of her completely. It was only for a second, then he sighed and pulled her sharply against him, but it felt like a moment's rejection and she hated it.

'My mother won't object, not once I've talked to her.'

She put her arms round him and pressed her lips to his neck, wanting to arouse him and make him like he usually was. And soon he was kissing her; deep, passionate kisses that left her so breathless she had to pull away from him. He looked at her with half-closed eyes and she felt happy again.

'I hope you haven't got any more surprises for me like that,' he murmured.

In the end, she went home on her own.

'It's only fair to my mother if I speak to her first,' she insisted. 'Especially how she is at the moment.'

He had given in. Over the past few days she had begun to discover that however adamant he was about something at first, it didn't take too much to make him give in. Sometimes it felt like a game, trying to get her one way; a little power game that she always won and which, in an odd way, was essential to her.

Solange greeted her without the usual tears. She seemed more composed altogether and had removed the photograph of Christian from the hall table.

'Lawrence has unearthed some more about him,' she said. 'He went through the things he left here. I think he's had lots

153

of affairs with young girls – he was certainly,' she paused, 'active in that way.'

Josephine frowned at her. 'I don't really want to hear all this, Mother. He's gone – that's all I want to know.'

Solange's eyes filled with tears for a moment. 'And I nearly lost my children over him.'

Josephine took a deep breath. 'Well you might be gaining some family. I've got something to tell you.'

Solange's eyes widened. 'You're not pregnant are you?'

'No of course not.' Though it's not through anything you taught me, she felt like adding, annoyed at her mother's quick assumption.

'I have wondered about you,' said Solange. 'Living in that house with a man of his age. Lawrence thinks it's strange you never want to come home as well.'

'He loves me,' she burst out suddenly. 'He loves me and he wants to marry me.'

'But you're only sixteen. And he's . . .'

'He's thirty-four, but that's nothing to do with it. You were expecting Lawrence when you were my age, and daddy was forty. You were happy – that's what I want to be.' She broke down in tears. 'I want to marry him.'

Solange took hold of her and rocked her back and forth. 'Oh, Phina, this is all my fault. I drove you away. You've never been really happy since Daddy died, have you? Now I've pushed you into this.'

'You haven't,' she sobbed. 'I want to marry him.'

'But you must think about it, darling. I married your father because I loved him. I'm not saying you don't love Ross, but do you love him in the right way?'

'I do love him.'

'Then why all these tears?' Solange held Josephine's face between her hands, but it only made her cry all the more because it seemed that they had never been so close as at this moment, and somehow it was all too late. 'I've been so selfish.' Solange began to cry herself. 'All the time you were so unhappy and I only thought about myself. And after Christmas . . .' She stopped and laid her cheek against Josephine's. 'I let you and Lawrence go and . . .'

Josephine clasped her round the neck and cried almost hysterically. 'Don't talk about it, please don't talk about,' she sobbed.

They sat together until they heard the taxi that brought Louisa home from school come into the courtyard, then began frantically wiping their faces. Solange was the first to compose herself, but when Louisa ran straight into the kitchen calling for Nella, she put her arms round Josephine once more.

'Will you do just one thing for me, darling? I won't stop you if you really want to marry him, but promise me you'll wait a little while – until Easter maybe. And promise me you'll get married from here, in church, a proper wedding.'

Josephine nodded through the remains of her tears, and Solange smoothed her hair and kissed her cheek. 'When am I going to meet him?'

'Soon. I'll bring him to stay. You will like him, I know you will. He's so nice.' She smiled and shrugged. 'He's just so nice.'

Solange gave a little sigh, as though something still bothered her, then Louisa was coming across the hall shouting: 'Is Phina here?'

Josephine stayed nearly a week, and in those few short days she recaptured things she had thought were lost for ever: walks up to the quarries in the damp autumn air, paddling about on the edge of the river in gumboots with Louisa and, best of all, the quiet peace of Waylands. The courtyard at dusk: the soft twitters and rustling as her mother's birds settled down for the night, and the bats floating in and out of the lofts, silent as shadows.

It felt as though she really had knocked two years off her age, not just told Ross about her lie. But on the train back to him she was nervous, feeling that she had to step suddenly forward again.

She walked from the station, taking a detour to collect Tessa from her grandparents who had picked her up from school.

'I'm glad you're back,' said Ross's mother. 'This toing and froing is too much for Ross to cope with when he's so busy at work. He wasn't himself at all this morning when he brought Tessa round. Or maybe it's this break up with Cheryl.' She gave a little sigh. 'He always seems to get mixed up with the wrong girls.'

Josephine busied herself buttoning Tessa's coat, wondering what his mother would say when Ross told her the truth about his breaking up with Cheryl.

They got back before Ross, and Tessa was settled at the kitchen table with a plate of fish-fingers when he came in. He pulled his sweater off and kissed Tessa briefly on the head. His hair was powdered with brick-dust, his T-shirt shadowed with damp, and he raised grimy hands towards Josephine as though to say, I won't touch you like this.

But even in that silent gesture she knew something was wrong, and when she asked what he wanted to eat, he shrugged and went off up the hall.

'I'll have a shower first,' he called over his shoulder.

She followed him to his bedroom and stood in the doorway.

'I can start cooking while you're in the shower,' she said, trying to catch some sign on his face to indicate what was the matter.

He started to pull off his T-shirt and she had a sudden longing to go to him, wrap her arms round him and know that everything was all right. But for a moment the blatant masculine power of him seemed threatening and she held back.

He threw his T-shirt on the floor and beckoned to her. His expression also seemed slightly menacing, but she went up to him, her face raised in question. He put out his hand and ran a finger down her neck and along her collarbone.

'Where's the locket you used to wear when you first came here?' he said.

She froze; no answer would come.

He moved his finger back up her neck and lifted her chin.

'I remember it because Tess was always wanting to open it, and I used to think how sweet you were never minding how many times she asked about the picture of your father.'

'It's—' she began, but he cut her off.

'I won't make you lie to me – there was a phone call here for you last night.' He dropped his hand and took a deep breath, looking away for a moment. 'I was just surprised.'

'It was someone I met months ago.' Keep calm, she told herself. 'I broke the chain of my locket when I was with him once and he put it in his pocket – I'd forgotten all about it.'

It was true, she had forgotten about the locket, forgotten that after she'd torn it from Nicky's bedpost and broken the chain for the second time, he had hidden it from her.

'What did he say?' she asked.

'He asked for you, but he wouldn't leave his name. He said to remind you that he still had your locket and what did you want him to do with it.'

'Did he leave a number or anything?'

'No. No, he didn't.'

'Well, I'm not worried about the locket, and I've got lots more photos of my father.' She shrugged and folded her arms across her chest, putting a barrier between Ross and the telltale storm that was going on beneath her ribs.

'How long were you seeing him?'

'Oh don't start questioning me, Ross. It's all over – it has been for ages.'

'Are you sure?'

'Yes! Yes of course.' She glanced up at him. 'I've told you before – I don't want to talk about it.'

'Perhaps we should.' His voice softened slightly. 'For everyone's sake.'

'What do you mean?'

'I think you got into something you couldn't handle – am I right?'

'No.' She put her hands to her ears. 'I don't want to talk about it, do you hear?' Her brows drew together and she bit back sudden tears. 'Never.'

He put out a hand but she ran off back to the kitchen, knowing he wouldn't pursue any of this in front of Tessa.

But when he came in a little while later, he sat down at the table next to her and put his arms round her, regardless of Tessa watching them. He rested his damp head against hers and helped himself to one of the fishfingers that she'd just cooked for herself.

Tessa laughed and he smiled across the table at her. 'Do you love Josephine?' he asked her.

'Yes!' said Tessa, loudly. 'And I don't want her to go away again.'

'I love her too,' he said, kissing her on the cheek, then holding an arm out for Tessa. 'Do you want her to be your new mummy?' he said once she was cuddled to his side.

Tessa nodded, a little less exuberant now, as though she wasn't quite sure what he meant. 'I won't have to stay with Nanna will I? I want to stay with you,' she said, her voice turning into a whine.

'Of course you'll stay with me.' He hoisted her on to his lap, then turned back to Josephine and whispered against her ear. 'I'm sorry.'

'It's all right,' she murmured, staring down at her plate, her whole body tense with the effort of controlling the turmoil of emotion churning inside her.

'I just can't bear to think of you with anyone else,' he murmured. 'Last night – when he asked for you – I wanted to reach down the phone and grab him by the throat.'

'Daddy, what are you saying to Phina?' Tessa asked, pulling his head round to her.

'What a horrible jealous bloke I am,' he said, tickling her. 'Like you.'

'Don't – you'll confuse her,' said Josephine, unhooking his arm from round her and starting to eat again, though every mouthful seemed to stick in her throat.

'Have you fed Spikey yet?' said Ross.

Tessa slapped a hand to her mouth. 'Oh, no,' and rushed off to call him.

As soon as Tessa was out of earshot, he turned back to Josephine. 'I'll buy you a new locket,' he said, pushing back her hair and kissing her ear.

'I don't want a new locket. Now let me finish eating and then I'll get you something.'

'And I don't want anything to eat – except you.' He took the fork from her hand and singled out her third finger. 'We'll go out on Saturday and buy you a ring. Then we'll go and tell my parents.'

She realised that she hadn't yet told him what her mother had said and her promise to wait until Easter before getting married.

'Here, you finish this.' She pushed her plate in front of him. 'It's obvious you're not going to let me.'

'No, I'm not.' He leant round to kiss her, slipping his hand up beneath her sweater and pushing his thumb inside her bra.

She hauled his hand away. 'Stop it, Tessa will see.'

He leant back in his chair, studying her. 'Was he the first?' he said quietly, his face serious. 'Was he? Tell me.'

She jerked her head away from him. 'Are you going to go on and on about it?'

'I just want to know if you still think about him. Do you?'

'No,' she said, staring across the room.

'Well, what are you going to do about your locket?'

'I've told you. Nothing, nothing at all.' This is how I was with my questioning and my jealousy, she thought. This is how it begins.

'Swear to me,' he said, suddenly. 'Swear to me that—'

'Stop it!' she shouted at him before he could finish. 'You'll ruin everything. I told you I love you and that's all that matters. The past is not important.'

But she knew that it was and she knew that, if she didn't stop it, the past would creep up to spoil the present and there was only one thing she could do about it.

Chapter 12

She put on worn jeans and a thick grey sweater – mustn't let him think she had dressed up to see him. But looking at herself in the mirror, she thought, why am I doing this? I don't have to try and manipulate his thoughts – it doesn't matter to me what impression he gets. She opened the wardrobe again. The demure velvet dress with the pearl buttons was right at the back along with most of the other clothes she had brought with her from Waylands. Few of them got worn now. She fingered the pale blue suede skirt that he'd bought her, then took it out and changed into it. It looked awful with the grey sweater. In growing agitation, she changed that too and put on a tight black one of soft angora, sank on to the bed and pulled on long black leather boots. Ross liked her in this outfit; she dressed to please him now. Finally, she twirled her hair into a loose knot on top of her head, snatched up a fur-lined denim jacket, and went downstairs, resisting the temptation to look in the mirror once more.

A fine drizzle was falling and she caught a bus, getting off at the stop near the turning to Sapphire's. As she approached the café she heard the church clock begin to strike. It seemed to go on for ever, each chime sounding louder than the one before, as though the bell-tower were striding down the road to meet her.

I have to look in the window, she told herself. He could be there and if I miss him this trip will be wasted and I am never going to do it again.

She stopped and looked between the frilled curtains, and it felt like she was already back in that house leaving reality

161

behind, because he was there, sitting over in the corner, his leg stretched into the gangway, Sapphire behind him, her hands on his shoulders.

And when Sapphire chose that exact moment to look up, her painted face and great bulk like a crazy cartoon, the detachment from reality felt complete. She saw Sapphire's lips form her name, then Nicky was looking at her as well.

She walked in, pushing her hands into her pockets and tossing back her head.

'How lovely to see you, darling,' said Sapphire, holding out her arms for a moment, then letting them drop to begin massaging Nicky's shoulders.

'Hello, Sapphire.' She cleared her throat. 'Nicky, can I speak to you?'

He looked up at her, his head to one side, the corners of his mouth curved in the tiniest smile. He pushed a chair towards her with his foot. 'Go ahead.'

'You're looking amazingly well, darling,' said Sapphire. 'Couple of pounds heavier maybe.' She gave one of her deep chuckles. 'Isn't she looking adorable, Nicky?'

'It's her new lover, Sapph.' He craned his head up towards Sapphire, flexing the biceps of his good arm and making an obscene gesture as he spoke. 'A builder,' he said in a mocking loud whisper. 'He must be keeping her happy.'

She looked straight at him, searching for words that would hurt him as he was hurting her.

'Well, I'm very pleased for her,' said Sapphire. 'She deserves someone a lot nicer than you. You've done the right thing, sweetheart.'

'Oh, I'm sure I have,' said Josephine with another flick of her head. 'And I'm sure Nicky's found plenty of company to keep him just as happy.'

Nicky pushed off Sapphire's hands and stood up. 'Actually, I've been completely celibate since you walked out on me,' he said. He put a hand between his legs. 'I've nearly forgotten what it's for.'

'Look, if you can't talk to me in a civil way, then I'm going. And don't make any more calls about my locket, you can . . . you can do what you like with it. I couldn't care less about it any more.'

Sapphire chuckled again. 'That's it, my darling – you tell him.'

'Shut up, you old pervert,' said Nicky. 'Come on then, if you want to talk we'll get out of here.'

Outside the drizzle was still falling; it looked like early evening rather than midday.

'Fuck this,' he said, pulling up the collar of his leather jacket and grimacing up at the sky. 'Come on,' he repeated and went limping off up the road.

He rarely swore and she felt a little sense of triumph, sure she had annoyed him by remaining composed when he had tried so hard to upset her. He didn't say another word until they were at his gate, then he turned to her, smiling, the rain glistening in tiny drops on his hair and lashes.

'I'm glad you've come,' he said. 'I wanted to show you what I've been doing.'

'I'm not here for one of your tours. I just want a quick word with you and then I'm going.'

He smiled again and pushed open the gate. 'Well, you can have your quick word while you look,' he said.

She knew he was mocking her but was determined to remain calm: this mustn't deteriorate into a row.

He led her down to the studio, flicking on a series of lights from a new panel just inside the door. The effect was amazing. The whole ceiling had been painted to resemble a midnight sky, with bulbs strategically placed to create a galaxy of twinkling stars. There was even a crescent moon that glowed pale yellow.

'Watch,' he said, his finger on the panel again.

The moon became full and bright, then slowly narrowed back to the sharp pointed crescent.

'It's brilliant, isn't it?

'Yes, marvellous. Nicky, can you listen to what I've come to say?'

'Let me dry your jacket.'

'No.' She stepped away as he went to take it from her shoulders. 'I'm getting married – I don't want him to know about you.'

His expression remained exactly the same. 'Can you notice anything else I've done?' he said. 'The fire-escape door.'

She automatically looked towards the far wall; the door had been bricked up.

'It's for security. I had to remove the first few steps. I've got a new entry to it now.'

'Nicky, will you listen to me?'

'I am.' He stared at her with the half-smile that she knew so well. 'So you're getting married.'

'I don't want him to know about you,' she repeated.

'Well he does. I've spoken to him, haven't I?'

'What did you say?'

'Not much.' He looked at her from beneath his lashes, as though it amused him. 'I told him you'd be very disappointed if he didn't pass on my message and he said, keep away from her or I'll break your fucking neck, and slammed the phone down. No wonder you don't want him to know about me.'

'You don't understand. You don't understand feelings like that – you never cared about me enough.'

Again his expression showed not a flicker of emotion, and she turned to go, knowing that if she said one more word, her composure would crack and she'd be in tears.

'Don't worry, I won't tell him anything. I'll erase the past six months from my mind.'

She ignored him and walked towards the door.

'Josephine.'

'Yes?' She stopped but didn't turn round.

'Don't touch the doors or you'll get a massive electric shock.'

A cold zip of fear kept her from moving. She stared at the pair of innocent-looking louvered doors. A thin cable ran along the top of the frame and disappeared into the wall, just as it did in the upstairs rooms.

'I don't believe you,' she said, still without turning.

'You didn't really think I was just going to let you walk out of here, did you?' He came up behind her. 'Or forget about the past six months?'

She swung round. 'Then why didn't you phone me before?'

'You walked out. I've never chased after anyone.' He looked in deadly earnest now. His hair hung in wet streaks round his face and his eyes glinted hard and gold as the rings in his ears. 'How long have you been sleeping with him?'

She didn't answer but looked towards the door again. 'This is one of your tricks, isn't it?'

'Try it then. It's enough to kill you.'

She hesitated and he caught hold of her wrist. With his strapped arm clasped round her wrist, he dragged her to the door.

'Stop it! Stop it!' she shrieked.

He forced her fingers down on to the metal handle and she screamed with fear. Nothing happened. The door came open a fraction. He let her go and burst out laughing.

'You bastard!' she shrieked at him.

He raised his eyebrows with surprise and laughed all the more. She screamed it at him again, then drew back her arm and slapped him round the face. He didn't flinch and she slapped him again, harder, her face streaming with angry tears as she raised her hand to hit him once more. This time he stopped her.

'Don't cry,' he said, putting his arms round her, his body still shaking slightly with laughter. 'You know it melts my heart.' He bent his head to rest his forehead against hers, his voice growing softer. 'Sapphire told me you cried when you phoned her.'

'Well it's too late to worry about that now,' she said, twisting away from him.

'What meaningless words you talk.' Nicky took her face between his hands, wiping away the tears with his thumbs. 'This is nothing to do with anything else. This is just me and you and now.'

She saw his eyes close, his lips part, and the room seemed to come spiralling in around her as he pushed her back against the wall and kissed her. And as soon as he touched her, running his long fingers over her body, unhooking her skirt and plunging his hands down to the back of her thighs to press her tightly against him, he was right: it was just the two of them.

There was an unfamiliar urgency about him. It was the first time he'd made love to her while she still wore most of her clothes, and he didn't stop to switch on the music as he used to. But standing with her back against the barre while he moved his fingers against her and then into her, she felt as if she would die with the pleasure of it. And when he'd brought her to the brink, so that her stomach leapt with ecstasy, he took his hand away and whispered: 'Once more, Josephine? Shall we love each other once more?' She could only murmur his name but he smiled and squeezed his hands round her waist, tilting her hips towards him. 'I knew you'd come back to say goodbye.'

And just as she had that very first time, she watched their reflections in the mirrors: saw the dark shadow of her hair as it escaped from its knot and tumbled over his shoulders; saw his body moving against hers, slow and measured at first, then faster, until her head swam and she could see nothing except the flicker of lights on the ceiling. And at one point, when he had his arm clasped round her waist, almost lifting her from the ground, she knew that she was crying, but didn't know why because she was thinking, nothing will ever feel as good as this again.

The barre dug into her back; Nicky collapsed against her, his face pressed into her shoulder. The seconds stretched into minutes, until finally he straightened up and gripped the barre either side of her. 'I've had no one else since you left.' His face was very close to hers. 'That's the truth.' She lowered her head but he tilted her chin with one finger. 'Speak to me, Josephine. Why all the frowning? Where's that lovely smile I used to see?'

She reached up and tugged at the sides of his hair. 'Why did you do that? You know I don't take the pill.'

He shrugged; his face changed slightly. 'How do I know? I don't know what your new arrangements are.' He stepped back to zip up his jeans and buckle his belt, looking at her as he did so. 'You weren't worried about it a few minutes ago.' For a moment, he was the same Nicky who had kicked that chair towards her at Sapphire's. She turned away and began to straighten her own clothes, miserably self-conscious. Then she heard him give a loud sigh and he came and cupped her face in his hands. 'Don't be sulky, Josephine, don't spoil it.' He kissed her lightly and smoothed back her hair with both hands. 'Come on, we'll go upstairs. I'll find your locket and you can have a shower.'

She shook her head, swallowing hard against a welter of tears and guilt. 'I'll just go,' she muttered.

'Don't be silly. What if he's there when you get back and takes you straight off to bed? He'll know.' He sniffed playfully at her. 'He'll smell me on you.'

'Don't!' She shoved him away. 'How can you say things like that? How can you act as if . . . as if . . .?'

He kissed here again, then bit gently at her lower lip. 'Come on.' He took her hand and held it against his chest, bending his head to smile into her face. 'Don't run away angry or you'll break my heart even more.'

And she told herself she went with him because he was right, she must wash away all traces of him. It was the sensible thing to do, go upstairs and scrub him away. They were out on the fire escape; the steps were slippery in the rain and she clung to his hand and wondered why ever he'd brought her up this way. But why did he do any of the things he did?

In his bedroom, the curtains were still pulled across as usual and he threw himself on the bed and closed his eyes.

'Come and sleep for a while,' he murmured, stretching out an arm towards her.

She wished she could. How she longed to curl up and sleep and erase the last hour from her mind. But it wouldn't alter anything, wouldn't alter the fact that before long she must go back and face Ross, just as she had had to go downstairs on Christmas Day and face her mother.

He raised his head a moment but she walked away, wandering round the room. On the dressing table was a photograph of Nico. She had never seen it before. He was dressed in school uniform, but his resemblance to his father – the mass of hair, the beguiling smile and the glitter of gold at his ears – looked so incongruous against the smart blazer and tie that it made her smile for a moment. She picked it up. On the back, in neatly childish handwriting, it said, 'With love and a thousand kisses, from Nico'. As she replaced it, she noticed her locket lying there, the chain tangled and broken. Heaped on the other side were a pile of cassettes. Two embossed invitation cards protruded. She could only read the odd words: 'Gala Performance' and 'Your company is requested'. She sighed and turned away. Three separate parts of his life, and all that she had amounted to was the broken gold chain.

He was sleeping now and she got undressed and went into the shower. She would go before he woke, and on her way out she would throw the locket over the fire escape into the jungle of nettles beneath. She leant her head against the tiled wall and lingered there until the spray of water turned cold.

For a moment she thought the church clock had begun its horrible chiming, but realised that it was music and that Nicky must be awake. She wrapped herself in a towel and reached up to turn off the water.

He came to stand in the doorway, his hair standing out from his head, his face deathly white and creased with sleep.

'I thought you'd drowned,' he smiled.

'What a good idea.' She was about to step out but he barred her way.

'Don't marry him,' he said.

'What – and be your weekend visitor once more? Get out of my way, Nicky.'

'Don't marry him,' he repeated, stepping into the shower cubicle fully clothed and turning the water back on. 'Or I'll drown us both.'

'You're mad.' She was laughing and crying all at the same time, and he held her head under the jet of water and kissed her lightly on the lips.

'What happened to that guy in the picture?' he said. 'Tell me it again.'

'The nymphs took him to their underwater grotto and he was never seen . . . Stop it!' she yelled as he turned the water up more. 'It's freezing . . . and I'll never get my hair dry.'

He laughed and kissed her again and she couldn't help laughing too because he still had his boots on and they were beginning to fill with water.

'So you don't really want to drown?' he said, tilting her head under the spray until the water began to fill her eyes and nose as well.

She reached out for the soap and quickly lathered her hands, then rubbed them in his face.

'God!' he gasped, letting her go and rubbing at his eyes. 'You've got a vicious streak in you.'

'Serves you right.'

It was like the summer when they'd played their games all over the house and, like the summer, he came after her as she ran back into the bedroom, the soaking wet towel held around her. She screamed as he pulled her on to the floor, then rolled her in his arms on the deep soft pile of the carpet. And soon they were locked together in a frenzy of kisses and she had her mouth open wide for his tongue and her legs wrapped tight round him.

'Wait,' he whispered, lifting from her and unbuckling his belt and the leather straps from his arm. 'I don't want to damage you.'

'I don't care.' She sat up to kiss him again as he began to strip off his soaking clothes.

'I do.' He pulled off his boots, showering water across the floor, then touched her cheek. 'I'm a gentle lover. Not a fiery little nymphomaniac like you,' he said, pushing her back down.

She laughed. Nothing he said or did mattered – or what he didn't do once more; she just wanted him.

He pushed his hands up under her breasts and ran his tongue slowly round each nipple in turn. Then ran his fingers over her hips and down her thighs, trailing them so lightly over her skin that her nerve ends were drawn like shreds of metal to a magnet. She pulled him against her, but he held away and bent to kiss a path down her stomach, ending on the inside of her leg, at the very top, where he sucked at the skin until it tingled with drawn blood. She opened her legs and he moved his mouth. The rush of pleasure was so instant and intense that she felt herself jolt away from him.

He drew up to lie beside her, his face in the wet tangle of her hair.

'Do you know, Josephine,' he murmured. 'You're the most responsive girl I've ever made love to.'

And still she didn't care what he said; it all seemed part of the spell he cast over her, these things he said and did.

He lay on his back and pulled her on top of him. She felt voluptuously weak and warm and stretched her arms above his head.

'But you're selfish,' he said, kissing her armpit, then tickling her there with his thumb.

She flinched away, laughing. 'No I'm not.' She drew a hand down and slid it between their damp bodies, coming to a halt as she reached the hard jut of his pelvic bone. 'I'm not selfish, am I?' she said.

'Yes you are,' he murmured.

She moved her fingers slowly sideways until she felt the first thin line of hair down his stomach.

'Say I'm not.'

'You are – a little bit.'

Again she moved her hand, spreading her fingers in the coarser hair between his thighs and finally taking hold of him. He closed his eyes with a smile.

'All right, you're not.'

She raised her body above him, letting her legs fall either side of him. 'Well I am,' she said, dropping down on him. 'Totally.'

His hips rose to meet her and she put her hands flat on the carpet above his shoulders, watching the beads of sweat break out on his brow and the colour flow into his face. His breathing grew faster and he wrapped his arms round her and turned her over on to her back for the last final thrusts.

While they lay there still joined together, their breathing gradually slowing back to normal, the church clock started to chime.

'That fucking clock,' he said, lifting himself from her.

'I've never heard you complain about it before,' she said. 'And I've never heard you swear so much.'

'Oh, I have got one or two faults, you know.' He reached over for the sodden towel and wiped himself with it, then handed it to her.

'Yes, I know.' She looked at him, her face grave. 'That's twice.'

'Go and run up and down the fire escape,' he said.

She got up and went back into the shower. When she came out, he was sitting on the bed, still naked, a dry towel round his shoulders, a hair-dryer plugged in beside him.

'Come here, I'll dry your hair,' he said.

She went and sat in front of him. He had his leg stretched beside her; it was the first time he'd ever left it exposed like this. She sat without speaking while he rubbed at her hair with the towel then switched on the dryer.

'So you didn't tell him about me?' he said suddenly.

She shook her head and he leant his chin on her shoulder. 'And you won't tell him about this afternoon?'

'No!' She swivelled round to face him, pushing the dryer away. 'How could I? How could I do that to him?'

'More of your little secrets.' He smiled. 'Did you ever sleep with him when you were seeing me?'

'You know I didn't.' Sudden misery overwhelmed her. 'You know I didn't want anyone but you. Why do you always try and hurt me?' She broke down in tears and buried her face in the duvet. The minutes ticked by. She felt the bed move as he got up, heard him getting dressed.

'Haven't you got to collect the little girl today?' he said.

Josephine imagined Tessa waiting for her, upset because she hadn't come, and she cried all the more. How could she walk out of here and act as if nothing had happened?

He came back to sit on the bed and pulled her up by the wrists. 'You can do one of two things, so you'd better make up your mind. You can go back and tell him that you're not going to marry him, or you can say, goodbye, Nicky, it's been a wonderful farewell and we're parting friends.'

'I wish I was dead.'

'Why? Because you've cheated on him, or because you can't have us both? Now get dressed before you're late.'

'You've got no feelings, you don't understand.'

'I have a million feelings you know nothing about.' His voice sounded unusually cold and he eyed her with chilly detachment. '. . . So you wish you were dead, do you?' he said in the same tone.

'Yes, yes, I do,' she sobbed burying her face again and remembering how Ross had comforted her when she'd said the same thing to him.

'The trouble with you, Josephine, is you like playing the games but you don't like the consequences. Now let's play the real thing, shall we?'

She turned her cheek on the duvet and watched him stretch across the bed and pull open the drawer of the bedside table.

'We'll see how sincere you are.' He straightened up, holding what looked like a narrow metal comb; but as he held it in front of her, a razor-thin blade shot out of the end. With a little swipe, he cut through the denim of his jeans, checked to see if she were looking, and ran the blade across the exposed skin of his leg.

She watched, mesmerised, as a thin line of blood seeped to the surface. 'Here you are, do it yourself.' He held the knife out to her. 'Practise on me if you like. Let's see what you're made of, Josephine.'

She drew back from him. This was a Nicky she didn't know; his face devoid of expression; no sign of the sudden laughter. Fear came creeping over her.

'No?' He raised his eyebrows. 'You surprise me. I thought this would appeal to you. Too much for you, is it?' He held the blade to his wrist. 'Shall I show you how? I've shown you so many other things, haven't I?'

'Don't,' she whispered.

'Don't,' he echoed. 'Not very often you say that, is it?' Still he didn't smile but stretched out on his stomach, holding the knife between his fingertips. 'Let's see who's going to die first,' he said. 'Hylas or the nymph.' Then he threw the knife at the picture. It sliced into the canvas right in the middle of a water lily and he sprung off the bed and pulled it out, then slashed at the picture, ripping it apart.

'Here.' He picked up her locket from the dressing table and tossed it on to the bed. 'Don't forget to take it with you this time.' With that, he was off down the fire escape.

She dressed, wiped away the tears as they fell and went down the inside stairs. Music came up from the studio at a deafening pitch and she stood in the hall, tempted to go down and say goodbye, make an attempt to part friends. But what good would it do? Better to leave now with his hostility fresh in her mind. She'd spent the afternoon doing stupid and dangerous things, betraying the person she'd promised to marry. Fresh tears streamed down her face and she wrenched open the front door and ran off down the garden path.

On the way to collect Tessa, she got herself under control, and by the time Ross came home, she had the semblance of a smile back on her face. But it wasn't easy to keep it there. And when he came up and put his arms round her soon after Tessa had gone to bed, she felt the tears well up again.

'Have you washed your hair?' he said, pressing his cheek against her head. 'It feels lovely and soft.'

'It's the rain,' she murmured, ducking away from him to gather up some doll's clothes Tessa had left on the floor.

'Have you been out then?'

'Just to get Tessa.' She bent her head over them, arranging them in a neat pile.

'Yeah, I know, I meant anywhere else – you look dressed up.'

She shrugged. 'No.'

'Leave that. Tess should put her own things away.' He pulled her up and put his arms round her again, running his hands down over her hips and lifting the hem of her skirt. 'Let's go to bed.'

She caught his wrists. 'Don't. My period's started early. I'll sleep with Tessa if you like.'

He put his hands on her shoulders as though he was about to shake her. 'Don't insult me like that.' His voice was raised and he did shake her slightly. 'Do you think just because I can't make love to you I don't want you in my bed?'

He stared hard at her and the tears threatened once more. She wasn't quite sure why she'd added the last sentence to her lie; she yearned for him to hold her, longed to fall asleep with his arms wrapped round her.

'You've got some very funny ideas about love, Josephine.

You've got funny ideas about a lot of things,' he finished, his voice softening. 'Why the hell did I fall in love with someone like you?'

He sank into an armchair and pulled her on to his lap, and she curled there, her head against his shoulder, trying to block out what she had done to him.

'You won't ever stop loving me, will you?' she murmured after a while.

'Nothing will make me do that,' he said, hugging her closer.

'Would you love me whatever I do?'

'Why, what are you thinking of doing?' he said, jokingly.

'Please just say it.'

'You're the strangest girl,' he said, kissing her cheek. 'Whatever you do,' he added. 'Except if you were unfaithful to me.'

Chapter 13

That night, in a sudden yearning to be back home again, she persuaded Ross to take a few days off work so that they could go to Waylands for him to meet her mother.

He looked a bit daunted as they drove up the long gravelled drive and through the brick archway into the courtyard.

'My God, Phina,' he said. 'I didn't realise it was this big.'

But he was soon himself again and within the first half-hour he'd sat down with her mother and said; 'I love your daughter. I'll look after her and make her happy. I've got my own house and a successful business.' Then he'd stopped and smiled and added: 'What more can I say?'

Josephine watched her mother and knew that she was touched by his words and charmed by the open, honest way he spoke.

'Well, you've said the right thing first,' she smiled.

By the end of the first day, he'd also been round the house, advising her about repairs and all sorts of things that Lawrence hadn't managed to organise. Josephine knew he wasn't doing it to impress, it was just the way he was. And, shortly after their arrival, Louisa had taken charge of Tessa. She was a few months younger than Tessa but bigger and more confident, having been left much to her own devices since Josephine had gone. They had soon disappeared together upstairs, and didn't show up again until they were called for tea.

'Tessa doesn't want to sleep in the end room,' said Louisa firmly. 'She's frightened on her own.'

When Ross told her not to be silly, she started to whine, and Josephine said she could come in with her as Louisa now slept in with her mother. Louisa immediately said she would as well, so it ended up with the three of them together.

'You'll have to have a word with your mother about the sleeping arrangements when we come again,' said Ross. He'd been assigned Lawrence's old room.

Josephine laughed at him. 'My mother doesn't approve of people sleeping together before they're married.'

It had turned into an exceptionally happy few days. Sleeping in with Louisa and Tessa, she'd had time to pull herself together after that afternoon with Nicky; time to try and wipe the episode from her mind before Ross made love to her again. And, being away from London, spending carefree days doing childish things, had made her sure that she wanted to marry Ross. He fitted in so well at Waylands; it felt so right being there with him. She looked across the table at him one morning at breakfast, and knew that she couldn't bear to be without him. And when he looked back, his eyes full of desire after another night apart, she smiled at him, longing to tell him how much she loved him.

But on their last day, checking the little red cross in her diary, that afternoon with Nicky came flooding back. There was still no sign of the stomach cramps that plagued her each month, and she was always so regular. She told herself that she might have got the date wrong, but either way she still had something to worry about. If she was mistaken with the dates, Ross would realise she'd lied about her period starting early and want to know why. But if nothing happened – she couldn't even bring herself to think about this possibility. What had been a nagging worry suddenly grew to monumental proportions. In a panic she decided to stay on a few days on her own. She gave the excuse she wanted to see Lawrence. Ross had to get back to work and Tessa to school.

That morning, she and Ross drove into the village to get some shopping, leaving the girls with her mother. On the way back he branched off down a track and pulled up.

'I just need to kiss you,' he smiled, taking her in his arms. 'We've hardly been alone since we got here.' After a few seconds he drew away from her. 'I wish you'd come back with me,' he said, running a hand through his hair.

'It's only a few days.' She didn't know whether to change her mind, what to do for the best. She put her hand absently against her stomach, her mind blank for a moment, drained with thinking too hard. Then Nicky's words came unbidden into her head: you like playing the games but you don't like . . . She glanced at Ross and imagined what it would be like without him.

'You look worried,' he said.

She stared at him a moment, then wound her arms round his neck. When he kissed her again, she pushed her tongue into his mouth and slid her fingers under his shirt-collar to massage his neck.

'Don't tease, Phina. That's not like you.'

'Let's go for a walk,' she said suddenly, placing her hands on his shoulders.

'So that I'll cool off?'

She didn't answer, but hopped out of the car and climbed over a wooden gate to one of the long grassy avenues of the pine forest. It was one of the newer plantations, the trees only halfway to maturity and the path not rutted with the comings and goings of the machinery used to cut the timber. Here and there groups of hardwood trees stood amongst the pines, breaking up the military-style ranks and making little havens where the grass grew thick and lush.

A little way along she took his hand and led him off the track and into one of these little glades.

'We used to say these were fairy glades,' she said, standing under the dripping, almost leafless trees. 'Especially if they had rings in the grass.'

'The fairies would need wellington boots today,' he laughed.

Despite the watery sun which had made an appearance at lunch-time and was now shining down quite brightly between the skeleton of branches, the ground was soggy with recent rain.

'Yes, they would,' she laughed back, looking down at her flimsy shoes and the hem of the long Indian cotton skirt she had on.

'And you're mad coming out like that,' he said, gathering her in his arms and lifting her from the ground.

As he went to put her down, she clung to him, her arms tight round his neck, pushing her tongue between his lips once more. He opened his mouth and slid his fingers up through her hair, then took a step back to lean against a tree and draw her close to him.

'Are you all right now?' he whispered.

She nodded and stared up into his face and he let out a short gruff breath and looked around them.

'It's too wet here. I can't take you back home with your clothes soaked through.'

She put her lips against his ear. 'We don't have to lie down.'

She knew by the way he held her that she'd excited him more than ever, but again he stopped.

'But I haven't got anything with me, I—' She cut him off with a hand over his mouth.

'It won't hurt this once,' she whispered.

He began to kiss her again and she knew that he wouldn't stop now. They changed positions so that her back was against the tree and he murmured was she sure she wanted this? And she said, yes, over and over, because it was no longer just to make her feel safe, but because she had never felt so aroused by him before.

When he and Tessa drove off the next day, she felt an overwhelming sense of loss as she watched him go. It was almost a physical pain. She'd never felt anything quite like it before.

'What's the matter with you,' said Nella, as she came back indoors. 'You've got a face as long as a week of wet Sundays.'

'I wish I'd gone back with them,' she said, her eyes filling with ridiculous tears.

Later on, she walked up to the quarries, the first time she'd been there for ages. It was sunny again and she wandered about, trying to sort out her feelings and wondering if she had done the right thing yesterday. Right for whom? a little voice seemed to ask her. She felt lonely and confused. If only she'd gone back with him.

She came to the hollow where her father had fallen that awful day nearly three years ago, and sat at its edge, looking down into the drift of dead leaves at its bottom.

'I'll never deceive him again,' she said aloud. 'I promise I won't. Please let everything be all right and I won't do anything wrong ever again.' She pressed her forehead against her knees and cried silently for all the mistakes she'd made.

That evening she phoned Ross.

'I just wanted to tell you how much I've missed you today,' she said. 'And how much I love you.'

'That's the first time you've ever said that without me asking you,' he said softly.

They chatted for half an hour, batting words of love and suggestive remarks backwards and forwards down the line.

'I hope nobody's listening in on us,' she giggled.

'Well, if they are they'll know that Josephine Jarrouse likes it standing up under a tree with—'

'Shush!' she hissed at him, laughing and holding her hand over the receiver.

'Was it really the best ever?' His voice had grown quieter.

'I'll tell you when I see you.'

'You'll have to go on the pill if we're going to carry on like that.' He sounded serious now.

She took a little breath and said: 'Would you mind if I was pregnant?'

'Of course I wouldn't mind, but I wouldn't want anyone thinking that's why I was marrying you. I'm going to tell my parents tomorrow,' he added. 'Just in case.'

It was Miran who revealed that his parents didn't entirely approve.

'He told them you were really sixteen and they think you're too young for him,' Miran said to her. 'But they'll get over it. I do as well,' she added with a laugh. 'But I'd rather it was you than Cheryl. She thinks you've been after him for ages. She once said you were always running around cooking for him or waltzing round the house in your nightie.'

Josephine was amazed by this remark; she wanted to reply, I was madly in love with someone else a few weeks ago, I hadn't even given Ross a thought. But that would sound awful, and of course Miran was like Ross and believed she had spent the summer weekends with her mother. Sometimes the lies weighed heavily on her heart, but there was no way she could tell Ross the truth; he was already jealous enough. He never wanted her to go anywhere without him, and became aggressive if another man so much as glanced in her direction. It didn't fit his easy-going nature, and she felt almost trapped by it sometimes. But then she would remind herself what it felt like, how it magnified and distorted things. And with this reasoning would come thoughts that she didn't want; memories that she had tried to banish from her mind, and that bruising feeling of guilt that was never far away.

She filled her head with other things. Ross planned to redecorate and refurnish the bedroom that had been hers, so they could move into it together, and he let her choose all the colours and furniture. And there were all the preparations to be made for their wedding in Easter. Two weeks after their first visit they went to Waylands again to discuss it with Lawrence, who was going to help Solange organise everything.

The following weekend they went to Ross's parents for lunch on Saturday. Tessa was staying there the night as they were going out with Miran and her boyfriend. Miran's salon was doing well, and she wanted to take them out for a meal to celebrate their engagement.

There had been other outings, more of Ross's relations to meet and, as Josephine helped Tessa pack her overnight bag, she felt a surge of weariness followed by a sudden wave of nausea.

'You forgot Bobby,' said Tessa, unzipping the bag to stuff a fluffy pink rabbit amongst the other toys that had to accompany her to bed each night.

'Sorry.' Josephine flopped on the bed, a hand to her forehead, sweating with the force of the attack.

A minute later Ross was calling upstairs to see if they were ready and she took a deep breath and followed Tessa down.

It was a bright cold day, and the nausea subsided a bit as they went out to the car and a chill breeze cooled her face. But, in the heat and chatter of Ross's parents' house, it returned in full force.

Ross was in great spirits. That week he'd put in a price for the renovation of a sixteenth-century farmhouse for a pop star, and thought the chances of getting the work were very good. He'd made the contact through his mother, who did part-time dressmaking for a company that produced costumes for the stage.

'There'll be a bonus in this for you and Dad if I get it,' he said as he talked to his mother about it over lunch. 'I'll pay for you to go away for a few days.' Josephine knew Ross was worried about his father's health but she was feeling too ill herself to join in the conversation. As soon as she started to eat, she was overwhelmed with nausea.

'It's on the Suffolk border,' Ross went on. He turned to Josephine now. 'If I started it in July we could stay at your mother's for the summer holidays. It'd be nice for Tess with your sister.'

She nodded and tried to smile but had to leave the table and rush to the bathroom. Within seconds she vomited up all she'd managed to eat. She washed her face and went down again but just the aroma of the sponge pudding that Ross's mother had put on the table sent her back upstairs.

This time Ross followed to ask if she was all right. She shouted, yes, she'd be down in a minute, and heard him go into the kitchen with his mother. As she came downstairs, she heard the tail end of their conversation.

'I know it's none of my business, but you're just storing up more heartache for yourself, and upset for Tessa as well.''

'You don't know what . . .' Ross stopped as her footsteps creaked on the stairs and he came to meet her.

'Do you want to go home?' he asked.

'Yes, if you don't mind.'

The goodbyes were brief and once they were in the car, Ross said: 'My mum said I'm selfish and irresponsible, trapping you into motherhood at your age.' He paused and gave a little smile. 'Is that what I've done?'

She nodded. 'I'm not sure, but I think so.' She looked down, preparing herself for another lie; it got harder and harder to lie to him. 'I'm only a couple of days late but . . . What else did she say?'

'That you'll get fed up with babies and married life and in a few years you'll be looking for the excitement you've missed out on.' He pulled out into the road, looking over his shoulder. 'Is that right as well?'

'If that's what you think, then don't marry me,' she said lightly.

He glanced at her. 'It's not what I think, and even if it was it wouldn't stop me from marrying you – nothing would.' He reached across and took her hand. 'Especially not now. Nothing in the world's going to stop me marrying you.'

By the evening she felt completely recovered and even began to work up an appetite as she got changed to go out. She put on a close fitting bright red dress with short skirt and narrow shoulder straps, and pinned up her hair.

Miran complimented her on how good she looked, and she knew the waiter 'had given her more than a glance or two behind Ross's back. It made her feel confident and happy. Not that she wanted admiring looks from other men, she didn't. It just fitted the feel of the evening, made her feel special and optimistic and, most of all, secure.

'Well, here's to you two,' said Miran, raising a glass of the champagne she'd ordered for them. 'And thanks, Ross, for helping me with the salon.'

Josephine smiled and clinked glasses with Ross, then leant over and kissed him on the lips, looked into his eyes and did it again.

'You've come a long way from the shy little thing you were when you first came here,' said Miran, looking at her sideways.

'A lot's happened to her since then,' said Ross, slipping his arm round her shoulders and kissing her cheek. Josephine laughed and gulped down a mouthful of the champagne, then remembered that Ross had said she shouldn't drink alcohol now. She whispered to him that she wouldn't have any more and he kissed her again.

'I think we'd better let these two go home,' said Miran. Then she leant back in her seat and clapped her hands. 'Except that I've arranged a surprise for you.'

Ross frowned and looked at Josephine. 'I don't like the sound of that,' he joked.

'Nothing dreadful, I promise,' said Miran as she led them out to the cab she'd ordered. 'I've just organised a few of your friends to meet us so we can have a real celebration.' She put her arm through his. 'An excuse for you to get thoroughly pissed up for a change. You've done nothing but work for the past few years.'

Ross laughed. 'That's not strictly true, but if you're paying, Miran, I shan't argue. Where are we going?'

'The Rising Sun.'

'No.' It came out far too quickly.

Ross looked at her, the smile frozen on his face. 'What's the matter?'

Only one excuse came to mind: she felt ill again. But she'd been in high spirits for the last two hours: it would sound invented. Her brain raced, desperately trying to think of something.

'Don't you want to go?' said Ross.

'We're going, it's all arranged,' butted in Miran, pushing them towards the cab. 'I thought you'd like it there,' she added, half indignant.

'I was only joking.' Josephine took Ross's hand, her stomach doing somersaults as she remembered how Nicky had once said, 'You're the only girl who's ever kept me in on Saturday nights.'

By the time they walked into the pub her heart was thudding crazily, and she kept her eyes averted from the crowd at the bar. But as Ross led her over to a far table where a group of his and Miran's friends sat waiting for them, sending up a little cheer as they approached, she knew he was there.

The next half-hour was torture. She sat with her back to the bar, frightened to turn round, and all the while she had to be sociable, listen to the jokes, the good wishes for their future – all of which got louder as glasses became empty and were immediately refilled. At one point, when the laughter was at a peak and Ross was involved in a friendly but very loud argument, Miran leant across the table and said: 'You know who's at the bar, don't you?'

Josephine had to turn and look. She caught just a glimpse of wine-dark hair, then turned back to Miran.

'He's hardly taken his eyes off you since . . .' Miran broke off as a drink got knocked over in front of her. There was swearing and more laughter, and one of the crowd started to sing to the music that was blaring out at full blast above their heads.

Somehow she got separated from Ross. He leant over to ask if she was all right, his voice barely audible above the noise, his eyes bright with alcohol.

'Of course she is,' said the woman sitting next to her. 'I went out with Ross when he was eighteen,' she shouted in Josephine's ear. 'Is he still sex mad?'

Josephine glanced at her watch. Another ten minutes and she'd tell Ross she wanted to go – if she could get him away.

The woman leant over to tell her something else.

'Excuse me.' Josephine got up and made her way to the Ladies. Somebody followed her in and she glanced round, startled to find Alice there.

'Nicky wants to speak to you,' she said. 'He's waiting along the passage.'

'I can't, I'm . . . I'm here with—'

'He only wants you to go and talk to him, for God's sake,' said Alice. 'That's the least you can do.'

She was surprised at Alice's tone, surprised at the hint of accusation.

'Please,' Alice coaxed. 'Or he'll think I haven't tried. I'll watch in case your boyfriend comes,' she added, pulling her towards the door.

The dimly lit passageway led past the Ladies' room and out to a rear car park. Nicky was leaning against the wall by the back entrance. He was wearing an emerald-green silk shirt and white jeans, his hair shining with henna-coloured lights. The shirt had full sleeves and gathered yoke and the jeans were skin tight; he could have been dressed for the starring role in a ballet.

'You look wonderful,' she said without thinking.

'So do you.' He stared into her face. 'I just wanted to ask how you were, that's all.'

'I'm fine.' She fixed her eyes on the wall beside him.

'And everything's all right?' he persisted.

She stared out into the darkness of the car park and wondered what his reaction would be if she said, no, it's not all right. I think I'm pregnant and it's probably yours but I've convinced myself it's another man's because . . .

He broke in to her thoughts exactly as if he'd read them. 'I would want to know if it wasn't.'

'I told you, I'm fine.'

'Look at me and say it.'

She raised her face to him, blanking out all thought. 'I'm perfectly all right,' she heard herself say.

They stood there in silence for a few seconds and then he said, 'Just make sure you think of me sometimes – close your eyes in the dark and think of me.'

She clenched her fists, silently crying, don't, don't, don't, and took a step backwards because she knew that if he touched her, if he took her hand and said, come back with me, she would forget her promise, push aside all thoughts of Ross and go with him.

He smiled and straightened up. 'I hope you'll be very happy with him.' The spell was broken and he walked off.

She stumbled back to the bar, went straight to Ross and said she wanted to go. But he pulled her on to his lap, hardly listening.

'I want to go now,' she insisted. 'If you don't come I'll go on my own.'

He tried to cuddle her but she pulled away and got her coat. By the time she'd put it on, he was on his feet, looking slightly unsteady and starting to say his goodbyes. Most of the others were in the same state and didn't seem to take a lot of notice of their early departure, though she did hear someone say, 'She's got him right where she wants him.' But she didn't care; she had to get away.

Back at home, she made him black coffee because she hated him like this; it was so unusual and she desperately needed him to be his normal self. By the time they went to bed he seemed only mildly intoxicated and, when she wriggled out of the red dress, he commented that soon she wouldn't be able to wear things like that. She stared at herself in the mirror, then ran her hands down over her stomach and imagined what it would be like when she was bloated and huge. The thought repulsed her and suddenly the whole idea of being pregnant repulsed her.

'I told you, it's not definite.' He was in bed and she looked over her shoulder at him. 'And I want you to keep taking precautions just in case – because I don't want a baby yet.'

In the light from the bedside lamp, she saw his face change, as though she'd said it purposely to hurt him. She got into bed and curled up away from him, stricken with a feeling that made her want to hurt him even more. When he put his arms round her, she sat up and swung her feet to the floor.

'If you don't leave me alone I'll go and sleep in Tessa's bed.'

He lay on his back staring up at her as though he were confused by her behaviour, and she didn't move because she was confused herself.

'Is it because I've had a few drinks?' he said after a while.

She shook her head and wrapped her arms round herself against the chill night air.

'Then what's the matter?'

'I don't know.' She almost shouted the words. 'Just leave me alone.'

He propped himself on an elbow and tried to touch her, but she pushed him away and after a few moments he said: 'Either get back in bed or clear off to Tessa's room.'

She hugged herself tighter but didn't move.

'Did you hear me?' His voice was calm but she knew he was getting annoyed with her. When she still didn't move, he shook her arm. 'Josephine!'

'And did you hear me?' she flung at him. 'I said leave me alone!'

He pulled himself upright and took her by the shoulders.

'You try my patience at times, do you know that? I do everything I can to make you happy but . . .' He broke off and gave her a shake. 'You try to test me, don't you, see how far you can push me?'

'No, I don't.'

He shook her again. 'I haven't got endless patience, you know, and I can't switch on and off like you can.'

'Get off me.' She tried to prise up his fingers but he gripped her tighter. Then all at once he let her go.

'Let's stop this before it gets out of hand,' he said. 'Now get back in bed.'

'No.' She moved out of his reach and he pulled the duvet over his head and turned away from her.

'Right, I'll go up to Tessa's,' she said. She walked over to the door and stood there. 'And I'll stay there all night!' she shouted.

'Stay there all week,' he said from under the duvet.

She ran back to the bed and caught hold of his hair, tugging at it to make him look at her. He leapt out of bed and she thrust her hand in front of his face and pulled the engagement ring he'd bought her halfway up her finger.

'If I take it off I'll never put it back on,' she shouted at him.

'Here.' He grabbed her hand and pulled off the ring and threw it on the floor. 'Let me do it for you.'

'I hate you.' She burst into tears. 'I hate you.'

'Why have you done this?' he shouted, clenching his fists at her.

She put her hands to her ears and screamed again that she hated him and that she didn't want to marry him. The words came tumbling out; she didn't want to say them but she'd lost control and couldn't stop screaming at him. He raised his hand to slap her but at the last moment he drew back and she stopped screaming.

For a moment neither of them moved. They stood there staring at each other, then he lifted her up and took her back to bed. He pushed her down quite roughly and knelt over her.

'Did you hate me tonight in the restaurant when you kissed me?' he said.

She twisted away from him but he pinned her arms above her head.

'And what about that day in the pine forest?'

She closed her eyes.

'Did you hate me then? Did you?' he persisted, dropping his head to kiss her neck. He gripped her wrists with one hand and pushed up her nightie with the other, running his hand down over her breasts. 'How much did you hate me then?'

She didn't resist when he lowered himself on to her but he treated her quite roughly, as though she had. And something in her felt changed; she wanted him more than she ever had before; more than that day in the pine forest; more than she'd ever imagined possible. Her response to him soon became totally abandoned. And for the first time, she felt herself heading towards the same peak of excitement that she'd known only with Nicky. She knew that she was begging him not to stop, and at that final, almost delirious moment, she dug her teeth into his shoulder.

She opened her eyes. The room spun a little. Ross buried his face in her hair and whispered, did she still hate him? and she held him tight and said, no, she didn't hate him, she'd never hated him. He didn't question her any more, and she knew instinctively that she had pleased him so much that he would forget the way she'd behaved.

They lay entwined together and he kissed her face very gently over and over and, before dawn, he made love to her again as passionately and fiercely as before. When daylight and the distant hum of traffic announced that morning had arrived, they were exhausted and lay dozing in the tangled bed for another hour.

'I'll get you some tea,' he said sleepily, kissing her forehead and unwinding her arms.

And after he'd brought in the tray, he crawled around on the floor until he found her ring and came to put it back on her finger.

She didn't say a word, because any attempt at explaining what had happened last night would lead her into territory that she had no wish to explore; she knew only that her feelings for him had moved into another dimension.

Chapter 14

Life was like a roller-coaster during the months leading up to Easter. They went to Waylands for Christmas and brought Solange back to London with them for the New Year to meet Ross's mother. It was supposed to be a treat for her and Louisa; Ross was going to have time off work and take them out sightseeing, but Josephine was ill and they hardly went anywhere.

The doctor had confirmed she was pregnant and told her that the nausea she was suffering would wear off in its own time. But there were whole days when she could eat nothing without vomiting, and the thought of even getting into a car or train made her feel ill. She told them to go without her – all she wanted to do was curl up and sleep – but Ross wouldn't leave her.

He was unendingly patient in caring for her, and although Solange remarked, I knew I shouldn't have let you leave home, when she first learnt about the baby, she soon changed her mind. And on the day she left to go home, she said to Josephine: 'Ross always acts as though he's lucky to have you, but I'm beginning to think it's the other way round.'

'Yes, I know,' smiled Josephine. 'I know I'm lucky.' And for a moment she imagined herself with Nicky in the state she was in now; imagined his reaction to someone who spent whole days grey and sick, unable to do anything but drag around the house with tangled hair and eyes red-rimmed from vomiting. Whatever his reaction, she was quite sure it wouldn't be to wash her face, brush her hair, then settle her down on the sofa with a pile of cushions while he rushed down to the shops because she'd just thought of something she might be able to eat.

She'd thought less and less about Nicky since that evening at the Rising Sun. Being ill had helped. Like travelling and food, sex had become almost abhorrent to her during her worst spells; Ross only had to touch her in the wrong way and she'd become tearful. He remained as patient as ever, although he'd been under a lot of stress himself as his father had died shortly after Christmas. In February, Josephine decided to go home for a couple of weeks to take the strain off him.

She came back for her birthday. Not only was she feeling much better, but she was also missing Ross desperately. Car travel still made her sick so she came by train. He was waiting at the station and Josephine threw herself into his arms and cried with happiness.

Ross held her away for a second to look at her. 'It feels like you've been gone for a year,' he said, then gathered her up again, lifting her off her feet and kissing her until heads started to turn in their direction.

'What do you want to do for your birthday?' he asked, setting her on her feet again. 'Tessa's with Mum, we'll go wherever you want.'

'I want to go home to bed with you.'

He laughed and whirled her in his arms again.

Going back to the house alone together, it felt like the time when she'd agreed to marry him, when she had danced with him and experienced a thrill of anticipation about spending the night with him but couldn't really love him totally because of Nicky. And do I now? she asked herself as she got ready for bed. Am I cured of whatever it was that possessed me for all those months?

As she pulled off her sweater he came up behind her. 'Here's your birthday present,' he said, slipping a narrow gold chain round her neck.

She lifted her hair and watched in the mirror as he fastened it. It was a tiny gold locket encrusted with pearls.

'It's beautiful. Thank you,' she said, touching her fingers to it.

'I thought you'd like it. It's Victorian. Now you need never worry about getting your old one back.'

'No,' she murmured.

He ran his hands down over her breasts, then splayed his

fingers round the tiny swell of her stomach.

'Anyway, we're bound together now, aren't we? Nobody can come between us, can they?'

'No,' she murmured again.

But a few months later, during the early hours of her wedding day, she allowed herself to go back to him once more.

It was that magical time just before dawn: yesterday finished, the new day not yet begun. Caught between dreams and waking, she pushed open the black iron gate.

Flowers bloomed alongside the path and she smiled, remembering how the garden had always been full of weeds. But inside the house, nothing had changed: the hallway stained with damp, the narrow staircase down to the basement studio. And music. Pulsating up the stairs, loud enough to shake the walls. Music for dancing, music for dancers with bodies like steel and silk. Then soft, and words to slice away at dreams. The familiar rush of excitement came as sharply and powerfully as ever.

She opened her eyes and watched the first sliver of dawn creep between the curtains and knew she mustn't go on with this – soon she would be in church, vowing to love someone else until death do us part. He had said that to her once; that day she would have died for love of him. She closed her eyes again, wanting to go back, wanting to go down those stairs. Careful not to fall – too steep to manage with closed eyes. Then open them, look up to the glass domed ceiling and round the walls all covered with pictures of him. The doors to the studio stand open – but he isn't there.

He will be sleeping – of course. Sleeping his heavy drugged sleep of deadened pain, drowned in the softness of that huge bed, the great thick curtains doubled across because he does not like to wake early. It is easy to get from the studio to his bedroom on the second floor; easy to skip up the slatted iron treads of the fire escape. The music echoes up from below, threatening to overtake her and waken him. She starts to run, wanting to be first. In his bedroom, so silent and warm, she creeps barefoot across the carpet to stand beside the bed. Soon he will wake, push back the wild hair from his face and say again, so you're getting married?

And how can she tell him? She stares down at him, wanting to touch him, but instead she says his name, then lifts up her nightdress and stands there in front of him, a hand against her stomach. He says nothing but raises his arm to open up a hollow of warm darkness, and she climbs in, already sick with desire for him.

She woke in sudden sweating panic and sat bolt upright. The room was full of gentle early sun now – sunshine and warmth for her wedding day. Her wedding day. She sank back on the pillow, one hand on her stomach as it had been in her dream, and the other tangled in the chain of her new locket.

But later, as Josephine walked up the aisle of the little Norman church with Lawrence, the dream had faded, and all her early morning fantasies had slipped away with it. This was real and now; she had everything she could wish for. And when Ross turned to look over his shoulder at her, she was flooded with aching love for him. Miran had cut his hair and tamed his curls with gel so that they were smooth and gleaming, and his skin, never without a faint tan, glowed with health against the stark white of his shirt.

'Nothing is quite like your wedding day,' her mother had said earlier as they were about to leave for the church, holding her at arm's length, her eyes filled with tears. Then she'd hugged her and cried openly. 'Not long ago I was plaiting up your hair for your first day at school – now you're getting married and I'm going to be a grandmother.'

Solange had cried again during the ceremony and even more when they left to go to the country hotel where they were to spend a couple of days before returning to London. They had decided against going away for any longer; not only was there Tessa to consider, but Ross was tied up with a big contract. They planned to have a long holiday after the baby was born.

'My poor mother,' said Josephine as they drove away. 'She gets so upset about everything.'

'I suppose it's the divorce as well,' said Ross.

Josephine nodded, not wanting to talk about that.

'Never mind. Now I've got that Suffolk job to do, we'll go and live with her for the summer holidays.'

'She'll love that. We'll have the baby and Tessa – she'll be in her element. She once told me she wanted ten children, but she couldn't have any more after Louisa.'

'Well, I think six is a good number.'

'What!'

He laughed. 'I'm sure I've mentioned that to you before.'

'You have not.'

'Well, it's too late now.' He hugged her. 'You belong to me now, you have to do what I say.'

But as they settled down to married life, it was quite the reverse. He went out of his way to do whatever he thought would make her happy.

At first she whiled away the days with Tessa. He gave them money to go shopping and have their lunch out, or they would sit watching the television or videos. When Tessa went back to school and Josephine became bored on her own, he went to great lengths to teach her how to do simple bookwork for him. Figures had never been her strong point, but she was a fast learner and enjoyed doing something different. Soon she was sitting out in the yard office with the elderly man who kept an eye on things and who answered the phone for Ross. Josephine liked the company, the people coming and going; it felt as if she had a job. Other days she would take a bus and visit Miran's salon, watching the stylists at work on clients' hair and wondering if she could train to do something like that.

But of course there was the baby. Sometimes she wished she wasn't pregnant, all those weeks of feeling ill. Now she could no longer get into her clothes either. Ross gave her money to buy new ones, but she refused to buy maternity clothes and instead bought stretch pants and huge sweaters and T-shirts. Whatever she wore, he said she looked beautiful, and whatever she wanted, he got for her.

She was happy – but sometimes she wondered what kind of happiness it was. Thinking about it disturbed her. It felt as though she had grabbed at things she thought she wanted and discovered they were not quite what they seemed. Once, staring in the mirror at herself and hating what she saw, she cried aloud at her image and shouted, what the hell do you want then? *To be with him.* It was no more than a whisper in her head and she clamped her hands over her ears and ran downstairs to Ross. With his arms round her and the half-amused, indulgent look on his face, she felt reassured. This was what she wanted: Ross, who loved her so devotedly, who would love her for ever and never make her unhappy and who asked nothing more than that she love him back in the same devoted and uncomplicated way. This was happiness; of course it was. All other thoughts must be sealed away; the past must be forgotten.

But early one evening, when Ross had gone to the sitting room to watch the television and she remained in the kitchen with Tessa, snatches of a news report caught her attention and she realised it was about Nicky.

She went to the door and listened.

'Angry scenes outside the theatre led to Frey . . .'

'I need more icing,' said Tessa. She was busy decorating some little cakes Josephine had helped her to make earlier.

'. . . and being warned that next time he appeared before the court it would mean . . .'

'Phina, I need more—'

'Yes, all right.' She looked round and smiled in case her tone had sounded sharp; she never lost patience with Tessa.

'. . . Miss Martinez was not in court but her husband, the musical director, Carl Reinhold, told the judge that his wife had gone to great lengths to meet Frey's demands regarding his son but had been continually . . .'

'Phina, please do it now or it's going to go all wrong.'

'Just a little, little minute.' She went along to the sitting room and stood in the doorway, just in time to catch footage of Nicky leaving court. He was flanked by the woman Romana and another man who led him to a waiting car. He looked as wild as ever, throwing back his head and laughing at something one of the reporters asked him, then making an obscene gesture before getting into the car. Next came an older, smartly dressed man who stopped to say to the reporters, 'Would you leave your child with him for a weekend?' He threw up his hands as he also made towards a waiting car. 'He's turned my wife into a wreck, a wreck . . .'

'Do you want another cup of tea?' she said, her eyes fixed on the screen, her heart pounding with relief that Nicky hadn't spoken.

'No thanks, darling,' said Ross.

'Frey denied charges that he ran his finger across his throat in a threatening gesture at Miss Martinez, and spat in her husband's face while high on amphetamine sulphate. However, witnesses say . . .'

Ross craned round to look at her. 'I thought I was getting a cake.'

'You are.' She went to perch on the end of the sofa and he

slipped an arm round her waist and turned back to the television.

'. . . from a family of East European circus performers, Nikolay Frey shot to stardom in the television series "Dancing with the Magician". But despite its enormous popularity, plans for a second series faltered amidst rumours of drugs and black magic and were finally abandoned when Frey sustained multiple injuries in a horrific motor-cycle accident.'

'No wonder they don't want the kid to see him,' said Ross, flicking over channels.

Josephine said nothing; something had gone cold inside her.

'Mind you, it can't be easy for that other bloke bringing up someone else's child.'

'Why?' she said very quietly.

'Well, he must be a constant reminder of his wife and that Frey guy – the majority of cases of child-battering happen in situations like that. Some men can't accept other men's children – I don't think I could. It's all to do with jealousy.'

'I'm bringing up Tessa . . . I love her.' Her mouth had gone very dry. 'I'm not jealous.'

His arm loosened and he looked up at her. 'It's different for women – they don't feel jealousy so powerfully. Anyway,' he shifted in his seat and looked away, 'Karen's dead. And you know very well that I never loved her like I love you.'

Yes, she did know that; never for a second had she felt any jealousy in that direction – or in any other, because she was totally confident of Ross's devotion to her. But how would that devotion stand up should he discover what had happened on that rainy day last November?

She began to imagine what would happen if she bumped into Nicky in the street; it was unlikely, but possible. Or it might be Alice. It would only need a chance word, a phone call from Nicky, and Ross would soon put two and two together. He had never mentioned that call about her locket again, but she was sure he had Nicky's distinctive husky voice ingrained on his memory. It would take so little to destroy her happiness.

She began to stay indoors most of the time. The nausea returned and she couldn't eat and then her blood pressure rose and the doctor said she would have to go into hospital if it went any higher. On a rare visit to the shops, she fainted, and Ross had to be called from work.

He was beside himself with worry and one morning when

she woke, breathless and vomiting, he phoned his mother to come over with her until he got back from work.

It was the last thing Josephine wanted, and she stayed in bed, hoping that Hannah would leave her in peace.

She did for a while, bringing her up tea and then going downstairs to do some ironing. But when it was time to go and meet Tessa, Hannah came upstairs once more.

'I've done all the ironing,' she said.

'Thanks,' murmured Josephine. There had been a huge pile but she hadn't felt like doing it over the past few days because it had been so hot. Ross had told her to leave it, they'd wear unironed clothes.

'Why don't you get up now?' Hannah said. 'Come with me and get some fresh air. You ought to go out. Ross says you never even go down the shops now. Pregnancy's not an illness,' she added.

Josephine raised her head a fraction. Go away, she wanted to scream at her. You don't understand, nobody understands.

'Well, you ought to get up before Ross comes home.' Her tone was frosty now. 'It's not fair to worry him like this. He's had enough to put up with in the past.'

'I know that.'

'I don't think you do. I don't like to say it, Josephine, but I think you take advantage of him.'

'I don't.' Tears overwhelmed her but she burrowed under the duvet so Hannah wouldn't see.

'I'm only saying it for your own good. If you keep trying to get your own way, your marriage won't last.'

Go away and leave me alone, she screamed silently into the pillow.

But when Hannah came back with Tessa, Josephine was already up and said she felt better and that Hannah might as well go. For some reason she couldn't bear the thought of her being there when Ross came home.

Tessa was always full of things to tell her about school and, on the odd occasions when Ross collected her, she would come bursting through the back door, calling, 'Phina, Phina', before she did anything else. But today she looked sulky and wouldn't even say goodbye to her grandmother properly.

Josephine made her a drink and then went to curl on the sofa because she was feeling faint. Tessa followed her in and Josephine held out an arm to her.

'Come and tell me what you've been doing then.' She smiled at Tessa's cross face and collapsed ponytail. 'Who did your hair this morning? Daddy?'

'Yes.' Tessa gave a little sniff and pulled out the rubber band.

'What's the matter?' Josephine patted the place beside her. 'Come and tell me.'

Tessa came reluctantly, but would only perch on the edge of the sofa.

'I don't want to go and stay with Nanna for ages and ages,' she said, scuffing her heels on the carpet.

'You haven't got to.' Josephine tried to get hold of her but she pulled away.

'Yes I have – Nanna said – when you go and get that baby in hospital. I don't want a horrid baby here, anyway.' She marched off towards the kitchen. 'And I don't want to touch your horrid tummy any more. And you tell lies,' she shouted out. 'It won't be my brother because you're not my real mummy.'

Josephine stared after her, too stunned and upset to call her back. They'd been so careful in explaining about the baby to Tessa, letting her feel it move and even telling her to talk it. It seemed the last straw and, by the time Ross came home, Josephine was crying inconsolably. But she refused to tell him what was wrong.

'What can I do?' he said, throwing up his hands. 'I can't help if I don't know what's wrong.' He let his arms fall to his sides and walked over to the window and back. 'What do you want, Josephine? Tell me what you want.'

'I want to go home,' she sobbed. 'I just want to go home.'

'Home,' he said bitterly, 'is here.'

But at the weekend Ross took her to Waylands, and a few days later Josephine gave birth to a boy in the same hospital where Louisa had been born.

The baby seemed in a hurry to get into the world; not only was he early but he arrived with record speed for a first baby. It was the hottest day of the year, and Josephine complained about the heat more than anything, and kept asking that the windows be opened.

'I think you're overdosing on that gas and air,' she heard a nurse laugh. 'There aren't any windows in here.'

She looked at Ross, his face dripping with sweat, and

pleaded with him to open the windows, but he just smoothed the hair from her forehead and rubbed his hand up and down her arm.

They moved an electric fan close to her. Its gentle whirr was like the sound of wind through summer trees. She closed her eyes and imagined she was riding up through the pine forests, the horse's hooves kicking up dust from the sandy track, and the smell of resin pungent in the heat. If only she was. If only she could go back that far. Escape from this prison of things she did not want: a baby she did not want, Ross she did not want. She let out a strangled cry of pain – a whole life she didn't want.

The nurse was saying, it's a boy, and then there was a massive silence and Ross was holding her hand so tightly, that her rings dug into her fingers. The nurse left her side almost knocking over the fan. She heard the doctor say, come on, you little devil, and Josephine raised her head a fraction. All she could see was the doctor half turned away with the nurse at his elbow, but she knew they were panicking, knew there was something wrong. She let her head fall back and closed her eyes again, unable to look at Ross. He was still as a statue, his hand still gripping hers, and all she could think was, if it's dead I hope they don't show him. I don't want him to know what it looks like – I don't want to know myself. I don't want to know anything about it. I want them to take it away.

Instead, they were handing it to her and she gave a little cry, convinced they were handing her a dead baby. But as she looked down at it, she saw that its mouth was wide open and realised it was yelling quite loudly. And as she touched the matt of thick black hair and looked into its little screwed-up face, she felt instant and overwhelming love for it. Her mother had said, don't worry if you don't love it right away, not all mothers do and you're so young, but she did, more than she had ever loved anyone. She looked at Ross and smiled and everything seemed changed completely.

They called the baby Christopher Louis, the second names of both their fathers. Ross's first because he particularly liked the name and because of his father dying. When he'd suggested it, Josephine had worried that it might upset her mother, especially if they shortened it to Chris. But she kept quiet, knowing how Ross hated her even to mention Christian.

With the divorce due to be finalised, Solange too seemed to want all memory of him wiped away and was succeeding very well, especially now that she was surrounded by children. Ross had brought Tessa to Waylands with them, and Solange had taken her under her wing, showering affection on her to prevent her being jealous of the baby. There were no more outbursts and she seemed content and happy, playing with Louisa and lapping up the attention she got from Solange and Nella.

Ross was besotted with the baby. He took a week off work to be with them, although there were plenty of willing hands to help. He started the Suffolk job in late July, planning to finish by September in time for Tessa to go back to school. His mother had agreed to pop into the London house on alternate days with the cleaning lady to keep an eye on things and feed the cat, and his yard was manned by the old gentleman who did his accounts. He set up a temporary office in the old storeroom at Waylands, where he laid out plans and organised a workforce of local tradesmen.

The fierce heat of July had eased a little by August, and the weather settled into a pattern of long summer days starting with dew-soaked grass and ending with balmy, scented evenings. Louisa and Tessa spent all their time outside: Louisa wallowing in the superiority of knowing the hundred and one games that could be played in a huge garden with trees and outbuildings, summerhouse and swings; Tessa completely enthralled by all these things that she'd never experienced. Nella and Solange harvested crops from the little vegetable garden and sat on the back lawn, shelling peas and slicing up runner beans for the freezer. And Josephine just lazed about watching them, while the baby slept under his sunshade, waking only when he was hungry.

Ross worked long hours through the week to complete the job on time. But at weekends he spent the days outside with them, relaxing in the sunshine, playing with the girls or stretched on a blanket with Josephine, the baby tucked between them. And at night he would hold her in his arms, pressing gentle kisses over her face and neck, moving his lips softly over her skin until finally they covered her mouth and he'd draw back halfway through a long, hungry kiss. She neither encouraged nor rebuffed him, and only once did he suggest she relieve his frustration in another way. And when she hesitated, he immediately told her to forget it, but said that she'd better get herself on the pill before they were able to make love again or she'd probably end up pregnant straightaway.

Some nights, lying awake after she'd fed the baby, she would get out of bed and sit on the windowsill, just as she used to before she left home. They were in Lawrence's old room which overlooked the front courtyard, and she would watch the bats flit from loft to loft in the moonlight and wish things could stay exactly this way for ever. She felt peaceful, both emotionally and physically, as though she were floating on a warm lake whose surface was completely free of ripples. Then a pleasurable tiredness would overtake her and she'd creep back to bed and curl against Ross, and even in sleep he'd draw her close to him.

And one of these nights, he murmured, half asleep still: 'You're restless tonight, darling. What's the matter?'

'Ross.' Her voice was low but vaguely questioning, and he came fully awake and turned on his side to face her.

She lay silent for a while, not sure whether to go on. If you cannot tell the truth, then don't say anything, her father used to say. Would half the truth do, she wondered? Would it do if there were no lies?

'Ross,' she began again. 'You remember that night you took me out to dinner, the night I said I'd marry you?'

He kissed her lightly on the lips. 'And the night you first slept with me.'

'Well, you asked me something – and I wouldn't talk about it.'

He rolled his head away on the pillow and, after a few moments, he said: 'I know what you're going to tell me – I guessed.'

She was puzzled, but said, 'I want to explain.'

'And I don't want you to.' He put his hand over her mouth but she pulled it away.

'But if someone else told you about it . . .'

'Phina, I don't want to hear. I heard enough that time he phoned about your locket.'

'I wanted to be honest with you,' she said. 'Because I love you.'

He had his arms round her instantly, then took her hand and held it tightly against his chest. 'Phina, I've got everything I want. I'm totally happy. Don't spoil it by telling me things I don't want to hear. Whatever you did before is nothing to do with me. I've got no right to say anything about it and I don't want to know.' He lifted her hand and kissed her palm. 'Just as long as you're always faithful to me and always love me, that's all I want.'

The next morning, watching him with the baby while she drank the tea he always brought her in bed, she wondered why she had felt that sudden need to tell him about Nicky, how she could have felt insecure enough to think it important to undo past lies. Having the baby had secured his love for her like nothing else could. She sipped her tea and watched as he coaxed the baby to smile up at him. How quickly the days were going. It was September tomorrow. Soon the summer would be over and they would be back in London. She sighed and he looked up.

'It's a long time since I heard you sigh like that,' he said.

'I was just thinking how nice it would be if there was a button we could press that would stop time.'

He laughed. 'I expect everybody in the world has thought that at some time or another.'

That evening, the feeling of melancholy that had hit her when she thought of returning to London, came creeping over her again. It was past eleven and she was achingly tired. In an effort to make the baby sleep through the night, she had decided to stay up and give him a late feed.

Although the days remained as warm as ever, the nights had gained a chill and Ross had lit a fire in the sitting room so they could sit up and watch television to keep them awake.

He had just put another log on and it crackled away sending sparks up the chimney.

'It reminds me of winter with a fire,' she said, her voice betraying her feelings.

Ross turned to look at her but she didn't want him to see she felt sad and she lowered her gaze to the baby. His little fist was clenched against her breast and his dark lashes fluttered slightly as he sucked. There was a contented flush on his face and she stroked a finger gently against his cheek to make sure he wasn't too hot.

Suddenly Ross said: 'You don't want to go back, do you?'

'I don't mind.' She looked up at him and smiled. 'I know we can't stay here. I know you've got other jobs – and there's

Tessa's school, and your mother, and all your friends.' The ache of tiredness seemed to move right into her heart, where it said, and I owe it to you not to be selfish.

He came round behind her and put his arms very gently round her shoulders, careful not to disturb the baby.

'There are some things you can fool me about, but this isn't one of them,' he said, kissing her lightly on the cheek.

'Maybe not.' She forced another little smile. 'But I won't mind. We can come back to Waylands for holidays.'

'We won't go back.' He straightened up, his hands resting on her shoulders. 'I'll look for a cottage or something round here. If I can find somewhere to renovate we can stay here while I do it. Tessa's happy here, she can change schools. And you'll be near to your mother.'

She twisted her head round to look at him. 'What about work?'

'There's a chance of more work where I am now.' He shrugged. 'And if that doesn't come off, I'll just have to travel backwards and forwards until I can sort out a way of handling everything.'

'But . . . but I know you like living in London best.'

'I'll get used to living in the wilds.'

She knew he was smiling even though she was gazing down at the baby once more, but she could feel her own lips turning down and her eyes filling with tears.

'It's for me, isn't it?' she murmured.

'Of course it's for you. Everything I do is for you.'

She blinked hard, but a tear escaped and splashed on to the baby's face. He was nearly asleep, but his little head jerked and he sneezed, then lay there staring up at her as though he wondered what was going to happen to him next.

More tears came, distorting Josephine's vision, so that looking down at the baby's face his eyes appeared lighter, shimmering bright gold beneath his thick lashes. She blinked again and lifted him up against her shoulder to rub his back. Ross craned round to look at her as though he sensed her tears, then took the baby and went to sit opposite, his eyebrows raised in question.

'Don't let him fall asleep,' she said, brushing a hand across her face because the tears refused to stop. 'He hasn't had enough yet, he won't go through the night.'

Ross propped the dozing baby on his knees, holding him

upright between his palms, but continued to look at her, his face full of concern.

'Oh, take not notice of me,' she said, wiping at her face again. 'I'm just tired . . . and you're always so nice to me.'

He gave a puzzled smile. 'But that's how I should be – how could I not be nice to you?' He kissed the baby's fluffy head, then brought him back to her and laid him in her lap.

And when her tears had dried, she looked down into his face again – but he was fast asleep and his eyes were tightly closed.

PART 3

Last Dance

Did you miss me?
Come and kiss me.
Never mind my bruises,
Hug me, kiss me, suck my juices
Squeezed from goblin fruits for you,
Goblin pulp and goblin dew.
Eat me, drink me, love me.

Christina Rossetti

Chapter 15

'No, leave them a minute.' Ross put out a hand to stop her. 'Look at him trying to copy them.'

'They'll be late for school,' said Josephine.

Still Ross held on to her, laughing as Kit toppled over and rolled about on the lawn, his legs in the air.

They all called him Kit. Tessa had started it by saying he was like a little kitten. And he was in some ways: he had boundless energy and limbs like rubber and when he was tired he would just flop down wherever he was and curl up to sleep. And like a small appealing animal he knew instinctively how to catch attention; one laugh at his antics and he was away with a repeat performance.

'Won't be a minute,' shouted Louisa. 'I'm teaching him to do an arabesque.' She hauled him upright and Tessa pulled his leg out behind, but as soon as they let go, he toppled over again.

'Come on or we'll be late,' said Josephine.

Normally Ross would have gone by now, but he had a meeting this morning and was going to drop them all off and take her car for the day. Knowing he hadn't got to rush, they had got up later than usual.

Tessa looked up but Louisa, always the leader and the most defiant, ignored her. Josephine went marching down the lawn and gathered Kit up in her arms.

'He has to practise,' said Louisa, hands on hips, 'if he's going to be in the show.'

'He's not going to be in any show,' said Josephine, carrying Kit off towards the house, while Tessa ran up to Ross. 'He's too young.'

'He's only got to run round the stage and flutter down,' said Louisa, skipping along sideways. 'I'll be next to him.'

They were indoors now and Ross put a hand on Louisa's head. 'Stop chattering and go and get in the car.'

Louisa brushed his hand off. 'You're mean,' she said, standing in front of Josephine. 'He likes doing it. You never let him do anything.'

'Car,' said Ross sharply, pushing her after Tessa.

Josephine sat Kit on the draining board and wiped a flannel over his green-stained hands and knees. 'Have you got a kiss goodbye for Mummy?' she said.

He wrapped his arms round her neck and obediently pressed his lips to hers, then she lifted him up and held him towards Ross to kiss before taking him upstairs to her mother.

Solange looked after him while Josephine went to work in the antique shop that Lawrence had opened two years ago, shortly before Kit was born. It was their father's old shop, and he'd opened it up again because he hadn't been sure what he wanted to do with his life after leaving university. At first it had been a hobby, but soon business had built up and he'd become engrossed in it. Josephine had started to help him out for a few hours each week, until recently when she'd been going in every day after taking the girls to school.

Ross had them settled in the car by the time she went outside. Over the past two years he'd come to treat Louisa much as he did Tessa; living in such close proximity they had soon become like sisters. His business had grown enormously, and he commuted between the London house, which Miran was renting from him, and Waylands, doing work in all the counties between. There had simply not been any time to look for a cottage and, although they lived in with Solange – and often Lawrence, who came and went between girlfriends – privacy was never a problem because there was so much room.

As they pulled up outside the school, Tessa leant over the seat and kissed Ross, then Josephine. Louisa also kissed Ross but ignored Josephine.

'She's such a madam when she can't get her own way,' said Josephine as they drove off.

'Is she still on about this show?'

'Yes. It's their stupid ballet teacher – Miss Beryl or whatever her name is. She told them they can have their little brothers and sisters as leaves in some woodland scene. I told them that

Kit was too young, but that wasn't good enough for Louisa.'

'Oh, let him go with them. As long as he's happy.' He laughed. 'He'll probably do it all wrong and steal the show.'

Josephine didn't answer but rummaged in her bag for a comb. She took the girls to their ballet class once a week, but after the first time would never stay to watch them. Most of the other women did, chatting together in an adjoining room while their children danced. That had been bad enough; she knew none of them but they knew her, she could tell by the look on their faces and the way conversations came to a halt when she was around. Rumours about Christian had spread much further than the village and, although the girl he was supposed to have raped had since left, she knew that the gossip went on long afterwards.

But worse than this was the sight of those little girls and the few boys, clad in leotards, hands on the barre, toes pointed. And the music. It affected her in a way she was quite unprepared for. Ross always had a radio on wherever he was, she hardly noticed it, but the combination of those little dancers and the music conjured up so many memories.

But Kit loved it. Egged on by Louisa, he had cried to stay with them while Josephine went off shopping to pass the hour away. At first she'd said no, but a couple of the women had offered to look after him, and she'd felt it would be churlish to refuse; she knew they already thought her stuck up. So now, every week, Kit watched entranced, then spent hours with Louisa and Tessa while they practised what they'd learnt.

But she wasn't going to have him in the show. She flicked the comb through her hair, craning over to inspect herself in the mirror.

'I hate getting up late,' she said, flooded with sudden irritation. 'It's such a rush.' She ran her fingers through her fringe, then looked at herself again. She'd had all her long hair cut off. The longest layer still reached her shoulders, but the top and sides were much shorter and framed her face in soft black fronds.

'Do I look all right?' she said.

'You look lovely,' said Ross, without taking his eyes off the road.

'You didn't even look.'

'I don't have to,' he said, turning to smile at her.

When they pulled up outside the shop, Ross caught her arm.

'Now don't forget to tell Lawrence about August.'

'Yes, I know,' she said, looking at her watch to show he was detaining her.

'And mention what we were talking about.'

'All right.' Her tone verged on snappiness and she didn't look back as she hurried across the pavement.

Ross brought the subject up again as they got ready for bed.

'Did you tell Lawrence?'

'Yes. He says he can manage without me for a couple of weeks.'

'But that's only while we go up to London. He'll have to look for someone permanent.'

She didn't answer.

'I don't want to make a big thing of this,' Ross went on, 'but he ought to know where he stands.'

Josephine was sitting at the dressing table plucking her eyebrows. She moved her eyes up the mirror to see if he were watching her. 'I'm not sure if I want to give up the shop yet.'

There was a long silence, long enough for her resolve to harden. The shop had opened up a whole new way of life to her. Talking to customers had helped cure her shyness with strangers. People wanted to chat when they were buying antiques and she found all the things she'd learnt from her father came pouring back. And she loved the shop: the sign over the door that said Jarrouse Antiques, the musty smell, the patina of polished wood and the feeling of times gone by.

'Well you're not going to leave a young baby with your mother.'

'Ross,' she said without turning round, 'I'm not pregnant yet – and that's something else I'm not sure about either.'

'But you agreed. Why the sudden change of mind?'

She swung round. 'I haven't changed my mind. I just don't feel ready yet.'

'You don't want to leave the shop, that's what it boils down to.' He went through into the adjoining room to check Kit as he always did last thing. When he came back he got straight into bed and she heard him sigh, then the sound of the springs as though he were settling down to sleep. She glanced over her shoulder and found him propped on an elbow watching her.

'To be honest, I wish you'd never started working in the shop,' he said.

'Why?'

'It's changed you. You never used to spend all this time looking at yourself.'

'I'm not looking at myself, I'm plucking my eyebrows.'

'There's nothing wrong with your eyebrows.'

She flung down the tweezers and went to get into bed. 'So I've got to ask your permission about how I look now, have I?' she said, yanking back the duvet.

He immediately reached up to pull the light cord, as though he wanted to shut her out.

'Hang on,' she said, stopping him. 'I haven't taken my pill yet.'

'A new lot,' he said, turning to watch her, then snatching the packet from her hand. 'Just the right time to stop.'

She knew that he wasn't playing about, knew that he had done it to provoke her, and she folded her arms and looked away from him. 'Don't be childish,' she muttered.

'Oh, I see. When you want something it's called, because Ross loves you, but when I want something it's called being childish.' He threw the packet across the room and got out of bed, snatching up his jeans.

'Where are you going?'

He tapped his fingers against his head. 'I've got things in here I need to think about and I want to do it on my own – away from a wife who considers going to work more important than her marriage.'

'You're being ridiculous – and selfish. I love the shop.'

'You love all the attention you get there, you mean,' he said, storming off.

She'd never seen him like this in the whole two years they'd been married, though she'd known this business about the shop had been boiling up for weeks, ever since Lawrence had joked about someone fancying her. They had a lot of dealers come into the shop, most of them men, and it wasn't the first time someone had shown an interest in her.

The sound of the back door being unbolted came up through the open window and she went to look out. He was walking down the lawn. The sight of his solitary figure just visible in the dark made her feel suddenly guilty. What had she called him? Ridiculous and selfish. He was neither of those things and yes, he was right, whenever she wanted something he gave it to her because he loved her. Now she'd made him

211

unhappy over the only sacrifice he'd ever asked of her.

She got out of bed, checked on Kit and went after him.

He was right down at the bottom of the lawn now, almost hidden in the mist that had drifted up from the river. The grass was sodden with dew and silky between her toes. He didn't hear her until she was right behind him and she slipped her arms round his waist before he could turn. She felt him take a deep breath and then he put his hands over hers.

'I'm sorry,' she said. 'It's me who's being selfish.'

'I've tried not to mind about the shop,' he said. 'But I feel it's taking you away from me.'

'What do you mean?' she said quietly.

He rubbed his hands along her arms. 'Most of the time I feel we couldn't be happier, but . . . sometimes I feel there's a little part of you I can't get at.' He paused. 'A bit of you that belongs to someone else.'

She moved back a fraction. 'I didn't know you felt like this.'

'I've always felt it. I knew when you married me that you didn't love me totally, but I thought time would change that – and it has – but now and again . . .' He broke off and pulled her round in front of him. 'Now and again I catch a look on your face that says things I don't understand.'

She put her fingers to his lips. 'Don't, Ross. You're seeing things that aren't there. There's no part of me that belongs to anyone but you.'

'Do you remember you tried to tell me once? Soon after Kit was born you wanted to tell me about him but I wouldn't listen.'

'Ross, stop this.'

'Just tell me one thing – do you ever think about him?'

'Of course not.' She slipped her arms round his neck. Ross had never asked for a name and she was never sure if he knew; the vague 'him' told her nothing. And deep down she knew it was still dangerous territory; the more time that went by the less risk there was that he would ever find out what she had done. 'Let's compromise,' she said, wanting to change the subject. 'If I agree about the baby, will you promise not to mind if I carry on at the shop while I'm pregnant.'

'All right.' He put his arms round her waist and lifted her off the ground, laughing quietly into her hair. 'If last time is anything to go by, you'll feel too ill to work.'

'I'll carry on regardless.' She hugged him. 'Anyhow, it was the way Kit was conceived that made me so sick.'

'In the pine forest,' he murmured. 'Perhaps I should carry you off there now.'

She gave a little shriek and wriggled free, dashing off across the lawn and collapsing with laughter on her knees as he came after her.

'I'm soaked! Look at me.'

He crouched beside her. 'It was wet that day. Do you remember?'

She didn't answer, just tilted her head back so that he could kiss her.

'But it doesn't matter tonight,' he whispered. 'We haven't got to go back and face anybody.'

'Dew's good for your skin,' she whispered back.

'Is it?' He pulled off her nightdress and rubbed his hands on the grass, then began to massage her breasts with his wet palms.

Josephine, Ross and the children went up to London in early August. Normally they stayed in the house with Miran but this time they went to his mother's as Ross was going to put in some new kitchen units for her. And she was always complaining she didn't see enough of Tessa and Kit.

Kit seemed to have drawn her and Josephine together more, although they'd had a bad moment after his birth when Hannah had remarked on how surprising it was that his skin was so light.

'What did she think?' Josephine had said angrily to Ross. 'That I was going to produce a black baby?'

'It was your mother's fault,' said Ross. 'She told my mother that she had no idea about her parents and how much mixed blood there is in South America.'

Kit's skin was no darker than Ross's, even though his hair was nearly as black as Josephine's. He had Ross's curls and Josephine's generous lips. But his eyes were his most striking feature: they were a tawny amber in colour, and when he smiled they slanted upward giving him an oriental look. Everybody said what an attractive child he was. It was all too easy to make a fuss of him and they had to be very careful that Tessa did not get left out and that she spent time on her own with Ross. On the second day of their visit, Ross took Tessa over to his yard with him, while Josephine and Kit went with Hannah to deliver some costumes that she'd altered.

The woman Hannah worked for sold and hired costumes for all kinds of stage and film productions and had her premises in an old Victorian warehouse.

'They've got some fascinating stuff here,' said Hannah, leading Josephine and Kit through a maze of partitioned and curtained-off rooms to a large office.

Josephine wrinkled her nose. It did look fascinating, with the piles of costumes and stage accessories heaped everywhere but, despite the lofty ceilings, the smell was overpowering. It was a mixture of stale perfume, hot bodies, cigarette smoke and, strongest of all, the burnt herb smell of cannabis.

'It's awful, isn't it?' said Hannah. 'I don't know why Leila lets them smoke in here. It clings to everything.'

A girl came to greet them as they walked into the office. 'Do you mind hanging on for five minutes?' she said. 'Leila's out the back with someone and I know she wants to see you about those rabbit costumes.' She smiled down at Kit, holding her hands out to him. He went to her immediately, just as he went to everyone.

'Isn't he adorable?' she said, sitting at her desk and lifting him on to her lap. 'What's your name?'

'Kit,' he announced, fiddling with the stack of bangles she wore.

'Tell Celia your proper name, darling,' said Hannah.

He thought for a moment, then said, 'Christopher.'

'Christopher what?' said Hannah.

Josephine went to the far side of the room where there was a long couch covered in fringed shawls and heaped with magazines. Once Hannah started showing him off, the questions went on for ever. She heard Hannah say, show Celia how you dance, and saw Kit slide from the girl's lap and point out each foot in turn, then twirl round. She buried her head in a magazine.

'Have you ever thought about signing him up with a child model agency?' the girl called across to her.

Josephine shook her head. 'No, I haven't.'

'You ought to. They can earn a lot of money. He's so pretty, he'd do really well.'

Josephine smiled and shook her head again. 'My husband wouldn't want him to model.'

'That's my son,' Hannah went on. 'He's got a little girl as well. He . . .' her voice died away, drowned out by a man's loud laughter as he came through from another room, pushing aside the curtain that hid the door.

'Like hell you will, you crazy lying bastard,' he called over his shoulder.

Josephine glanced up.

'Oh, I beg your pardon, ladies,' he smiled, bending to tickle Kit as he passed Celia's desk.

Kit gurgled with laughter and clambered back on Celia's lap.

'I'll see you later, Celia,' said the man, then called over his shoulder again. 'Are you coming, Frey? I'm not like you, I don't have all day to doss about here.'

Josephine's head jerked up again. A second later Nicky appeared from behind the curtain.

He saw her at once and came to a halt. It was more than two and a half years since she'd seen him, and his striking looks struck her so forcibly that it was like seeing him for the first time. Her mouth went dry and she couldn't speak, only watch as he came towards her.

'I'll catch you later,' he said to the other man without taking his eyes from her.

She managed to smile. No need to get in a panic; they hadn't parted on bad terms. A vivid image of that night in the Rising Sun rose up before her: standing in that passageway, knowing it had to be over. She smiled again but no words would come.

He had on jeans and T-shirt and his body still looked fit and muscular, but his limp was noticeably worse. And his face was thinner, the cheekbones jutting too sharply. The mane of hair was the same, longer and brighter if anything, and streaked with colour like the plumage of some exotic bird. But beneath it his skin was unhealthily pale and his eyes shadowed with pain.

'How are you?' he said, coming to stand in front of her. 'Happy?' he added, his voice pitched lower.

She nodded. 'Yes, yes, I am thank you.'

'What are you doing here?'

She licked her lips. 'I'm with my mother-in-law. She's a dressmaker.' She indicated Hannah who was looking across at them.

In the moments that followed it seemed that everything

happened in slow motion. He turned and looked at the group of Hannah, Celia and finally Kit, smiling politely at Hannah before returning to stare at Kit.

'Is he yours?' he asked.

She nodded.

'How old is he?'

'Two.'

She watched as he went over to them and perched on the corner of Celia's desk.

'So you're two, are you?' he said, putting a finger under Kit's chin.

Kit shrank away from him and clung to Celia.

'Is that all he is?' said Celia, looking at Hannah for confirmation. 'He talks as well as my little nephew and he's three.'

'And he was only two last month,' said Hannah proudly.

Nicky was still staring at him and he buried his face against Celia.

'He's frightened of you,' said Celia. 'Come on, Kit, say hello to Nicky.' She jigged him up and down on her lap. 'Show him how you dance. He likes dancing.'

But Kit put his head on her shoulder and would only look at Nicky out of the corner of his eye.

'It's all right, leave him,' said Nicky.

At that moment, a woman came from behind the curtain and led Hannah off with a string of apologies. Nicky came back across the room and sat on the couch, so close to her that when he stretched out his injured leg, it brushed against her.

'So you're happily married,' he said.

'Very.'

He glanced towards Celia; she was busy playing with Kit, although she did look towards them now and again.

'And you never told him?' His voice was low again and he had his arms resting on his knees and his head turned to her so that there were only inches separating them.

'We don't talk about the past.'

He ran a hand through his hair and stared into her face. 'But it's not just the past, is it?'

'Look, my mother-in-law will be back in a minute. Please don't . . .'

'Why didn't you tell me?' His voice was almost a growl. 'How could you not tell me.'

'I don't know what you're talking about.' She glanced at

Celia; as she did so Kit happened to look up and caught her expression. He came running to her, his face anxious, and stood there, arms resting in her lap.

Nicky reached out and stroked his head. 'So you can dance, can you?'

Kit stood frozen to the spot. Two women came into the room and Celia became engrossed in conversation with them. Kit looked over his shoulder, then turned back to them, his eyes on Nicky. He took a quick little breath. 'I can be a leaf,' he announced as though Nicky's question had made a connection in his brain.

'You can be what?' Nicky looked amused and bent his head to Kit. 'A leaf?'

'With Lulu and Tess,' he said breathlessly, avoiding Nicky's gaze.

'It's just a show my sister's in,' said Josephine.

'And Tess – the little girl you used to collect from school – and take to ballet lessons.'

She nodded, clasping her hands together to stop their shaking.

'Does he go?'

'No, he's too young – he won't anyway.'

Nicky put out a finger and coiled it in the profusion of ringlets that hung down the back of Kit's neck. Kit stared up at him then put both hands on Josephine's knee and gave an excited little jump.

'Where does he get his curls from?' said Nicky.

'From his father.'

He shook his head very slowly. 'You know he's mine,' he said.

She couldn't answer, could only watch while he lifted Kit on to his lap.

Kit looked apprehensive but didn't protest, and after a few moments he put a probing finger on one of the leather straps that bound Nicky's arm.

'Do you like them?' said Nicky.

Kit nodded. The straps were different from the ones she remembered; they were adorned with tiny gold chains and buckles. There was something more decorative about him altogether, something glittery and crudely magnetic.

'Are you going to be a dancer when you grow up?'

Kit nodded again and gave a shy smile.

'He doesn't know what you mean,' said Josephine. 'Please put him down.'

'Then I'll have to ask him again when he's older, won't I?' He undid one of the straps and put it round Kit's waist. 'A belt for you,' he said.

Kit patted it and beamed. 'Belt for me,' he repeated.

'Where are you living?' said Nicky.

'With my mother. Miles from here,' she said, turning her head away from him.

'I can soon find out.'

She jerked back round. Celia was laughing with the women, no longer watching them. 'He's not your son,' she said. 'Believe me, he's not.'

He studied her from beneath his thick lashes. 'Do you think I can't see for myself? Do you really think I can look at him and not know? You may have deceived your husband, but you can't deceive me.'

Hannah returned now. Nicky stood up, lifting Kit with him and making a great show of cuddling and kissing him. Then he took him to Hannah.

'He's beautiful,' he said. 'Just like his mother.'

Hannah raised her eyebrows at Celia and took Kit from him. He came back to Josephine and bent his head close to hers.

'Bring him to the house to see me.'

'I can't do that.'

'You can and you will.' He straightened up and without another word was gone.

Hannah looked across at her and pulled a face. 'What was all that about? Do you know him?'

Josephine shook her head and shrugged, then picked up another magazine, bending her head over it.

'He's always like that,' said Celia. 'He thinks he can do as he likes – especially where women are concerned.'

'Wasn't he on the television at one time?' said Hannah.

'Yes, a few years ago,' said Celia. 'He was a dancer. He teaches now, or so he makes out – nobody knows what he's up to half the time. Sometimes we don't see him for months on end, then he turns up and he's everywhere. He's as weird as they come.' She laughed. 'And that's saying something considering the types we get in here.'

On the way back, Josephine took the leather strap from Kit's waist. He wanted to carry it but she pulled it from him and put it in her bag.

'Oh let him . . .' Hannah began as his lips turned down ready to cry.

'No, it looks ridiculous.'

Hannah's mouth tightened and she patted Kit's hand. 'Nanna will find you something nice when we get home,' she said.

Josephine barely heard her; the echo of Nicky's words drummed out everything else.

Back indoors, she agonised over whether to ask Hannah not to say anything, but decided not to; it would only add importance to what had happened. And anyway, Hannah was well aware how jealous Ross could be over the smallest incident, and would probably not bring it up.

Keeping quiet proved right. Hannah hardly mentioned where they'd been except to say that she had just one costume to do while they were there so could spend all her time with them.

But that night, as Ross undressed for bed, Kit woke up and pointed to the belt of his jeans. The three of them slept in the same room at Hannah's.

'I want . . .' He patted his waist. 'Mummy, I want that.'

Ross put the belt on a chair. 'What does he want?' he asked.

'I don't know.'

Kit leant over the bars of his cot. 'Mummy, I want it.'

'What do you want, baby?' said Ross, lifting him out.

He pointed to Josephine's bag on the dressing table.

'Mummy's bag?'

Kit shook his head and began to cry.

'He's tired,' said Josephine. 'He doesn't sleep properly here.' She stopped short of saying, let's go home, please let's go home. I shan't sleep here either now.

Ross sat on the bed and Kit stuck his thumb in his mouth and let his head fall on Ross's shoulder.

'You look tired as well,' he said.

'Yes I am. It's all this travelling about with your mother.' She ignored the arm he held towards her and climbed into bed. After a while he put Kit back in his cot and joined her. He kissed the back of her neck but she pretended to be asleep.

Chapter 16

Kit woke as soon as it was light, shaking the bars of his cot and then trying to climb out. Ross got up and brought him into bed with them.

'This won't get us a new baby, will it?' he laughed, tucking Kit down between them.

Josephine lay there with her eyes closed. She'd hardly slept at all. Nicky's words and Nicky's face had been before her in the dark most of the night.

'You're a nuisance,' said Ross, making Kit shriek with laughter as he tickled him. He stopped a moment, catching hold of Kit's waving arms to lean over to her. 'You're very quiet.'

'I didn't sleep all that well.'

'No, I thought you didn't. I'll try and get this new job set up as quickly as I can so we can go home.'

'Perhaps I could . . .' she half turned, about to say perhaps she could go home on the train with Kit. But he would want to know why. The one thing she mustn't do was arouse his suspicions.

'Perhaps I'll have a sleep later,' she finished lamely.

'I won't take any more work on up here once you're pregnant,' he said. He lifted Kit into the air. 'Come on, sunshine, we'll get up and let your mother get some sleep.'

She watched while he dressed Kit, pausing now again to catch his stumbling baby talk. It was almost too painful to imagine what it would do to him if someone suggested Kit might not be his.

By that evening, she was so tired and strung up that she

went to bed at the same time as Kit. As she was getting undressed the phone rang. The next thing she knew, Hannah was coming up the stairs.

'It's for you. I think it's that man who was at the costume agency.'

Josephine stared at her, speechless.

'Ross is busy doing my cupboards, but if he asks I'll tell him it's your brother.' Hannah looked at her coldly. 'I'm sure there's some perfectly plausible explanation but—'

'Of course there is,' Josephine broke in.

Kit had woken and Hannah went to lift him up. 'I'll wait with him for you,' she said.

The phone was at the bottom of the stairs. Above her, Hannah sat with Kit; along the hall, Ross was hammering away in the kitchen.

'Why are you doing this to me?' she said as soon as she picked up the receiver. For a moment she thought he wasn't there, then she heard a low sigh and he said her name in such a way that she knew he was smiling as he spoke, even knew the expression on his face. He would be stretched on the bed – she'd seen him make calls before and he always stretched out on the bed with the phone on his chest.

'How did you get this number?'

'Questions, questions,' he said. 'I can find out anything.' His voice was barely more than a whisper and she lowered her own voice, looking anxiously towards the kitchen.

'What do you want?'

'You know very well. Bring him.' The line went dead. She replaced the receiver and stood there with both fists pressed to her mouth, listening to Ross and Tessa laughing together in the kitchen.

The following evening he phoned again. They were eating dinner and Hannah called her out to the hall, then went back to the table without a word.

'Yes?' she said, her eyes on the open door to the dining room.

'I've just been speaking to your mother. She tells me you come to London quite often.'

She felt shocked, trapped, and then angry.

'OK, go ahead, wreck my marriage,' she said. 'Do you want to speak to my husband? Is that what you're planning to do?'

'Can he overhear you? Is that why you're talking so quietly?

Would you rather I called later – midnight maybe. Tell me a time, Josephine, because I am going to call you every day until you come here.' He put down the phone just as he had before.

'Lawrence,' she said briefly as she went back to her meal. 'I put something by for a customer. He couldn't find it.' She filled her mouth with food.

Ross started to question her as soon as they were alone in bed that night.

'I know there's something wrong,' he persisted when she would give no explanation.

She lay silent and desolate in the darkness, and knew there was only one thing she could do. Kit was sound asleep at last; he too seemed to have sensed her mood, and had cried and protested for hours when they put him to bed.

'Come downstairs,' she said finally. 'I want to tell you something.'

He followed her down and into the kitchen; it was the furthest room from Hannah's bedroom.

'Shall I make some coffee?' he said, his face full of concern.

She shook her head. 'Ross – I don't know how to begin this. I should have told you before but I couldn't.'

'You're worrying me to death.' He gave a little smile. 'It can't be anything that awful, can it?'

This is what it feels like, she thought, to be standing at the edge of a cliff and know that soon you have to jump. And if you don't, someone will push you.

'That summer when I was first working for you, I was seeing someone.'

The smile left his face. 'We've been through all this before. Why are you bringing it up again?'

'Because I want you to know the truth.' Tears were stinging her eyes now. 'I made a mistake and I hid it by lies.' She stopped as they overflowed.

'This is going to be about your stepfather again, isn't it?'

'No.' She frowned with surprise and brushed a hand across her face.

He took a deep breath and looked away and then back at her. 'I always knew you lied about him. I knew there was more to it than what you told me. That time he phoned about your locket . . .'

'Ross, it wasn't him; it's nothing to do with him. It was Nicky Frey.'

He stared at her, his face blank.

'You remember. They used to call him the Magician. It was him I was seeing.' Now I have to jump, she thought. I have to tell him because he's going to find out anyway. She leant back against the fridge and ran her palms across its smooth cold surface. 'He's been phoning me. I saw him when I went to the costume place with your mother. He thinks Kit is his son.' Her voice died away and she looked at Ross.

He didn't move. He didn't speak. But stood there as though he was trying to make sense of what she said. It was like a film where someone is shot but doesn't fall down.

'You carried on seeing him after you said you'd marry me.' His voice was quiet, hardly breaking that explosive silence.

'No, no I didn't.'

'Are you going to explain?'

'I went to tell him I was getting married. I had to. I'd been staying with him every weekend. It was over but I had to tell him.'

He waited; his breathing seemed to fill the room.

'I don't know how it happened. I don't know why I did it.'

He crossed the space between them in two strides and hit her. It was no more than a slap round the face, as though he wanted to shut her up.

She put a hand to her cheek and looked at him. 'I never meant to hurt you.'

He hit her again, so hard that her face burned and her ears buzzed, but still she stood there and looked at him.

'All this time . . .' He raised a clenched fist towards her, then banged it against his chest. 'All this time you've been lying to me.' He raised both hands now, as though he wanted to drag her head from her shoulders. She flinched away from him and his arms fell back to his sides, and she could see by the movement in his throat that he was swallowing over and over and his eyes were filling with tears. She watched helplessly as they slid down his cheeks, and it devastated her. Ross, whose whole life was based on happiness and laughter, and she'd made him cry.

'I could kill you,' he said, his voice strangled with misery. 'I could kill you.'

'Kit is your child.' She couldn't stop her own tears now; it felt as though a stranger stood in front of her and she put her hands over her face and sobbed helplessly.

Abruptly he turned away and went to stand by the window, gazing out into the darkness, his hands gripping the sill.

'Kit is yours,' she repeated. 'Believe me, he is.'

He bent his head to stare down at the floor.

'He's mistaken,' she pleaded. 'You have to believe me.' She took a step towards him but he swung round and she stopped dead.

'Where does he live?' he said.

'No, Ross, I don't want you to go there.' She put a hand on his arm but he shook her off.

'Get away from me.'

She thought he was going to hit her again and she backed away. 'Please, we have to talk.'

'All I want to hear from you is where he lives.'

'I can't tell you . . . I don't know what it's called.'

He grabbed her by the hair. 'You go there all summer, you go back there again and again, and you tell me you don't know. You're a liar and a cheat.' He took a succession of angry breaths. 'You lied to me from the moment you stepped inside my house. You even cheated on your own mother.'

She tore away from him, sobbing hysterically. 'Don't you think I feel bad about that?'

He went to grab her hair again, but his hand dropped away at the last moment. 'And how do you think I feel?' he shouted, wrenching open the door. 'How do you think I feel?'

She listened to his footsteps going round the side of the house. A door opened upstairs and she heard Hannah walk across the landing and then Kit start to cry. With shaking hands she dashed cold water over her stinging cheeks and went up. Hannah was at the top of the stairs with Kit.

'I knew this would happen,' she said. 'I knew it would come to this.'

Josephine took Kit from her without a word and went and crawled into bed with him. All night she waited for Ross, listening to every sound, hoping and hoping he would come. But he didn't, and towards dawn she fell into an exhausted sleep.

When she woke, she could hear him downstairs with Hannah. She lingered in bed, not sure what to do, and then she heard the car start up.

'He's taken Tessa with him,' said Hannah when she went down. 'I'm going over to my sister's today,' she added, lifting

Kit into his high chair and pouring cereal into a bowl for him. 'I'll take Kit with me if you like.'

'No, I want him with me,' said Josephine, slumping down at the table.

'It's up to you.'

The atmosphere was awful. She knew Hannah was avoiding looking at her because of her bruised and swollen cheek. Ross had probably never done such a thing in his whole life. She wanted to shout at Hannah, don't worry, I deserved it; I'm a cheat and a liar and not nearly good enough for your son. Instead she jumped up and snatched Kit from his high chair and held him on her lap. Kit sat there, still for a change, his face watchful, his eyes flicking from one to the other of them.

After Hannah had gone, Josephine took him out to the back garden and sat on the lawn while he clambered about on the little climbing frame Ross had made for Tessa one summer.

It was very hot, oppressively so, and beyond the rooftops a mountain of inky cloud was building up. In the distance, lightning flashed in long, ragged streaks. Music poured from an upstairs window next door, the twang of electric guitars cutting harsh swathes through the sultry air. Kit jigged up and down to it as he stood on one of the bars. Josephine watched him for a while, staring at his bright little face, her head aching with the heat and the throb of her bruised cheek. Then she lay back on the grass and closed her eyes.

The thunder jolted her awake. The music had stopped and for a moment she felt completely disorientated, imagining she was on the long slope of lawn at Waylands and that the bob of dark curls in front of her was Louisa. She heaved herself up on her elbows. Kit saw her and did a little somersault round one of the lower bars.

'Careful,' she murmured.

He did it again, then stopped to smile at her from beneath his long lashes, his expression arch with childlike seduction.

'We have to go out,' she said suddenly, getting to her feet. 'Hurry, Kit, we have to go quickly.'

He scrambled from the climbing frame and ran to her with outstretched arms. She took him into the house and pulled off his play-soiled clothes, then dressed him in fresh white dungarees and brushed his hair. In her haste, she caught at tangles, and he screwed up his face and hunched his shoulders but didn't complain.

There were buses every few minutes from the end of the road and it was only one change. She got off the stop before the one she used to, not wanting to go on that walk past Sapphire's. Kit was flagging after the first hundred yards; he wasn't used to long walks on hard pavements, especially in such heat.

'I want drink,' he said.

She caught him up in her arms. 'Soon, soon. It's not far.' But it was. She got lost, just as she had that first time she'd tried to find the house on her own, and went round in circles, carrying Kit for short stretches and then putting him down to walk. And then there it was; the long brick wall, the dark alleyway and that grey church tower looming up behind.

The gate was different: taller, blocking out any view of the garden, and along the top of the wall were pieces of broken glass, the colours glinting like sharp jewels in the sun. And inside the garden there was colour too. Tall groups of dappled foxgloves rose under the trees and their lower branches were coiled with white bryony.

There was a new intercom system on the front door and she pressed the button and cleared her throat ready to speak into it. A red light came on but nothing else happened.

'It's me, Josephine,' she said, tentatively, her head bent towards the light.

The door swung open and she felt sudden annoyance. Why did he have to do things this way? Why did he try and unnerve her and put her through all this? The house was completely silent and she stood in the hall holding Kit's hand and wondering where he was. The studio. It had to be the studio. She lifted Kit to take him down those narrow stairs and for a moment she had visions of the dream that had come to her the morning of her wedding: the flowers, then the empty studio and her climb up the fire escape. But it wasn't like that; he was waiting, holding open the louvered doors, his sleepy face half hidden by the ragged lion's mane of hair.

'Little Josephine, who used to wake me with kisses,' he said, stepping back to let her in.

'I didn't have to come, so don't . . .' She broke off and took a deep breath. 'I've told Ross. I've told him what you're saying, so don't try and threaten me, he knows everything and there's no point in . . .' The words came tumbling out too quickly. 'Look, I've done what you asked, I've brought Kit, so please leave me alone, please don't wreck my marriage.'

He was listening, his head to one side, his arms wrapped round his bare chest as though he were cold. 'Calm down,' he said. Then he reached out, and with a little click of disapproval, touched a finger to her bruised cheek.

'He was so upset . . . he said he could kill me. He wanted to know where you live and I'm frightened if he comes here that . . .'

'Shush,' he put a finger to his lips, then bent to Kit. 'He looks just like Nico did at two,' he said, turning to smile at her.

Kit backed away from him and clung round Josephine's leg. 'I want drink,' he said looking across at the fridge over in the corner.

Nicky's smile widened. He put his mouth to Kit's ear and whispered something to him. Kit nodded and took his hand. Josephine watched them walk over to the fridge, Kit standing there hopping from one foot to the other, while Nicky took ice cream from the freezer compartment. She saw him put the ice cream in a glass and top it up with fizzy drink from a bottle and give it to Kit.

'Watch him with that glass,' she said.

Nicky looked over his shoulder, stared at her for a moment, then lifted the bottle towards her. 'Do you want some?'

She shook her head, irritated and disturbed by his behaviour, the way he was acting as if it were perfectly normal for Kit to be here with him. How well she remembered this act of his, that deceptively calm way he had of ignoring what he didn't wish to know.

'Nicky,' she began, trying to get his attention. 'If he comes here, please say you'll tell him you know Kit is his.' He remained with his back to her, staring down at Kit. 'I've never asked you to do anything for me before, have I?' she persisted, her voice rising on a note of desperation. Kit eyed her over the top of the glass, his lip rimmed with ice cream. 'Have I?' she repeated.

Nicky put the bottle on top of the fridge. 'He's mine,' he said.

'So you're determined to wreck my life. You're bitter because your own life's wrecked, so you want to wreck mine. That's it, isn't it?'

He turned to face her now. His lips were twisted in an odd little smile; she could see that she'd hurt him and she broke down in tears. Kit came trotting back to her, the glass gripped carefully between his two hands. 'It nice drink,' he said anxiously, lifting it to her as though it would stop her crying.

She drank some to please him. It was beautifully cool but too sickly with the blobs of ice cream floating about and she gave it back to him, smiling down at him through her tears.

'There, you drink the rest.' She took a deep breath. 'Nicky, I didn't mean that. Can we talk about this sensibly?'

He shrugged and turned back to the fridge, mixing another drink with fruit juice and ice cubes. 'All I want you to do is bring him to see me whenever you come to London. As long as you do that, I won't cause any trouble for you. You can tell your husband what you like.'

'And you think he won't know – you think I can just lead a double life, bringing Kit here and – and seeing you?'

'You'll think of a way, Josephine.' He gave the drink a final stir and brought it over to her. 'You're good at telling lies.'

'I'm good at everything wrong.' She pushed her hands up through her hair, trying not to cry again because of Kit. 'Thanks to you.'

'And I want him to have ballet lessons,' he said as though he hadn't heard. 'I'll pay for them. I'll pay for all he needs.'

'No.' She took a step away from him. 'No, I'm not coming here again – ever.'

He stared into the glass, holding it between his palms just as Kit was holding his, and she had the sudden feeling that he was going to harm her in some way. Kit had gone to sit on the cushions; he was still sipping away at the drink but kept rubbing a fist in his eyes and yawning.

She licked her lips and glanced towards the door. 'Will you do one thing for me? Will you call me a cab? I don't think Kit can walk all the way back to the bus stop.'

'I'll do anything for you.' His voice sounded dangerously sweet. 'Anything except deny Kit is mine.'

'I just want you to call a cab for me. Can you do it now please.'

Without a word, he handed her the glass and went off towards the fire escape.

She thought of leaving before Nicky came back but didn't want to risk any further confrontation with him. And anyway, Kit was looking sleepier by the minute. She sank down on the cushions with him and drank in long continuous gulps, then crunched on the ice cubes. They tasted peculiar – very bitter – and their coldness against her teeth brought back her headache.

'It's pouring with rain,' said Nicky when he came back. 'I've told them to come to the door – about quarter of an hour, all right?'

She nodded and ran a hand across her forehead. It was dripping with sweat although she was beginning to feel quite cold. Nicky sat down with them and pulled Kit on to his lap. 'Kit!' he said, taking the empty glass from Kit's hand. 'What an awful name. What would I have called you, eh?' Kit made no resistance but smiled sleepily as Nicky cuddled him and whispered things against his ear.

Josephine was beginning to feel too strange to care. Her head no longer ached but felt terrifyingly light, as if she were about to faint. She sat very still, fearful of the way her heart was pounding – one, two, three – as if it were marking off each second. Kit was slightly sick, bringing up a thin stream of frothy white liquid. She tried to find her handkerchief, but getting her hand inside the pocket of her skirt, seemed totally beyond her. Nicky stood up, lifting Kit with him.

'Shall we go and get you cleaned up?' he said, but Kit didn't answer; his eyes were focused somewhere far away across the room. 'I'll take him and wash his face,' he said, looking down at her. 'I shan't be long.'

She watched them go towards the fire escape door. Nicky looked back once and she could see Kit's head had fallen on his shoulder and knew she must let her own head rest somewhere or she would be sick herself. It wasn't the nauseous feeling of early pregnancy – she knew it wasn't that – but the sort of stomach-churning sickness you get with intense fear or excitement.

As she lay back, the midnight sky above began to move, swirling with thunder clouds. Almost at once they were scattered and shredded by a great rushing wind. It filled her ears and sent sparkling patterns across the sky. Giant drops of rain, big as puddles, began to fall, and she raised her head to call Kit from the climbing frame. He was laughing, his arms outstretched as he came running to her and threw himself on her and put his hands over her eyes. Next door, the music had started again. The notes floated across her skin like tiny burning pinpricks. Kit's hot little body pulsed with their rhythm. She held him tight, suddenly desperate to protect him, sure he was in terrible danger.

She sat up. Where was he? Oh yes, Nicky had taken him away. All round her the mirrors were crowded with strangers, their faces grotesque red masks and their limbs deformed and ugly. She shivered and wrapped her arms round her head. When she looked again, the faces had disappeared. She stood up; that was the easy part; getting up the stairs was a nightmare, and she had to go on all fours. On the first floor landing, she began to search for Kit, pushing open doors and wandering in and out of darkened rooms. It wasn't until she was up on the second floor, that it dawned on her where they'd be.

Nicky lay on the bed. Kit was face down on his chest, spreadeagled there like a collapsed puppet, his straggling ringlets jet black against Nicky's white skin. She stood there blinking in the dim light. Everything was as she remembered it: strips of slashed canvas still hung from the picture of Hylas, and the torn draperies were still tucked beyond the massive headboard of the bed. She stared across at the huge television, where cartoon characters jerked across the screen in a blaze of brilliant colour. Kit sighed and whimpered in his sleep and she went to look down at him. He was bathed in sweat, his cheeks flushed scarlet.

'What have you done to him?' She stared down at Nicky, then lowered her eyes to look at herself: her crumpled skirt and her bare legs speckled with dust and grime. 'What have you done to us?'

Nicky sat up, lifting Kit in front of him. He blew into Kit's face and gently patted his cheeks. Kit opened his eyes and smiled sleepily.

'See. He's perfectly all right. How could you think I'd do anything to hurt him?' He jiggled Kit about and began to sing to him in a low voice. Kit's head lolled from side to side, his face creased in drowsy pleasure.

'You could have come here,' Nicky said, looking up at her. 'This is how we could have been. The three of us, here.'

Yes, she thought, trapped in this house like a couple of toys, waiting for whenever you felt like playing with us.

'Drink,' murmured Kit. 'Want drink.'

'Here, take him while I get him some water,' said Nicky. Josephine sat on the edge of the bed and took Kit in her arms. He fell in a dead weight against her shoulder, and when Nicky came back with the water, he was asleep again.

Nicky put the glass down and opened the drawer of the bedside table. He looked as though he were searching for something. Her heart began to race as she remembered with sudden clarity what he kept there. He was going to kill them; or maybe just her. Not Kit, she thought, please not Kit, and she curled on the pillows, her body protectively round him. If she didn't look, perhaps it wouldn't hurt. Behind her closed lids she had a picture of him slicing the razor-sharp blade across his jeans, and the dots of blood like tiny rubies on his skin. That had been a rainy day too. She hugged Kit close, holding her breath. The cartoon video came to an end. And in the following silence came a sound that she'd heard so many times before: the rattle of tablets in a bottle. She opened her eyes and watched him shake some out, trickling them from one hand to the other like grains of sand.

'Look.' He held his open palm towards her. 'See how many I need now?'

She stared up at him and he smiled and emptied them into his mouth, then washed them down with the water.

'Where's my cab?' she asked, dimly aware that fifteen minutes must have gone by. Or had he said that? Had she dreamt about the cab?

'Soon,' he said, coming to sit by her. 'It'll be here soon.'

'What's happened to the clock?' She listened hard. Surely she hadn't missed those great, clanging chimes?

'That was a long time ago,' he murmured.

She eased Kit into a more comfortable position and closed her eyes.

'Stay here with me,' she heard Nicky say. She opened her eyes. His face was only inches away. 'Stay here with me,' he said again. 'I'll build you a little kitchen – whatever you want.'

It struck her as funny and she laughed. The sound echoed round the room, then was lost in the rushing torrent of rain that beat against the windows. 'Hark at that,' she said, finding it funny as well. 'I can't go home in that.'

'No.' He looked down at her, his eyes glittering bright as a bird's. 'You haven't got any feelings left for me, have you, Josephine?'

She shook her head, too tired to answer properly. And the pillow was so soft, the room so warm, that the urge to sleep became irresistible. She closed her eyes but couldn't sink the whole way into sleep because her heart raced too fast, and she was suspended, semiconscious and full of dreams. She imagined that Nicky was taking Kit away again; very carefully unhooking her fingers one by one. And when she reached out for him, her hands closed on emptiness. She panicked, clutching at thin air, but the next second he slid back into her arms, wriggling close against her. His hair was tainted with the smell of the studio, and she could feel the clockwork rhythm of his heartbeat and the dampness of his face against hers.

But he held her too tightly. He became like a demon, crushing her and suffocating her. She struggled to escape, aware that the only way to stop this happening was to wake up. But to wake up seemed impossible because she wasn't asleep. She began to scream and fight, but it only brought hateful pictures: all those stars, and the cold wind blowing across her body. She squeezed her eyes tight shut and stopped struggling, and when it was over, she cried herself into a deep sleep and dreamt she was laying naked and frozen on the ground up at the old quarries.

Kit woke her. He was pulling at her arm and whimpering like a child too weak to cry properly. Her head was pounding and she lay very still, delaying the moment when she would have to open her eyes and know for sure where she was.

'Mummy,' he whined. 'Mummy, I want drink.'

It was stifling hot but the moment she moved, she began shivering violently. Beside her, Nicky slept, or so she thought, because she couldn't bear to look at him.

She took Kit to the bathroom and washed him, then herself, splashing water everywhere because she was shaking so much. When she looked in the mirror, another face drifted in to view beside her own. She clapped her hands over her eyes, waiting for the images to go. Then she heard Nicky calling to say that her cab had arrived. She picked Kit up and went back into the bedroom.

Nicky was sitting up. Behind him a red light flashed on and off from the intercom box on the wall. 'What are you going to do?' he said. It seemed like that other time – how long ago was it? – when he had asked her to stay and she had wanted to but couldn't, because she thought Ross would be worried. Days and hours, past and present fused together for a moment. Then she thought of Ross again and how he had stood there last night with the tears running down his face.

'If you think . . .' Misery choked her. 'If you think that what you've done to me . . .' Kit rubbed frantically at her tears but she caught his hands, enclosing them in her own. 'If you think that what you've done will make me stay, then . . .' It was impossible to go on for a moment and she cried into Kit's hair. 'Then I feel sorry for you,' she finished in a broken voice.

In a blur of tears, she heard Nicky speak into the box, and as she left she thought she heard him call after her, 'I'm sorry, Josephine, I'm sorry.' But she couldn't be sure, because suddenly nothing seemed quite real. And as she went downstairs, she had the notion that perhaps, as she left this house, she would wake up and find herself back on Hannah's lawn, watching Kit on the climbing frame. But as she opened the front door she saw only the path and the dripping flowers, and the black gate, propped open to reveal the cab, its engine ticking over while it waited to take her back to Ross.

Kit was very subdued on the drive home. He sat there with his head against her, hardly moving. And she too sat very still. The shaking had stopped and she stared out of the window, watching in a daze as they drove through rain-soaked streets and wound in and out of the long processions of traffic.

She told the driver to stop at the end of Hannah's road: she was confused about the time, but her head was clear enough to know she mustn't take any chances. When they got out Kit was promptly sick on the pavement. He flopped down, his dungarees soaked and stained, and refused to move. The rain was pelting down even harder and she picked him up and hurried along towards the house. Just before they got there, he pointed to the Range Rover parked in the road, his little face brightening.

'Daddy,' he said, wriggling to get down.

The front door opened as soon as they were inside the gate and she watched as Ross came out and rushed to pick Kit up.

'Where have you been?' he shouted at her. 'Look at him. Where have you been?'

She followed him into the hall and stood there while he pulled off Kit's wet clothes. Kit was holding his hands to his head as though it hurt him, then he vomited again.

'To the shops,' she murmured.

'In this weather? Are you mad?'

'Don't keep shouting at me.' She leant against the wall.

Tessa came through from the kitchen but stopped and looked anxiously from one to the other of them.

'How long has he been like this?' Ross said.

'While we were at the shops . . .' she began, but he turned on her angrily.

'Are you lying to me? How long have you been out?'

'No – I don't know – what time is it?'

Tessa looked at the kitchen clock and said meekly, 'It's half past four.'

'Oh, God.' Josephine looked round at them. 'Oh, God,' she said again and ran off upstairs.

She was in the bedroom drying herself when Ross came up.

'Tell me where you've been.'

'I told you.'

He snatched the towel from her and grabbed hold of her hair, twisting her head round to face him.

'If you hit me again . . .'

'I'm not going to hit you.' He let go of her. He looked defeated, his voice tight with misery. 'I just want the truth – that's all.'

'I want to tell you the truth.' She closed her eyes and felt the tears squeeze out between her lids. 'I don't want to lie to you any more.'

He waited and she took a deep breath and looked up at him. 'I've been to see him,' she said finally. 'I went to reason with him, because I was frightened of what you would do if you went there.'

'And you took Kit?'

She nodded. 'He gave him some ice cream, that's what made him sick.'

There was a long silence, then, his voice deadly calm he said: 'And how many more times do you plan to visit him?'

'Ross, don't, please. I was just worried that . . .'

'You've good reason to be worried, because if you ever go near him again, I'll kill you . . . do you hear me?' His eyes shone with tears. 'I'll kill you,' he repeated. 'And when I find him, I'm going to kill him.'

The sound of Tessa crying came up the stairs. 'Daddy, come down,' she was calling. 'Kit's being sick again.'

Josephine was about to go, but Ross stopped her. 'Get your case packed,' he said. 'I'm taking you home. I'll see to Kit, you're not fit to look after him.'

His words made no impression on her; she felt numb. All she could think of were those lost hours and how she wanted to tell the truth but didn't know what it was any longer.

Chapter 17

On the journey home, she made a few attempts to talk to Ross, but he became agitated and upset, increasing speed in tune with his anger.

'We have to talk,' she pleaded. 'We can't go on like this.'

'I don't want to talk to you. I don't want to hear your voice and I don't even want to look at you. I'm taking you home, then I'm coming straight back.'

She glanced across at him and he immediately looked round at her.

'You've destroyed me, do you know that?'

His words hurt her but she said nothing, just climbed over on to the back seat with Kit, frightened to upset him further in case they had an accident. Kit was in his car seat, so deeply asleep that nothing seemed to wake him. They had left a tearful and confused Tessa with Hannah.

Solange accepted Ross's brief explanation that they had come home early because Kit had been unwell and would be best off in his own bed. But soon after Josephine had taken him upstairs, Solange followed.

'Are you coming down for something to eat? Ross says he doesn't want anything.' She looked concerned and stroked Kit's head. He had woken now and was sitting on Josephine's lap, thumb in his mouth and his other hand tucked under her chin. 'Or shall I bring you something up?'

'No thanks, I had something before we left.'

Solange looked closely at her. 'Have you been crying, dear?'

How she longed to pour out everything to her mother, get some kind of comfort. But she mustn't. Once you started spilling secrets it was difficult to stop.

'I'm just tired – I don't like being away. I'll put Kit to bed then I'm going myself.' She hesitated. 'I'm not sure what Ross is doing. He might go back tonight – he's very busy at work.'

Solange looked anxious but didn't question her, and Josephine took Kit to his cot and went to run herself a bath. Soaking in the hot water, she began to hallucinate. Fantasy shapes appeared in the steam and along the patterned tiles on the wall. She lay back and let her mind drift: perhaps this would be the answer; slip down into the water and let it wash over her head and pour down her nose and throat and fill up her lungs. The sound of Kit sucking away noisily on his thumb came through the open door, and she dragged herself upright, appalled at how beguiling the idea had seemed. And once she was in bed, sleep came quickly, soothing away all morbid thoughts.

She woke to find Ross's arms round her.

'You didn't go,' she murmured, her head thick with sleep.

His answer was to begin kissing her: fierce, hard kisses which hurt her lips.

'Ross, wait.' She twisted her head away. 'Don't, Ross . . . we have to talk.'

'Don't refuse me, Josephine,' he said, pushing up under her nightdress to caress the inside of her thigh. But his fingers dug too sharply into her flesh and when she pulled at his arm, his muscles tightened under her hand.

'So you're going to rape me as punishment, are you?' she said, swallowing against the desire to cry. 'You think that will solve things, do you?'

He ignored her and wrenched her nightdress up round her waist.

'If you do I shall never forgive you. Still,' she let herself go limp, 'you're never going to forgive me, so what does it matter? Let's end it the way it began, shall we?' Her voice rose with anger, she wanted to shout, let's end it with sex because that's what everyone seems to want from me. But she couldn't say it to him, and when he stopped and lay there with his head on her chest, she put a hand up and stroked his hair.

'I want to know you don't think of him. That's what he said – that time on the phone.' He raised his head, then let it fall again. 'He said, every time you fuck her she'll imagine it's me. And other things . . . I can't tell you.'

'Oh, Ross, I don't.' She clung to him, wanting to respond, wanting to erase those words from his memory. Nicky would have chosen his words for maximum effect; she knew full well what a talent he had for obscenity when he wanted to upset someone. 'I don't,' she repeated.

He rolled away from her and lay there breathing heavily, as though she had fought him away. She stared into the darkness; they would never get back to the way they had been; their happiness was wrecked now.

A few minutes later he got up, and had left for London before daybreak.

He phoned her, speaking briefly, coolly inquiring how she was and asking after Kit. She didn't ask when he was coming back but let each day drift by in a dull vacuum of loneliness; there was no chance of mending their marriage while his emotions burnt so fiercely. When a week went by without him phoning, she was seized with anxiety, thinking he might have gone to Nicky's house. But then he called again and wanted to talk to Kit.

'It's Daddy,' she said, holding the receiver to his ear, a lump rising in her throat as she watched the smile spread over Kit's face.

'Daddy,' he repeated, clapping his hands with excitement as though he thought Ross was about to come through the door. The smile widened as he heard Ross's voice, but he would say no more and she took the receiver from him.

'He misses you,' she said.

He didn't answer for a moment and, when he did, saying that he missed Kit too, she knew he was upset. But he stayed away another week, coming home the day before Tessa was due to go back to school. She had no idea what he planned to do but had steeled herself for whatever he had decided.

The awkwardness of his arrival was eased by Tessa and Louisa being reunited once more; they bounced off together like two puppies. Ross had scooped up Kit and stood watching them, holding Kit so tightly that he wriggled to be down and off with the girls.

'It's nearly his bedtime,' said Josephine. 'They'll get him excited and he won't settle.'

Ross said nothing; he hadn't greeted her in any way. Irritation rose in her and she went off after the children. If this was how he was going to be, there was no point in carrying on. But while she was putting Kit to bed, he came up.

'I've arranged to have the phone number changed,' he said.

For a moment, she didn't know what he was talking about.

'And I've warned my mother not to speak to him if he phones there.'

She nodded and sank down on the edge of the bed. Kit called from his cot and he went through to him. When he came back she was still sitting there, motionless.

'I want it to be as though he never existed,' he said, coming to stand in front of her.

'So do I,' she murmured. But for some reason the words made her feel unbearably desolate and she stared at her hands, clenched in her lap. 'You didn't go to his house then?' Her voice was hardly more than a whisper now.

'No. I wanted to – but I couldn't find it. I searched for hours.' He let out his breath in a great long sigh. 'Maybe it was for the best – I really wanted to kill him.'

The pattern in her skirt blurred before her eyes, but she bit back the tears because Ross would want to know what they were for and she could never explain.

'Why did you do it?' His voice was unexpectedly gentle. 'How could you have said you loved me, said you'd marry me, and then . . . Tell me the truth?'

I was crazy about him, I was madly in love with him. Simple explanations came pouring into her head. But none of them would do.

'I hadn't really got him out of my system when I said I'd marry you. I know that now. That's why it happened.'

'And then you found out you were pregnant?'

'No.' She looked up at him. 'I wasn't. It was after that time in the pine forest – with you.' She continued staring into his face. 'He can't have his own son, so he's convinced himself Kit is his. You have to believe me, Ross.'

He looked away from her towards the door, where the noise of Kit sucking his thumb rose loudly for a moment, then died back down to a low, contented rhythm.

'I love Kit. I don't want any doubts. Swear to me, swear on your father's grave.'

She folded her arms abruptly across her chest. How easy it would be to say it; they were only words.

'You have to trust me, Ross. Kit is yours. You said you

wanted it to be as though he'd never existed – how can we do that if you don't believe me?'

He crouched down in front of her and took her hands. 'I want to believe you. All I want is for us to be happy again. I've missed you so much.'

'And it's all I want – to be happy with you.' She blinked back tears but more came. 'Any lies I've told you, any secrets I've kept – it's only because I love you, and I didn't want to hurt you.' The tears fell faster than she could wipe them away, but he let her go on, as though he sensed that she must get everything out. 'Whenever I'm really happy, something always happens to spoil it,' she sobbed. 'Always, always, something goes wrong.' She took a long shuddering breath. 'I wish we could start again, I really wish we could – right from this very minute.'

'We can,' he said softly, wrapping her in his arms. She knew then that he was going to forgive her, but her heart still felt heavy and she cried against him for a long time.

'I'm tired,' she said at last. 'I feel as if I could sleep for days and days without waking up.' He smiled at her and she traced the curve of his lips with her fingers. 'Can we really start again?'

'Yes.' His face grew serious once more. 'If that's what you really, truly want. Is it?'

She nodded.

'And you'll never . . .' he began, but she pressed her hand over his mouth and shook her head.

'Let's never mention any of it again,' she said.

That night they made love for the first time in weeks. It was exciting after so much time apart and easy to convince him that there was no one but him in her thoughts.

Chapter 18

The lights dimmed, the babble of voices fell to a low hum, and the orchestra's discordant tuning stilled to silence as the curtains shivered and swung back to reveal a stage full of tiny ballerinas. In pink and white tutus they balanced there on one leg, each holding a silver wand. High, tripping notes came from a solo flute, and the audience began to clap.

The little dancers each turned a circle, and on to the stage ran a group of even smaller children dressed as elves, shepherded by a woman with a back as straight as a ramrod. In a voice as clipped as the staccato notes of the flute, she announced the anniversary show of her dancing school.

Josephine shifted in her seat and Solange leant across and whispered loudly, 'Are you all right, dear?'

'Shush, of course I am.'

All day Solange had been saying she ought not to go.

'You don't look well,' she'd said at breakfast when Josephine had mentioned her back ached. Then, ten minutes before they were due to leave, she'd said: 'Don't forget how quickly Kit was born. You could end up having this one on the floor of the theatre.'

'Stop fussing,' Ross had said. 'It's not due for another three weeks.'

'Kit was early, so could this one be.'

'Mother, I'm going to see Kit whatever happens,' Josephine had said firmly. 'Every five minutes he's been asking if I'm going to watch him, I couldn't possibly not go.'

'Don't be silly, he won't know if you're there or not.'

Ross had ruffled Kit's hair and said: 'Yes he would – you

know everything don't you, sunshine?'

And as the little group of elves began to weave their way amongst the fairies, she had the most powerful feeling that he did know. It felt as though an invisible thread joined them; as though he would only have to look out into the darkened auditorium and those slanting eyes of his would find her. Love for him overwhelmed her.

The back ache had returned in the cramped seat and was now accompanied by a dull pain in her legs. She placed an involuntary hand on her stomach, her eyes never leaving the stage.

It was over. The elves were making haphazard bows and curtsies. Kit spun in circles until one of the fairies caught him by the arm. People were laughing; either side of her, Ross and Solange clapped and laughed. She reached out and gripped Ross's arm.

'I think we'll have to go,' she whispered. 'I think we'd better hurry.'

As he led her up the gangway, she glanced back over her shoulder. The elves had disappeared, the spotlight followed one of the little ballerinas in her froth of pink and white, and she felt a great unease settle over her.

'Your mother won't ever let us forget this,' said Ross as he drove her to the hospital.

But she was caught up in another savage twist of pain and couldn't answer.

The baby, a girl, arrived with the same speed as Kit. As yet she had no name; it wasn't that they couldn't think of any, but Josephine stubbornly said she must see her first.

Ross brought Kit to see them the next day. They came unexpectedly and Josephine was feeding the baby. Kit looked horrorstruck, then burst into floods of tears, and would only be consoled when the baby was taken away and he could curl up beside her, thumb in his mouth.

'Did you like being an elf?' she asked him.

He nodded his head and snuggled closer to her.

'I'll be home soon,' she said. 'Then you can dress up in your costume and show me your dance again.'

'I went round and round,' he said, kneeling up, then standing on the bed to show her.

She glanced at Ross but he was absorbed in looking at the baby. Only once had she asked him if he minded Kit dancing, and then he'd turned on her, his expression carefully blank. No, why should I? he'd said. After that she'd never mentioned it again, and when Kit had started to join in the girls' dancing lessons, unofficially because the school's baby class, as they called it, started at three years, he'd still said nothing.

She hadn't been to London at all while she was pregnant. From very early on she had been ill again, plagued with sickness and fainting spells, and long-distance travelling was out of the question. Ross had looked after her just as patiently as before, their damaged relationship repaired by the expected baby.

On the day she was due to leave hospital, a nurse came round with the post. She handed Josephine a narrow box with a cellophane window and went to look at the baby.

Josephine stared at the perfect red rose on its cushion of white silk. Ross had twice sent her flowers during the four days she'd been there.

'Tell me, where did you get a man like that?' said the nurse in a soft Irish lilt. 'I'm after one of them sort meself, but I can't seem to find one.'

'They're very rare,' smiled Josephine.

'Well if you get tired of him let me know.' The nurse picked up the baby and smoothed a finger over her head. 'You're not going to get your daddy's beautiful curls are you, my darling?'

Ross was due shortly and Josephine finished gathering up her things, then went to the window to look down over the car park. She was just in time to see the Range Rover arrive and watched as Ross lifted Kit out, then took his hand to walk across the tarmac. Never once during the nine months since that awful row had he been anything but loving to Kit, and she had no fears at all that he would show any favouritism towards the new baby. He *was* rare; he was unceasingly loving and generous to her, and she must love him for ever in return.

She went back to sit on the bed, picking up the box with the rose and taking out the tiny card stuck on the end. It would say, I love you; that's all he ever wrote in cards he sent her.

For a moment she thought it was a mistake, that it was not meant for her. With shaking hands she picked up the envelope, read her name again – then read the card again. 'Call her Zuska,' it said.

By the time Ross and Kit came through the door, the rose lay crushed at the bottom of the rubbish bin, the stem snapped, the silken bed crumpled and the card torn into tiny pieces. But she could not stop the shaking in her hands and caught Kit up in a giant hug to disguise it, covering his dark head with kisses.

Epilogue

Josephine sunk into deep depression after the baby's birth. It wasn't just the short spells of sadness that she'd experienced with Kit, but whole weeks of physical and mental lethargy and fits of crying for no apparent reason.

The doctor prescribed tranquillisers which she soon gave up because they made her hallucinate.

Ross was his usual patient self, even on the days when she became hysterical over the most trivial things. And as before he gave into her, doing his best not to upset her and even agreeing to name the baby Zuska, though he always called her Suzy. Only once did he lose control and shout at her. It was the day she announced, completely out of the blue, that she was going to tell her mother what had happened with Christian. It developed into a great row, both of them hurling accusations, until she finally broke down, stabbing her fingers at her head and screaming at him that she was sick to death of living with lies. Go on then, he yelled back at her, tell your mother, hurt her like you hurt me. It's your favourite game, isn't it? You lie to get what you want, you don't care what you do, then when your conscience gets too much, you have a great time telling the truth. I can't tell the truth, she said with such a stricken look on her face that he feared she was cracking up altogether. But he too had reached breaking point and he slammed out of the house, needing to be away from her for a while.

When he came back she'd gone, taking Kit and Zuska. It was what he had always feared – not for any reason he could explain – it was just this feeling he had that one day he would lose her.

Three days later she was back, subdued and full of apologies but refusing to say where she'd been. It was the turning point; she became calmer, gradually recovering altogether, and even joking that if he wanted any more children they had better adopt because she wasn't prepared to put them both through months of hell again.

Their marriage grew happy and loving once more; the children thrived. But sometimes, in the depths of the night, he would hear her crying very quietly and he would pretend to be asleep because, for the few minutes that her tears lasted, nothing he could do or say would comfort her.